London Lovers

By the same author

The Novels of George Eliot: A Study in Form
The Appropriate Form: An Essay on the Novel
The Moral Art of Dickens
The Exposure of Luxury: Radical Themes in Thackeray
(*Peter Owen*)
A Reading of Jane Austen (*Peter Owen*)
Tellers and Listeners: The Narrative Imagination
The Advantage of Lyric
Particularities: Readings in George Eliot (*Peter Owen*)
Forms of Feeling in Victorian Fiction (*Peter Owen*)
Narrators and Novelists: Collected Essays
Swansea Girl: A Memoir (*Peter Owen*)
Shakespeare's Storytellers (*Peter Owen*)

Barbara Hardy

London Lovers

A Novel

Peter Owen

London & Chester Springs

PETER OWEN PUBLISHERS
73 Kenway Road London SW5 0RE
Peter Owen books are distributed in the USA by
Dufour Editions Inc. Chester Springs PA 19425–0007

First published in Great Britain 1996
First published in paperback 1997
© Barbara Hardy 1996

The author gratefully acknowledges International Music Publication
Limited for permission to reprint lyrics from 'Our Love Affair', © 1940
EMI Catalogue Partnership, EMI Feist Catalog Inc, USA. Worldwide
print rights controlled by Warner Bros Publications Inc/IMP Ltd.

A catalogue record for this book is available from
the British Library

ISBN 0–7206–1023–0

Printed in Great Britain by
Biddles of Guildford & King's Lynn

To
Mick & Charlie

Contents

Our love affair will be such fun
We'll be the envy of everyone,
We'll fight and quarrel
And tears will brew
But after the storm
Our love will shine through.

Our love affair was meant to be,
It's me for you dear and you for me.
Those famous lovers
We'll make them forget
From Adam and Eve
To Scarlett and Rhett.

And when our youth has had its fling
We'll spend our evenings remembering,
Two happy lovers
You'll hear us declare
Wasn't ours
A lovely love affair!

Our Love Affair

ONE

Wedding Groups

Yesterday I turned up our wedding photographs in Mother's album, to find my smile as sweet as any June bride's. On a blowy morning in early March I was surprised to be in St James's Church, Walter Road, about to get married to the boy next door. I stood inside the porch self-consciously holding Father's thin black pin-striped arm, while a smart navy-blue-suited Charlie stood at the altar with Percy Watkins, his best friend and best man, under the hideous green and yellow zig-zagged Lazarus where the blitz had smashed a Victorian Feeding of the Five Thousand. I speculated on their reasons for changing the miracle from a picnic to the revival of a corpse when the organ heaved mightily and we started to walk slowly and steadily down the aisle, keeping in step. Charlie turned his head, gave a discreet thumbs-up sign, and grinned. I grinned back and found myself wondering what on earth we were doing there. I was a vague agnostic, who detested the hell-fire rant and sentimental hymns of chapel, and Charlie was an old-fashioned Victorian Higher Critic, who read Rationalist Press pamphlets and hadn't been inside a church since he was thirteen. Of course it was because the mothers had ganged up on us.

My mother was a fervent believer, a Baptist Sunday school teacher who played the organ in Mount Zion, and Charlie's mother was a Church of England snob, who went to St James's twice every Sunday, wearing a smart costume from Belmont and an elaborate hat from Miss Terry's. She would pray for her husband and sons who couldn't be persuaded to go with her. I daresay she prayed for other things too, but that was what she used to say once every week to Charlie and Davie, and they quoted her with irreverent mirth. She and Jack Jones had been married in that very church thirty-five years ago. Their wedding photograph was framed, and hung over the black upright piano in the front room. Carrying a huge bouquet of carnations, roses, and maiden-hair fern, wearing a long veil with a trimming of orange-blossom over the brow, and a stern, though, as Charlie said, triumphant, expression, she towered majestically over Charlie's dad, who sported his thin Charlie Chaplin moustache and habitual look of resigned goodwill.

'Poor Dada', Charlie used to say, 'marrying Mam finished him. You can see the whole story in that terrible photo. She liked the taste and swallowed him in one bite. Mind you, I'm not saying it wasn't good taste on her part. The trouble was, she was ambitious, and he wasn't.'

I thought my own parents looked handsomer in their wedding group, also framed in black and gold, and over the fireplace in their front room. They looked so young I felt they didn't belong to me. They were also unsmiling. When I inquired, I was told that Deans, the Manselton photographers, discouraged their clients from smiling on the grounds that you didn't want a wedding group to look like a holiday snap. When you heard their watchword was 'Think of posterity', all was explained, though since the information came from Charlie's elder brother Davie, an unreliable narrator, or in his own words, a big kidder, the old firm may have been maligned. (Because of post-war economy, our photographs were taken by my brother Idris, so we were allowed to smile.) The veil and orange-blossom and bouquet were almost identical in both groups, but Charlie's parents had a small unhappy-looking page-boy, and four pretty little bridesmaids holding the long train, while my parents had one grown-up bridesmaid, Auntie Mary, dressed to the nines in satin and a feathered hat, and her married cousin Joyce as matron of honour. I found that term impressive when I was a little girl gazing at the veil and hats and white dresses and my mother told her story of the photograph, but I wasn't clear about the difference between maids and matrons. I thought a maid was someone who served or helped, and it was Auntie Mary who'd been in service, not Joyce.

My mother had left school when she was twelve, to follow her sister Mary as minder of the swarming brood of brothers and sisters when Mary went off to be a skivvy. Even though she'd been to the Greg school for their commercial course, my mother was jealous of Charlie's mother's top-dressing of High School accent, and her Training College education. I always thought Charlie's mother raised her plucked eyebrow at shabby Auntie Mary, and the Thomases' common relations in Greenhill and the Hafod. My father said she looked askance at the boys – my brother Idris, Uncle Bert, and Bert's sons Wally and Ronnie – as a set of old Reds, bent on seducing Charlie away from the Labour party and his admiration for Aneurin Bevan. For six months Idris had been a member of the Communist Party, called the Communist Party by the unpolitical, the Party by its members, and the C. P. by the politically minded who weren't in it, and Wally was studying Russian in his spare time. Ronnie was much maligned, being only interested in girls.

The mothers might have been surprised to know they had a lot in common: a Welsh god, frustrated intellect, ferocious ambition, and a determination that their son and daughter shouldn't disgrace the families by going to the registry office. They were at one in disliking the marriage. Neither thought the other's child good enough for her darling. Charlie's mother felt in her bones that I would never settle down to cook and clean and mend and be a good housewife and help her son's career, and my mother was heartbroken that I was getting married to a Swansea solicitor instead of finishing my Ph.D. and becoming a university lecturer in Oxford or Cambridge or even London. I explained patiently and clearly and frequently that nothing was going to stop me going on with my research and that I intended to have a career as well as marriage but she said nothing and looked gloomy. About a year later I discovered my aunts had convinced her that our sudden engagement meant I must be pregnant, so she could neither believe any more in my distinguished academic future nor dare to dissuade me from marriage.

The fact that the families had been next-door neighbours in

the Uplands for ten years didn't help. Both mothers would have preferred a glamorous stranger from London, or even North Wales at a pinch. The fathers were cynical, quiet men who kept their thoughts to themselves. My father did occasionally open his mouth in the family circle, preferably to one of us at a time, but Charlie's father, a Cardiff man who'd been snapped up by his wife on a holiday in Porthcawl, was totally silent.

Of course we had to get married, there was no alternative. For all the chapel sermons about sinners, nobody ever lived in sin in Swansea, before the sixties – if then. And this was only 1947. Children were frequently born two or three months after the marriage, which accounted, some said, for the gigantic bridal bouquets prominent in so many wedding groups. When Charlie's mother accidentally overheard him joking to Davie and me about big bunches of big blooms for big bellies, one Sunday after-noon when I'd been asked to tea, she rebuked him sternly. I admired her outspokenness. My mother would have pretended not to hear.

'Dada and I were married three years if it was a day when Davie was born. So don't be foul-mouthed. What will Florence think of you?' Charlie apologized and Davie changed the subject with a grin.

There were scandalous whispered legends of fornication and adultery, but sex was too furtive and wicked to be discussed in the family. A Martian overhearing all the Swansea conversations would have concluded that there were only engagements and marriages.

We thought of getting married secretly but it seemed too com-plicated. And we didn't really care all that much.

'It'll be a laugh, anyway,' Charlie said. 'Think of my mother kissing your mother. And imagine my father making a speech. The mind boggles. Well, mine does, and if yours is in proper order it will too.'

So we said 'All right', and tossed for church or chapel. To my relief, church won. Chapel had been the theatre of my theologi-cal ups and downs, but church had no associations. I'd only been in St James's a couple of times, once for an eisteddfod, once for a friend's wedding. Of course we didn't mention the gamble and our official story was that we'd agreed after amicable debate. It was a good outcome, because my mother was secretly tickled at the idea of an exotic ceremony in the posh church, with stained glass, the Prayer Book, the kneeling, and a college-trained organist to criticize or admire, while Charlie's mother, less polite and tolerant than mine, would have been rudely outspoken about the austerities of chapel architecture and ritual.

It was March because of the Income Tax. We were already having to think about money. That was marriage. Before we bought the ring somebody told Charlie you could get a discount for cash, so after we chose the narrow bevelled band of pale Welsh gold in Martindales, the posh diamond merchants in Oxford St, Charlie asked in his diffident way, 'Er – will there be – um – something off for ready cash?' and the salesman stopped smiling and said, 'One moment, sir, I'll ask the manager.' I felt ashamed, not of the asking, but of Charlie's obvious embarrassment at asking. Suddenly I wished I wasn't going to get married, or not so soon. It was only a month off now. It was the first domestic shopping expedition and the first twinge of intimate disapproval. The unctuous salesman came back and said yes, patronizingly, and we went off with the ring.

I still wear it, though the bevelling's worn away, except for one bit I can see because I know what it used to look like. After we split up I had periods of not wearing it, and when I stayed in a hotel with some man I disliked the way it conveniently turned into his ring. When Charlie died, ten years after the divorce, I kept it on all the time, though nobody noticed. I had refused an engagement ring, feeling or affecting a distaste for adornment, feebly straining for unconventional gesture after swallowing the idea of marriage. Now I wear the wedding ring with the moonstone Mick gave me, which I put on my ring-finger after he died.

My mother said, 'But Floss darling, why won't you wear a proper dress? And a veil? Oh, I always imagined you with orange-blossom in your golden hair, like me. Oh, what will Sarah Jones think!'

My father said they should leave me alone to do what made

me feel happy. So I held out and marched reluctantly and rhyth-
mically down and then up the aisle in tan flat-heeled shoes and
what was called a box-shouldered costume, in blue-green tweed,
which both mothers obviously thought was dreadful. My mother
said it was very nice, and Mrs Jones didn't say anything, but
their faces, one round and resolutely cheerful, the other long and
lugubrious, told the same story. Not much like a bride. I tried to
dispense with a hat but the prospect of hatlessness was as outrageous as the registry office so I gave in and bought a dark-
green felt which I hoped brought out a faint resemblance to Garbo.
Mrs Jones press-ganged all her relations into contributing cloth-
ing coupons so Charlie sported a suit made by Sidney Heath,
the poshest tailor in town, in which he looked long-armed, short-
legged, and square. I carried a small bunch of red roses which
kept me fidgeting all through the ceremony. I could never get
my arms at the right angle to carry it gracefully. Afterwards as
we walked to the vestry to sign the register, both sets of parents,
the brothers, and Auntie Mary in attendance, Charlie hissed in
my ear, 'My God, you're Mrs Jones now, just like Mother,' and I
didn't know whether to laugh or cry. I decided to smile and
Charlie gave me a kiss.

The wedding breakfast was at home, family and close friends
only. Sherry and port and beer and ham sandwiches and a three-
tier wedding cake. Idris and Davie were enthusiastic waiters, plying
the mothers with port until they started to cry. The speeches were
short, read from little bits of paper, except for Percy's, which
was full of extemporized wisecracks and loudly applauded. Everyone came to High Street Station to see us off. Charlie was in a
new Harris tweed sports coat and grey flannels, I was still in my
blue-green costume, which made a going away outfit unnecessary, as I had heard my mother explaining to an impassive Mrs
Jones. The mothers were still wiping their eyes and the fathers
looked solemn. We were off on our honeymoon. Babes in the
wood who didn't know anything.

It was a cold day, March coming in like a lion. As soon as
we'd got out of the church I started to take my hat off. I hated
hats and hadn't worn one for several years, since I stopped believing

in God and going to chapel three times every Sunday. My bran-new mother-in-law had her eye on me and, quick as a flash, shook her head in admonition. 'No, no, no, Florence love. The photos. Remember the photos.' So I pushed back the hatpin and pulled the hat on firmly.

There the photographs are, ours piled higgledy-piggledy in an old pink fibre suitcase by Charlie and me, my parents' copies given pride of place in my mother's leather-bound album with gilt edges, which I inherited when she died three years ago. There we are at the bottom of a pyramid of parents and brothers and aunts and uncles and cousins, the pathetic human pair, unable to go off alone into the woods or the dunes to mate. We are overwhelmed by ritual, with our new clothes and our square shoulders and big carnation buttonhole and clumsily clasped roses and bright brave camera smiles. We look about fifteen. We were twenty-one and twenty-eight. When Charlie proposed he said, 'I feel time at my back. Don't let's wait.'

I never showed Mick the wedding photographs. I don't even know if he had any. He and Ellen had married quietly, in Paris, away from families. I felt a mixture of envy and amazement at their escape. A week or two before he died he asked me to show him some photographs of myself as a girl and a young woman, and I took along a selection. He turned them over slowly. He looked for a long time at one of me with shoulder-length hair and lipstick and an open-necked linen dress. He said in his invalid-slurred voice, 'You were so lovely.' Then he held my face in his hands and pulled the skin down tight over my cheekbones to see it smooth and unwrinkled. As it had been for Charlie. I remember Charlie's skin against my skin. That feeling of unaccustomed touching nakedness was one of the honeymoon treats, but by the time I met Mick I'd grown out of those first thrills, forgotten all about them in new and more complicated desires and fantasy.

Mick and I never had our photograph taken together, so I can't tell if I'd feel sorry for the coupled images as I do when I look at our family's wedding groups. Once or twice he took some erotic photographs of me with an instamatic camera, for our personal fun and delectation, but he was a pornographer not a photographer.

He left them with me, for obvious security reasons, and after his death I tore them up and threw the tiny bits down the lavatory. They weren't to be looked at cold.

I have several photographs of him. The big one on my desk has the date written on the back and it's signed by the photographer. It was taken the year after we met, while he was giving a lecture. He's wearing a black and white shirt with a pattern inspired by the sign for the female chromosome, and a black silk tie with big white ducks flying over it. He is holding an open book in his left hand and his horn-rimmed spectacles in the right. It's an excellent photograph, taken at a moment of relaxed informality. I can see every fold in the bent sleeve of his coat, the grey tips of his curly side-whiskers, his dimple, the faint liver-spot on his forehead, and the almost invisible small bump under his right eyelid. He is smiling seraphically at the audience.

Charlie loved taking photographs of lakes and mountains and beautiful buildings and me and the children. There aren't many of him, because I was a reluctant photographer, though there are some happy snaps of him with Joanna and Susie on the sands at Oxwich, and standing by Arthur's Stone on Cefn Bryn. There are lots of me in the early loving days, swimming or sunbathing at Rhossilli and Llandudno, sight-seeing in Italy, lazing in Paris, walking in the Brecon Beacons, climbing in North Wales. There I am, as he saw me, against the background of the Worm's Head, the Great Orme, the towers of San Gimignano and Crib Goch, standing in front of the Ghiberti gates, by the roadside in the Black Mountains, climbing Tryfan, drinking coffee in the *Deux Magots*. There were some of me lying in bed, smiling at the photographer. The one I've still got has the covers pulled up to my neck, but there was at least one other he took of me lying naked on that bed. It seems to have disappeared. Perhaps he threw it away after the divorce. Perhaps he tore it into tiny bits.

They were taken in our first flat, the two small damp attic rooms in a house in Richmond Road, near Dylan Thomas's old house in Cwmdonkin Drive, with a wonderful panoramic view of Swansea Bay, and the old Mumbles lighthouse, no longer there. We used to sit on the battered old sofa watching dredgers and pleasure-steamers and big liners sliding along the horizon, looking to see if the Devonshire coast was clear, a sure sign of rain. Open sky and sea were contained by the big bay. We looked for hours at the stars moving across our window, knowing we were turning too. There was a sense of great space outside.

Inside it was a bit clammy. Once I thought the sheets were damp, and we took them off the bed and held them in front of the fire to find ourselves in a room full of mist. The only source of heat was the ancient portable gas fire, which gave off a fishy smell. Both our mothers disapproved, and for once they were probably justified as they sniffed and shrugged.

'And to think' my mother lamented, 'you're paying two pounds ten a week for two rooms. And two little small rooms. Dear, dear. And Floss not earning yet.'

'Come on, Mother', I said. 'They're going to let me keep most of the studentship, after all.'

'Well, Jane,' Mrs Jones reminded my mother, 'you know I said they could come to us. It isn't as if there isn't plenty of room in our house. And it's a quiet house, nothing to disturb their studying.'

'Well, Sarah,' my mother said, asserting herself, 'I think young people are better off on their own, though it was very kind of you to offer. And you know what they say about two women in one kitchen.'

'Well, Floss,' Charlie mimicked after they'd gone, 'if you weren't so headstrong you could have shared my Mam's kitchen and she'd have taught you how to make spotted dick and jam roly-poly and find the way to your husband's heart through his stomach.' The Jones family went in for heavy puddings.

I said, 'The mind boggles.'

We knew we were lucky, because our rooms were tucked away at the top of the tall narrow house, and our landlady was friendly and untidy and casual. Two of our friends, another newly married couple, had a nosy landlady who criticized them for not cleaning their rooms properly, and was always popping out as they came and went. We had a gas ring for cooking, the use of nice, slapdash Mrs Howells's oven for roasting and baking, and the messy family bathroom two floors below. I moved in three weeks before the wedding, against my mother's protests. She even offered me Auntie Mary for company. At last I had the room of my own, though I didn't appreciate it at the time. I couldn't wait for Charlie to move in with me.

One night after he had unloaded his usual rucksack of books from home to put on the shelves he was making with bricks and boards, he produced a bottle of whisky and some dry ginger. We drank from the heavy unbreakable glasses his mother had given us out of her vast store of household goods that might come in handy one day. I told Charlie she thought I'd break or wouldn't bother to dry and polish the proper thin wine glasses the Joneses drank their port from at Christmas. We drank each other's health in the thick glasses. We were celebrating our house, our first private space.

'Charlie, why do you want to be married?' I remember asking him, after several drinks. He took the question seriously. I was sitting on the floor, my head against his knee. He was in the ancient armchair. I looked round after he'd been quiet for a minute or so, and he smiled.

'Why? I want us to live together.... Sleep together.... Walk together.... Read together.... Share everything.... We might feel the god pass, together.'

Once, feeling close and calm after making love, I remembered what he had said, and asked him about this brush with god-head. He was shy of saying much. Rank atheist though he was, he had a kind of psychic sensitivity, though he never put a name to it. A skin too few, or an extra sense. There were times when you felt a thinning of the phenomenal world, something like that. He was shy of labelling experience. He had loved Greek and Latin history and poetry at school, and understood the gods' brilliant merging with mortals. Once visiting a client who lived near a famous haunted house in Boreham Wood, he had a funny feeling, and he was always warmest when we played the telepathy game. He once said my trouble was I couldn't see through a brick wall. Sometimes it seemed that he could.

I wasn't surprised when I dreamt about him immediately after he died. He was a very quiet voice on the telephone. It was a bad line and I could hardly hear him. When I asked him if he would be coming back, he laughed at the question in a very natural way, and said with his usual 'ers' and 'ums' that he was afraid he couldn't do that. I knew he was well beyond my reach. I dreamt about Mick too, but that was fleshly. He was back in touch.

That time in the attic I was insensitive to Charlie's gods. I had other fish to fry.

'Sleep together.' I echoed his words and began to cry.

Sobbing noisily, I told him I wasn't a virgin. I apologized. I made such a big drama that he had to respond with some sign of regret, but after saying he was sorry I was so upset, he added drily:

'Neither am I, but it didn't amount to much.'

I cried even more and said, 'It was awful. Don't worry. It was awful. It was boring. It was nothing. It was pointless. Every time.'

I started to go into details, but he didn't encourage my sexual memoirs, or offer his own. Long afterwards he said I had upset him because I'd been so distraught, and it was a bad start. I suppose I was modelling myself on Tess of the Durbervilles, but we ended up in bed, as we had both hoped or intended. It was neither boring nor nothing, though as Charlie said ruefully, 'Er . . . not too brilliant, but we'll improve.' He couldn't stay the night because though he had a latchkey his mother always knew what time he and Davie got in.

I once described Charlie's charming penis to Mick, at his urgent request, but I never told him about that night when we drank whisky and ginger and I went to bed weeping for my lost virginity. Or was it for the pleasurelessness of its loss? I never told Mick how much in love we'd been, either. Or about Charlie's gods, though I thought of them when Mick opened my Yeats to read one of his favourite poems, 'Parting', which amused him by its image of a woman's 'dark declivities'. It came immediately after one of Charlie's favourites, the poem 'Chosen', with its invocation of post-coital stillness:

That stillness . . .
Where his heart my heart did seem
And both adrift on the miraculous stream.

They loved Yeats for opposite reasons, Charlie for the mysticism,
Mick for the sexuality. Mick had once astonished Mrs Yeats, whom
he met at a party in Galway, by telling her he didn't believe in
ghosts.

Mick once asked me why my marriage hadn't lasted. I said
flippantly that I wasn't the marrying kind, but then I didn't think
anybody was. It was a question I'd often asked myself. We were
too young or not young enough, too Welsh or too unWelsh, too
clever or too stupid, too alike or too different, we didn't know
each other well enough, or knew each other too well. The last is
the likeliest reason. Perhaps we were too friendly, too like brother
and sister. Charlie said we spoke the same language, saying it so
thoughtfully that it didn't seem banal. Perhaps Mick and I did
well because we spoke different languages, but took pains to learn
to speak each other's language fluently, though always with a
slight foreign accent.

Once as we lay in the Hans Crescent bed, Mick said thoughtfully that it seemed accurate to say he was crazy about me. I
loved him saying it, but afterwards as I was going through the
afternoon's dialogue, I remembered Charlie's first sudden though
long-expected embrace, in a shelter on the Prom. We had walked
from Brynmill to Blackpill, then back again, and sat down to
look at Swansea Bay. The tide was a long way out.

'I love you to distraction,' he said. I remember the pressures of
his arms round me for the first time.

So we set up house in the attics. In the summer they were dry
and we didn't need the gas fire. We swam and walked in Gower,
visiting the beaches that had been mined and out of bounds during
the war, clambering to the end of the Worms Head, listening to
larks, and watching buzzards and kestrels on Cefn Bryn and
Llanmadoc Down. We went to Snowdonia for our honeymoon,
clambering along spiky Crib Goch and reaching the summit of
black Tryfan, but stopping halfway up Siabod to sleep on its grassy

aromatic slope. Siabod was Charlie's favourite mountain. The very idea of Mick having a favourite mountain was ludicrous. He was urban man, loving parties, gossip, literary conversation, social life of every sort.

On my honeymoon I ripped my new tan shoes climbing a tree in the grounds of our hotel. As Charlie said, unbridelike behaviour. It was my first experience of a posh hotel, and I felt snobbishly self-conscious, as if I were surrounded by people looking curiously at my give-away cautious table manners. Charlie was always more relaxed about things like that. Once at dinner there they served a savoury, after the delicious chicken fricassee. I'd never had anything except a sweet after the main course, though I'd read about savouries in novels. I'd eaten Welsh rabbit, as my mother called it, or rarebit, as Charlie's mother called it, carefully cooked by my father, who was a good cook, unlike most Welshmen. Father's mixture was brown with beer, but this one was so pale that I thought it was custard and heaped it with caster sugar. I took a mouthful, and just managed not to spit it out. Charlie said obviously I wasn't cut out for high life. Life was full of laughs.

It was post-war austerity, and people didn't entertain much, but we would have friends and the brothers and cousins round to the flat for coffee and cake. And invite our parents for tea. Mrs Jones expressed complimentary surprise that my Victoria sponge was better than hers.

'Indeed it's light as a feather. Well done, Florence. Give credit where credit is due.'

I didn't tell her that was because I'd put in three times the recommended quantity of dried egg and half a cup of the free orange juice from the clinic given to me by my cousin Chrissie because the baby always spat it out. I remember making an orange cake, like one we'd eaten in Penryndeudreth, when we were on a climbing weekend before we got married. Charlie offered it to greedy Percy, saying 'This is special cake', and cutting through its glistening sugar top. We christened it Penryndeudreth cake. In our old gypsy days I liked occasionally making cakes and pastry, but we mostly lived on stews and fry-ups. We didn't do any cleaning unless one of the mothers was coming to tea.

When it rained we stayed in bed all day on Saturday or Sunday, and went to bed when Charlie came home from the office for lunch. We discovered sex together. It was our happy time. We liked the same music, the same poets, the same food, the same mountains, the same jokes, even the same Labour politicians. Not that there was much to choose there, Charlie said. He had been delighted by the 1945 election but was worried about the Labour party because it wasn't Socialist enough. Before he died he said we'd all underrated Attlee, and now I often wonder what he'd say about smooth, smart Tony Blair. The mind boggles. He'd understand why it became such an issue for me, deciding whether to leave the party or stay, and why I hung on, though unenthusiastically. He'd been there when the Tories defeated Labour in the autumn of 1951 and I wept. When I talked about English Socialism Mick would listen and sympathize but the subject was foreign. It wasn't part of his history, his growing-up, his class culture.

I finished my thesis, my supervisor liked it, and said he'd give me strong references for university jobs. Charlie started planning to save up and stand for Parliament at some future election. My viva went off like a dream, I began work on my first article, we went to France for our first foreign holiday, and came home to find I had an interview for an assistant lectureship in English at UCL. Charlie saw me off at the station, hugging me and wishing me luck. I was wearing my yellow New Look coat, a brown dress with a full skirt, and uncomfortably high heels. I was terrified.

The Professor of History, the Faculty of Arts representative on the appointments committee, looked at the box that said 'Married' on my form and asked what would happen if I got the job, since I was presumably married to someone who worked in Wales. I explained that of course we had discussed it. My husband would be able to find work as a solicitor, in London.

At first I felt jumpy, not in full control of what I was saying, but when the professor of English asked me whose prose style I most admired, I suddenly felt at home and said 'Hobbes' with conviction. I was reading *Leviathan*, which Charlie loved. I had been struck with its strong colloquial vocabulary and could even quote a sentence where Hobbes used the word 'gang' to describe a set of psychological associations. The professor raised his eyebrows and asked, 'Really? Hobbes? Not Swift?' but he sounded amused and then pleased when I said firmly, 'No, Hobbes.' I was hopeful, almost confident.

When the letter arrived offering me the job, I kissed Charlie, burst out crying, and accepted like a shot.

Mrs Jones was tight-lipped, my mother triumphant. My father knitted his brow, cleared his throat, looked at me, looked down into his cup of strong tea and said carefully he'd always known I'd get on, and he was never one for advising young people, but had I thought about waiting for something to turn up in Swansea or Cardiff, as it would be sure to, sooner or later? Because after all Charlie was very Welsh, a real Swansea boy, and though he knew I was fed up with Wales in lots of ways, he wondered if Charlie wouldn't be a fish out of water in the Great Wen. Charlie told Father it was a bird in the hand as well as a gift horse, and London was full of the Welsh, and though it was better to be Labour in South Wales, the English Labour Party needed real Socialists, and we wouldn't have to stay in the necropolis for good if we didn't like it.

He went to work for Percy's brother-in-law, who was the head of a firm of solicitors in Bloomsbury Square. He never did take to London. He was a fish out of water. He missed the hills and sea. He disliked the public schoolboys who were his colleagues and the barristers with Oxford accents. He never became a Labour M. P. We never saved a penny.

I published my thesis, we stopped climbing in North Wales, had our holidays in France and Italy, and drank wine instead of beer and shandy. We made lots of new friends, mostly through my work, academics and writers. We moved from Bloomsbury to Earls Court. There were lots of parties till Charlie said he felt like a fish out of water, and I'd better give parties when he was in Swansea, and go to other people's parties without him. So I did. I began to spend more time with colleagues and students than at home. I nearly had an affair, then I really had one. We had a trial separation, then a reconciliation. We tried to mend the marriage by having children. I wrote another book, I was invited to lecture in Dijon, Northwestern, and Moscow. I had another affair. Charlie had an affair with a colleague. I got a readership at Royal Holloway College. We got a divorce and Charlie went back to Swansea. I avoided seeing him till first his father died, then poor old Percy, and we met at the funerals. I had an easy menopause which at the beginning I mistook for a pregnancy, contemplated an abortion, and found I was lucky. I tried casual sex, then two semi-serious affairs at the same time. I lectured in Berkeley and Paris and Tokyo. Charlie remarried. I wrote articles for learned journals, reviewed for the *New Statesman* and the *Spectator*, published two more books and got a personal chair.

I tried to write a novel about growing up in Swansea, going to college in Aberystwyth, and getting married to a Swansea boy, but I couldn't. I didn't get beyond the first chapter. I could reinvent my grandparents and most of my uncles and aunts with loving care, but I couldn't write about my mother and father. They turned into music-hall Welshwoman and Welshman. I couldn't leave them out, like Auntie Mary. I couldn't do justice to my mother-in-law, whose woman's lot I could feel for, but whom I never liked. I tried to leap over childhood into late adolescence and marriage, pushing family into the background, but I couldn't change Charlie. I had to tell truth, not fiction. So I stuck to scholarship.

The girls went to university. By the time I met Mick I was a Londoner. Charlie was my ex-husband in Wales, till he died. Mick was my American lover in England, till he died, too.

TWO

Sharing Rooms

I was living without a man in the house, having the time of my life. I liked sleeping alone, in my own room. The first room I had to myself was only mine for three weeks, in the attic flat just before I got married. I slept in my parents' bedroom till I was two, then Idris was born and I moved in with Auntie Mary, my mother's elder sister. She lived with us, gratefully accepting bed and board from her married sister in return for help with the children and the housework.

'She never had a penny of her own,' my mother said when she died.

A spare woman, as I think of her, or an old maid, as the family described her behind her back, she left home at the age of fifteen to go into service. She was short and squat, with bobbed grey hair, and a heavily lined and bristly face which Idris and I found uncomfortable when we had to kiss her, as we did every night before we went to bed. After the kisses she always said 'Good girl', and 'Good boy', even when we'd been terrible all day, answering back, and giving cheek, and acting the goat.

'You know, Floss,' my mother would say, always loyal and doing her sentimental best to make us all love each other, 'she worships you and Idris. You're like her own. You're the son and daughter she never had.'

Mary was a subdued woman, who didn't talk a lot. In the evenings, when she wasn't washing up, scrubbing the kitchen floor for the umpteenth time, or jumping up and down from her

27

favourite hard chair to make a cup of tea, she would sit and knit, white or pink or blue baby-clothes for some first cousin once removed, brown or navy pullovers for my father or Idris. She was a great wireless fan, and I remember her laughing her little thin high quivering laugh at Tommy Handley and Arthur Askey, favourites with her and my father. She would beat time and wag her head when Askey sang his animal ditties, and I used to say that she identified with Mrs Mop but didn't understand why my mother sniffed with disapproval at her catch-phrase 'Can I do you now, sir?', though Idris disagreed, maintaining that Mary was a dark horse. Mary would always say it was very clever and made her laugh till she was bad. My mother approved of my snobbish withdrawal to read in the front room by the electric fire with false coal, because she didn't have time for comedians and used to snort, 'A lot of old nonsense!' or 'A daft lot, if you ask me!' or 'I don't know how you can listen to that rubbish, the lot of you. And our Idris ought to know better, a grammar school boy studying for his CWB!'

If we asked Auntie Mary to tell us a story she never responded with tales of her childhood, like my mother, adventures on the railway, like my father, or ghosts and devils, like my grandpa. She would say she was sorry but she could never remember stories. She never played Ludo or Snap or Tip-It or the Gibbs Ivory Castle game, with Giant Decay lying in wait for children who didn't clean their teeth with the right toothpaste. When we asked her to read to us, she shook her head, saying she wasn't a scholar. My mother took us aside and explained that she could read, but not very well. She'd been born a few years before my mother, when my grandparents had been very hard up, and she hadn't got much schooling.

'She's had a hard life, your poor Auntie Mary. She was only a skivvy,' my mother said in one of her occasional bursts of social bitterness. 'Worked her fingers to the bone, poor devil. She was in service.' My mother spat out the words 'in service' as violently if she was saying 'in prison'.

'She went to work for a farmer's family in Pembrokeshire, near Haverfordwest. Plenty of money and hard as nails. Proper old

Pems. They worked her to death. Dawn to midnight. Mind you, that's what they all did in those days. Girls were slaves. That's why I was always determined that you should go to the university, Floss. I say, I was determined. As well as Idris. Whatever the sacrifice. Though Nana said I wanted my head read. What was I saying? Yes, Mary. They let her come back up home from the farm to Swansea for a few days, because she was run down. Oh, she was bad. I'll never forget her when she came through the door. She was so glad to be back, she sat down in Father's armchair and cried as if her heart would break. She looked terrible. All skin and bone. My mother took one look and said 'No fear! She's not going back to that old farm, whatever you say, Will. I'm not having her get TB like poor Auntie Evie. I don't care what you say!'

The last sentence was purely figurative. Will wasn't saying anything. My grandmother, always called Nana, was head of the household and boss of our whole family, and Will invariably accepted her decisions. She'd been responsible for sending her eldest daughter into service, and she decided to let her come home. Mary stayed with her parents till my mother got married and had her first baby. Mary came to help her, and never left.

My mother escaped going into service. She stayed at school a couple of years longer than Mary, and was a bright girl, a great reader, and very determined. She inherited her mother's decisiveness at a slightly better time for a woman. She didn't have much schooling either, but she went to night-school to do shorthand and typing, got into the Wrens in the First World War, and worked as a typist in the Guildhall till she met my father. He had a clerical job with the GWR.

Auntie Mary was one of the last spinster aunts. I was fond of her, taking her for granted in a patronizing but affectionate way, but I hated sharing a room with her. She smelt of mothballs, snored, and always used the chamber-pot, even after we eventually had an indoor bath and lavatory put in. I used to open the window ostentatiously.

'She can't help it, Floss. It's what she's been used to,' explained my tolerant mother.

Auntie Mary's English was ungrammatical, she dropped her aitches, and she made noises when she drank her tea. I was ashamed of her when I brought my High School friends home, then more ashamed of being ashamed. She was proud of Idris and me, marvelling at our ability to read hard books, do homework, and pass exams, praising us as 'wonderful scholars', and rewarding us with packets of dolly mixtures or Mintoes. I was never sure where she got her money from, but I suppose my parents gave her something. Not that she spent much. She always had the same clothes, a series of shabby black knitted jumpersuits, protected by a pink floral pinny. She looked smart enough in my mother's cast-off hats and coats in chapel on Sunday evenings and Mothers' Meeting on Wednesday afternoons. Unmarried women weren't excluded from the Meeting. Mary had a green bottle of smelling-salts on the bedroom mantelpiece, and would let me have a sniff as a great favour when I begged hard.

'Only one sniff, now, Flossie. It'll go up your nose and you'll start sneezing and your Mam won't like it.'

She had a gilded text over her bed which Nana gave her when she left home to work, 'Thou God Watchest Me'. It was all very well for my auntie, but I wasn't at all keen on the idea of God's ever-open eye.

When I tried to write my novel about Swansea in the thirties I decided to leave Auntie Mary out. All I could say about her life seemed sad, and I didn't think she'd like being in a book, especially as she wouldn't read it. When I went to college she told me she felt lonely in our room without me, and I was astonished. She had never slept on her own before and was nervous. When they were children, they slept several in a bed, and when she was in service she shared a small room with the other servant.

When I went to college I still didn't have a room of my own. Student accommodation in wartime was crowded, and I had to share with my old school-friend, Annie Jenkins, in our digs in Portland Street, Aberystwyth. We were called co-diggers, like miners. I went back to share the room with Auntie Mary while I was doing my Ph.D. thesis and a bit of teaching at Swansea, impressing her with the books in the bookshelves Idris put up

for me in place of Van Gogh's *Sunflowers*, which I cut out of a
magazine and my father framed to put on the wall. When I was
little Mary would take me into her bed and comfort me if I got
nightmares. And if you have to share a bedroom as an adult, she
wasn't bad in spite of the chamber-pot. She went to bed at ten,
long before I did, and rose at half-past six, long before I did. My
mother said it was the pattern fixed by her days in service, when
she had to get up at five to blacklead the grates and light the fires.

From the cramped conditions of our small house I progressed
to the warm marriage-bed in Mrs Howells's attic in Richmond
Road, which I inhabited for those weeks before Charlie moved
in. Then we had a small flat in Bedford Place, handy for the
British Museum, and afterwards a much bigger one in Nevern
Square, where we had the children, and lived for the rest of our
happy and unhappy married life. After Charlie and I split up
our room became mine, but the flat was always full of my daughters
and their friends and boyfriends, not to mention relations coming up to see the big city. When I first took up with Mick, Joanna
and Susie were still at school, but independent streetwise London teenagers, easy to live with. In their holidays they usually
went somewhere with Charlie, and later on with Charlie and
Jean, and visited the grannies in Swansea or their cousins in
Porteynon. Later on they went to Europe and India with friends.
So there was more privacy for me. When my flat was too crowded
we went to Mick's in Hans Crescent or his college rooms in
Magnus. I never had a live-in lover.

At the beginning of my slow break-up with Charlie, before the
children were born, I went off to live with Timmy Rushton for a
couple of uncertain months. He was between wives, as he was
more than once. It didn't work. We were too different. I was too
restless, too fussy, too pedantic, too bonded to Charlie. I couldn't
adjust to Timmy's manners and mannerisms. He left lit cigarettes
balanced on the edge of tables, saying that he never forgot them
and nothing ever got burnt so what did it matter? I couldn't say
it seemed like vandalism in the mind. He peed in the bedroom
wash-basin, assuring me that piss was sterile, and only ammo-
nia. I couldn't stand his radio or records as background to meals,

his vague extravagances, facile enthusiasms, harmless boasting,
and knowing assertions about art and politics, usually nicked
from the Sunday papers. When I nagged, 'Hang on. Give me an
example', several times a day, he looked innocent and aggrieved.
He was quite a good mathematician, I was told, but kept his
intellect for his maths. He had a generous nature, but I couldn't
live with him.

We had some lovely times in bed, and once when I had a
nightmare, he reminded me of Auntie Mary. I woke up to find
his arms round me, and his reassuring voice saying it was all
right, it was only a bad dream. I'd woken him up with my trembling and tossing, so he'd held me and stroked me and told me
to calm down till I relaxed in his arms and woke up. Mary used
to say, 'Never mind, lovie, it's only a bad dream. You've got the
nightmare. Calm down, Flossie fach. Come and cooch down with
Auntie in the warm.'

I don't blame Timmy for anything. We were OK as long as we
weren't trying to live together. He wouldn't have been able to
put up with my sharp tongue and fussy ways for long. I was too
used to Charlie, who never generalized, said if he didn't know
something, was extravagant but knew where the money had gone,
didn't smoke and was very fastidious.

I couldn't sing as I moved round Timmy's flat, as I always
had at home and with Charlie. It was a big furnished flat in
Highgate, with heavy mahogany furniture, and worn fitted carpets.
Timmy said it was a measure of my lack of attachment to him
that I never moved my books and records and pictures. They
stayed in the old flat. Little hooks still pinning me to Charlie.
Sacred objects refusing to move into Timmy's territory. So when
I needed books, I'd go back and get them. When I knew Charlie
was in the office, I'd go and play Purcell or Dowland or Billie
Holiday on our record-player, and gaze at the reproductions of
Gauguin's Tahitian woman, his yellow Christ, and Romney's
portrait of Lady Hamilton. I never gave up my key. After a bit I
moved back and we tried again.

Now that was all over, the divorce was behind me, I'd got
over my promiscuous patch, was well into my third book, *Work*

in Victorian Fiction, and I had left UCL for the readership at Royal Holloway, which was taking in the first men students. I had enough money, and a chair to look forward to in the near future. On my walls there were one or two real paintings. The reproductions had faded or fallen to pieces. Charlie had taken his share of the books and records. I knew what I was doing.

I'd had enough of domesticated love. I'd had enough of tragic sex and grand passions. I occasionally saw Timmy, with whom I stayed on good terms, largely because of his sweet nature. We enjoyed an on-and-off sexual friendship with no jealousy, an extended fling we'd come to value but not overvalue. No hard feelings. Once in a while Mel Hammett, an American academic with whom I'd had a stormy affair, came over from New York, and though we never managed more than a weekend without tears and tantrums, we staggered on, with enough hopes and thrills to keep going. I took Mel too seriously, and Timmy not seriously enough. I tried not to think about Charlie, back in Swansea. There was the occasional one-night stand which I'd learnt to recognize and enjoy for what it was.

All was well except for an occasional irritating desire to have my cake and eat it, to have the room of my own and a steady lover and family friend. I tried hard to put that fantasy in its place as a pressure of history, the habituation to woman's place in a home. I resisted it. I went out a few times with Silas Barth, Liberal MP and television actor, a flamboyant character whom I briefly miscast as that steady lover and family friend. I occasionally brought someone back to spend the night, but I didn't really like doing that with the girls around. I didn't like leaving them on the spur of the moment, either, or for more than a night. Though I was happy, I was annoyed by my subtext, that hankering after permanence. At any rate after someone more permanent than Timmy or Mel or Silas, though not, definitely not, a life-mate, husband, or live-in lover. He was hard to find. I wasn't sure I wanted to find him.

When I was forty I decided that most people of all sexes, whatever they say, want one of three things: one-night stands, a new marriage, or the romantic adultery on which legal marriage thrives and twines like ivy. I didn't want any of them any more, but I found it hard to decide what I did want. Every variation seemed hurtful or under-nourishing, as I had to admit when I found myself imagining a steady lover. What I wanted was a decent relationship between equals, neither casual nor clandestine, domestic nor possessive, trivial nor heartbreaking. Serial monogamy, but you never call it that while it's going on.

I might not be a feminist critic in the strictest sense, but I was a feminist in my private life. I adored the room of my own. Its four walls contained vast space. Like Hamlet's nutshell, but not infinite. I was a modern woman, not a Renaissance prince. I loved my own company.

Once I was walking past some vineyards on a hill outside Dijon, where I was staying for a couple of weeks to give a lecture and seminars in the Faculty of Arts. It was a mild sunny day in early winter. It must have been 1965, because I'd postponed my departure to vote for Harold Wilson in the November election, which Labour won by a narrow margin. That was the news in England. The news in Burgundy was a bad summer, the failure of the grape. I was taking a morning walk before lunch at the *Prés aux Clercs*, a famous restaurant where Henri Talon, generous host, hypochondriac, and famous Bunyan scholar, recommended the *brochet*, which surprised me by taking its name from a weapon, like the English pike. The only time I'd eaten pike before was when Idris caught a big one in Llangorse Lake, put it in a tin, and sent it to me and Charlie in Bloomsbury to cook with claret and oranges from a recipe in *The Compleat Angler*.

It was the first time I'd left the children behind for a trip. As I looked at the bare vines and bright black earth I felt happy, for no particular reason. I had all the old worries about job and marriage and family. Should we stay together? Was it worse for the children to have parents who didn't love each other or parents who lived apart? Could I give up literary criticism and write my novel? Could I go and brain-drain to America and leave them all behind? Would the children come? How could I leave my mother, living on her own after the death of my father and Auntie Mary?

But in spite of the frets and frustrations, I was happy, exceedingly

happy. Suddenly in the Burgundian fields a line from a far culture shot into my head. It came from 'Daffodils': 'The bliss of
solitude'. Good old Wordsworth, I thought. I didn't know at the
time – I don't think anybody did – that the phrase wasn't
Wordsworth's but his wife's, Mary Hutchinson's, from the only
two lines of poetry she ever wrote. When I found out I rejoiced
in retrospect. It was quite right that my vision of random joy in
solitude was articulated by a woman. A wife and mother and
housekeeper, true, but we can all dream. She was described by
her famous husband as 'A perfect woman'. It takes a man's perfect woman, a perfect housekeeping woman, to appreciate the
bliss of solitude, accustomed as she is to its absence. Mrs
Wordsworth did not exaggerate. The word wasn't too strong.
Solitude could be bliss.

I wanted a lot more solitude than I'd ever had. I didn't want
to share a permanent pillow or a kitchen or a sitting-room. I was
disappointed when my friends got married for the second or third
time, like many of the women and all the men. When I was sixteen I said dogmatically to my shocked but sympathetic mother,
always torn between ambition and convention, that I was never
going to marry, never. I ate those words five years later when I
got married at twenty-one, but now in my retarded mid-forties I
was reverting to that first gospel of single blessedness.

I'd tried the old way, and now I could be alone. Except that
stupid desire was prompting the old dream of a faithful and
lasting love. As a dream, it was out of date. I'd served Nature's
purpose. I'd acknowledged that the world must be peopled. I'd
done my bit. When Charlie grinned and said, 'Let's face it, darling,
all those gorgeous curves are only a design for propagation', I
was furious. I only ever wanted to conceive when I was in bed,
but of course that was enough for canny old Dame Kind, hell-
bent on arousing and relieving the ache in an empty womb.

I couldn't turn my experience of desire and conception into a
political programme for single parenthood or infertility or pro-
miscuousness or lesbianism. I couldn't farm out my kids to Cam-
bodian peasants like Germaine Greer, or her ideal woman who
wanted to get pregnant and give birth, and be liberated. I just

did the best I could, with my partial, occluded awareness of history as my history. Charlie's marriage to Jean had lifted the weight
from my overtrained Welsh conscience and I was free. As free as
a Swansea girl brought up between the wars could ever be, I
thought. How free was that?

As Nana used to say, 'God is very good'. Mick turned up at
the right moment. He couldn't leave his incapacitated wife. He
couldn't ask me to marry him. He couldn't move in to my flat.
He couldn't take a permanent share of my pillow or my kitchen
or my living-room. But he could become the steady dream-lover.
He could be a friend of the family, though I never became a friend
of his, only pretending to when he had a few weeks left to live.

It had to be a secret ménage, but it was a ménage. He would
stay overnight and have drinks or a meal with us. He made friends
with my children, and enjoyed telling his jokes to Susie, who
loves jokes and remembers Mick's better than I do. When he
first called to drive me to his flat, there wasn't time for him to
look round, but on his next visit he said, 'Can I look at your
furniture?' He went quickly from room to room, then said, 'Yes,
I like your things better than mine.' I was pleased. He was at
ease in the household. Once he even bought a plug and chain to
fix in the bath, though the odd-job man got there first. But the
household goods and gods remained mine. We never shared them.
And he never played the role of substitute father, like the friend,
not a lover, who enraged the children by turning their music
down and telling Susie to put the top on the PLJ bottle.

'I like it here,' Mick would say, lying in bed or dressing in my
bedroom, looking out beyond my balcony. 'I like our garden in
the city.'

It was never really our garden. I don't think he came into it
more than once or twice, but sometimes he stood on the balcony,
looking at the spotted London planes, the fragile birch just outside my bedroom, the bright pink cherry and red chestnuts in
the spring. The garden was our view from my room. Or our
room. From time to time I admitted that it had stopped being a
room of my own, to become our room. But only from time to
time. Not for good. I could never make up my mind which I

wanted it to be, ours or mine. If I occasionally entertained fantasies about being a caveman's cavewoman, in my full waking I sometimes wished I was living in the middle of the next century. But very often I was content with my lot.

For a decade and a half we saw the garden together, at different times of day, often on Sunday mornings and Saturday afternoons, sometimes on weekdays, in all seasons. We met in middle-age and aged together, like an old married couple.

I gave a lecture called 'The Politics of Proposal'. There are three outrageous proposals in the English novel. Darcy asks Elizabeth Bennett to marry him though he finds her parents awful and has struggled against his desires. St John Rivers asks Jane Eyre to marry him because he needs a fellow-missionary and she is framed for labour not love. Worst of all, Richardson's Mr B asks Pamela if she would marry him if he asked her, to get an eloquent and eager reply. His proposal is provisional, as no proposal must ever be. Unlike Austen and Brontë who set up the proposals to put them down, Richardson doesn't recognize the incorrectness.

There were times when I saw Mick tempted to be Mr B, and held my breath. Once after a quarrel he followed me on to the platform at Oxford station, which he usually avoided. Urging me to kiss and make up, he said I knew we'd be married if he was free. Of course I said crossly I didn't know anything of the sort. In the end he solved the problem cleverly and gracefully. Perhaps correctly. We were in his room, after making love, and he raised his glass.

'Florence, I marry you. Here in Magnus college.' He didn't make it a request so I didn't have to accept or refuse. I didn't say anything. He looked into my eyes, saw something loving in them, and said, 'You're right to take it solemnly.' That was our ceremony.

Mick was never the host in my house. He was a guest with a latchkey, delighted to arrive, sorry to go, appreciative of bed and board, shop-talk and gossip. His wife's illness drove him into domesticity, his standards were low. You only had to make him an omelette or a salad or sew on a button to get grateful praise. He wasn't a substitute husband or the good guest. He was the perfect secret sharer.

THREE

Lovers Meeting

I looked up the date we met in my old green college diary for 1972. It was at a university lecture Mick gave in the University of London's Senate House on April the twenty-first, in a series called the Dale Lectures, endowed by a long-dead graduate now remembered only in the Vice-Chancellor's introductory speeches to the lectures. The date of Mick's lecture, curtly itemized as 'Dale Lecture', is there among all my other academic dates for the busy term. There are my classes on Dickens and Hopkins and Tennyson, tutorials with forgotten names, college and university meetings, a Senior Common Room party, a talk by Fredson Bowers, who made bibliography dramatic, a college dinner for George Steiner where he and Eric Hobsbawm told me off for not reading the papers – or was it for being proud of not reading the papers? – and a public lecture I'd given at Cambridge, at Muriel Bradbrook's invitation.

It was on Jane Austen, and at the party afterwards I'd enjoyed talking to Muriel, whom I always liked, and whose books on Elizabethan drama I'd admired as a student. I had run into her briefly on the frozen shore of Lake Louise, at breakfast in the sunny International House in Tokyo, with big gold and silver carp in the pool outside, and in Kyoto. I had described the ruling passion of Mrs Norris, the horrid aunt in *Mansfield Park*, as piglike greed, quoting what D. H. Lawrence said about our crude classifications of passion. She didn't quite agree with this way of putting it, she said mildly, with her totally concentrated and detached application of mind. I tried to explain what I had meant, and realized that I'd gone too fast, as usual. But she made me feel good, not bad, as real responsive argument does. And I met Tom Henn, who suggested I might go to the Yeats school in Sligo sometime, and talk about Yeats's stories. I said I'd never been to Ireland and had to admit I liked the tales a lot less than the poems. But he had me typecast as a critic of fiction and asked me if I'd read Olivia Shakespear's novels. I promised to read them, and he talked wonderfully about her and Yeats, and the short love poems referring to their attachment. He declaimed the one that tells about the beloved (Olivia in real life) going weeping away after seeing the old love's image (Maud Gonne in real life) in the speaker's heart. And one of the best short poems, repeatable in a breath or two, imaging indelible love-memory as a hare's forme, expanding passion in a small space, beginning with a face that had been Olivia's: 'One had a lovely face/And one or two had charm. . . .'

Henn also had charm, and the grand manner. No taint of the exclusiveness or condescension I snobbishly dislike and stereotype as Oxbridge. I told an old friend about this meeting, a psychiatrist who had been interviewed by Henn for his Oxford scholarship, and he said with amazement that for him Henn summed up the ingroup self-assurance and privilege of the old universities. But for me he was just eloquent and splendid, radiating welcome, fellowship and poetry. The opposite of horrible Sir Wallace Elliott, master of Magnus and friend of Mick's who summed up all I resented, and yet to crash into my social life. I'd read Henn's excellent book on Yeats and looked forward to meeting him again, but he was already ill, and died not long after.

It was a great party, and I enjoyed dinner afterwards with Muriel and with Graham Storey. They walked out and showed me the avenue of red tulips and white cherry-blossom – was it cherry or pear? – in Trinity College gardens. Even before I met Mick and felt my class-envy of Oxbridge compounded by my jealousy of his friends and colleagues, I always felt a mild bitterness at being outside the walls. But that visit to Cambridge was all pleasure, in spite of my nerves before the Jane Austen talk. It was friendship and conversation. It stays as part of that year's spring. I stayed the night with Gillian and John Beer, had good talk about the books we were writing, politics, and our children, and woke in the night to hear the Cambridge clocks chime three and feel a twinge of nostalgia for Mel, with whom I'd spent a weekend in Cambridge a year or two earlier. We stayed at the University Arms when he came over, missing Thanksgiving to interview Leavis for an American journal, and to see me. Now I had almost stopped hankering after Mel, and was pleased to find I felt no more than a twinge. That was the world before Mick.

I sometimes gave Patsy the diary to enter my academic dates, and the Dale Lecture is noted in her neat regular hand. The social entries are scribbled in my pencil or biro and as I flick through the rest of 1972 I see the first appearance of the familiar cryptic notes, 'No appointments' or 'Keep afternoon free' or 'MS', which start after Mick's party in mid-May and go on in all the diaries till 1987. But our beginning was that academic date. We started with work, not play.

We were introduced at the tea-party before his lecture by Randolph Quirk, who was taking the chair:

'Florence, do you know Michael Solomon?'

I got an impression of benign charm and warmth as we smiled and shook hands. Mick joked about his arrival as a Yank at Oxford, his narrow room in Magnus College, the glories of dessert in the Senior Common Room, the poorly attended optional lectures. My impression of warmth grew during his talk, though it was delivered in an uncompromisingly matter-of-fact and undramatized style, read with unselfconscious peerings at the script, and little fluffs and repetitions which didn't seem to embarrass him. I was to hear him lecture many times again, and grew fond of his manner, though it was not my ideal. I like lecturers who think aloud, or at least adopt the language of spontaneous thought, speaking new words with the hesitancy of improvization and not myopic reading. I grew fond of Mick's short sight too.

Two of his talks I especially remember. One was on George

Eliot's relationship with George Henry Lewes. As he read out a dedication of one of the manuscripts (was it *Daniel Deronda*?) to her 'husband', which had been coupled with Shakespeare's sonnet 'Let me not to the marriage of true minds', he paused as if overcome with emotion. He took his glasses off and gave them a wipe with his handkerchief. I felt moved because he was so moved, but he resumed cheerfully, and my neighbour whispered with a smile that he was having difficulty reading his script.

The other time we were at a conference in Denmark, talking about Victorian novels in a beautiful country house near Odense, at the end of a long avenue of pines, in snowy grounds by a frozen lake. Mick surprised me by talking instead of reading, and with affable ease. He was talking about the language of George Eliot's letters, and read some of her descriptions of Lewes, whom he never coyly called a consort or a husband, as one or two other scholars do. There was a nice phrase about Lewes being obtuse of palate, which reminded me of Mick himself. He had some fascinating material about George Eliot, or rather Marian Evans, using contraception, and about John Walter Cross, the younger man she married after Lewes died. Mick's speculations about Johnny Cross's jump into the Grand Canal on the wedding journey to Venice was biographical discussion at its most relaxed, clever, ironic, and funny. And Mick at his best. Afterwards he said he had done it like that to please me. We were so relaxed together too, on that trip, first in a small hotel in Copenhagen, and then in the sun and snow, so far away from England and Wales and America. I was so relaxed that I left my passport and a Victorian paste and turquoise bracelet in that house by the lake, and a chivalrous graduate student drove all the way from Copenhagen and back to get them for me.

On the April evening of Mick's Dale Lecture we left the lecture hall for drinks before dinner in the Vice Chancellor's room. I happened to walk along the corridor with the Vice-Chancellor, a scientist whose name I've forgotten. He smiled and whispered to me with exaggerated confidentiality:

'Now I think that was a very good lecture. Am I right? Was it a very good lecture?'

'Yes', I said, still making up my mind. Months later I reported the conversation to Mick as we were remembering our first impressions, and he liked the Vice-Chancellor's question.

At dinner I sat next to Mick. He pulled out my chair and slipped it under my bottom with the practised agility only found in American men. He didn't start calling me by my name, as Americans of both sexes always do, but quickly inserted 'Mick' before relating some anecdote, to invite me to call him by his name and let me know I shouldn't say Michael.

What did we talk about? His wife's book on Hawthorne's treatment of women, which she had spent years writing. She worked very slowly. When they got married she had made the decision not to work full time, to put family first. The book was published just before her illness was diagnosed as MS, and had been a great success. A friend and colleague of mine had died of the disease, after surviving thirty years, so I was able to listen knowledgeably. Ellen was still in an early stage with lots of remissions, but tired easily, and sometimes found walking difficult. We talked about Hawthorne. I hadn't read Ellen's book, not published in England. He urged me to get it, saying I'd like it as I was a critic of Victorian fiction. She made interesting connections with George Eliot and Thomas Hardy. We got on to Henry James, for whom I had a passion which Mick shared. We speculated about James's mysterious injury, then about his naturalization – was it loyalty to England or an alien's wartime inconvenience? – and returned to Mick's reversed brain drain, his immediate acclimatization to and love for Oxford, and the flat they 'd just bought in Knightsbridge so that he could go to the British Museum – was it still called that? – and Ellen could have lots of opera.

When he asked me about my marriage I said briefly I'd been divorced and lived in Earls Court with my two teenage daughters, and he told me about his children, all slightly older than mine. Somehow we got on to politics – perhaps through talking about schools. I tended to be aggressive on the subject of not exercising middle-class parental choice, except passively, by sending your children to the nearest state school. He assumed what many people who aren't politically conscientious about education do assume, that the school I'd chosen was an exceptionally good comprehensive. I quickly said it wasn't, just run-of-the mill, and anyway that wasn't the point. I treated him to my usual earnest Socialist speech, and he told me solemnly that he did care about politics and had once or twice been on demonstrations and distributed pamplets – was it opposition to the Vietnam War? Civil Rights? Integrated schools? I've forgotten. Mick was the most humane of people, a decent, conscientious citizen, but like most of my American colleagues he was a bit further to the right than his English – and certainly Welsh – equivalent.

For instance, we were never to agree about using professional influence. Mick believed firmly that one thing academics could do was 'help each other's children'. He was as surprised by my disagreement as I was shocked by his assumptions. He was comparing the poverty of university professors with the power and wealth of big business. I was comparing middle-class privilege with working-class disadvantage. But all that was to emerge slowly and piecemeal, in the following months and years. Looking back to our first conversation at the round pale ashwood table in the university dining-room, I see that we were interviewing each other and exchanging credentials.

A little group of us were making our farewells downstairs in the entrance hall of Senate House, and Mick asked the Vice-Chancellor the best route back to Knightsbridge. He had to collect some stuff from his flat before driving back to Oxford. I offered to show him the way. He could drop me in Knightsbridge and I'd go on by tube to Earls Court. I made the suggestion without ulterior motive. I hadn't fancied him, only taken a liking to him.

'There you are,' said the Vice-Chancellor, our Pandarus, 'Take Dr Jones home and she'll be your guide.'

We got into the car, parked outside Senate House, and I concentrated on navigation down St Martins Lane, Piccadilly and Knightsbridge till we reached Hans Crescent.

'Come in,' he said, 'I won't be a minute. I have to change out of these clothes and collect some books, then I'll drive you home.'

I looked round, and got an impression of a *chaise longue*, a small sofa, subdued elegance in a long narrow room. One of the

pictures was a dark, oddly lit landscape, with three hounds running towards a dark wood, and a grey sky with yellow light on
the horizon. Mick had picked it up in an auction because he liked
it, by a painter nobody had heard of. Sinister, I said. I was to
look at it many times, in many moods, with him, waiting for
him, and without him, after he dashed off to drive back or catch
a train, leaving me to take my time. Sometimes I would let myself in with the keys he gave me, hoping for his sake the next-
door neighbour wouldn't come in or out as I fumbled with the
lock of the house or the flat. Sometimes I would ring the outside
bell and Mick would let me in. I joked to him about his love-
nest, and he admitted it had turned out to be one. But it was
always their flat, their bed, with towels over the sheets, to be
carefully remade in their style, with the pillows over the sheets.

In the car that first night I asked him what friends he'd made
in Oxford. We were slowing down at a corner where there was
a bank, a shiny black-walled building which I was to know well,
many a time seeing my reflected legs walking briskly from the
tube to Mick's house, legs detached from body, always the same,
hastening love.

The only people he knew that I knew were Sally and James
Marsden. James had come to lecture at the University of London
Summer School when I'd been tutoring and we'd been friendly
colleagues ever since. Mick and Ellen had been to lunch with
them. When they were introduced to the Marsdens' eight-year-
old son, he had stared at Ellen, and said:

'I know about you. You're very ill, nearly dead.'

I found the story frightening, but made vague explanatory noises.
Robert was a difficult and strange boy; children could say awful
things. It wasn't the parents' fault. Mick sounded grossly offended
as he told the story, and brushed aside my excuses, saying resentfully the boy must have heard his parents talking. I didn't
ask him any more. He didn't say what they might have been
talking about, Ellen's illness, or Mick's domestic problems. His
touchiness about the incident, like his uninhibited recommenda-
tion of Ellen's book, made me cast him for the role of uxorious
husband. And in a way I think I was right. He had been an

uxorious husband, despite having a wife less keen on sex than he was. They had always done everything and gone everywhere together. He was a loyal admirer of her intelligence and her writing. He remained an uxorious husband to an invalid, taking great care never to let gossips catch wind of our affair, for her sake. He became my uxorious lover, if fidelity and attentiveness and possessiveness count. It's a pity there's no equivalent word for the unmarried lover's devotion.

As he slowed down to drop me at my house, I said I hoped they'd come and have dinner with me sometime when they came up for a London weekend. He said afterwards he'd been touched by my spontaneous-sounding invitation but had been wondering if he could kiss me. Instead, he grabbed my shoulder, thanked me, said they were having a party in two or three weeks, he'd send me an invitation, and hoped I'd be able to come. We said goodnight. I'd had a good evening, and as I undressed I thought I'd made a new friend.

Beginning with Charlie was like that too, I suppose. Friendly. We knew each other first when we were both still at school. He really was the boy next door, a few years older than me. I would watch him from our front room, going off on his bike with friends, and say hullo to him in the street. I would see him in Cwmdonkin or Singleton Park or on the Prom with girls. I would see him in Home Guard uniform. I heard all about him from my mother's serial narrative, over the years.

He was a nice boy, very clever, very upset when he was classed as C3 because of his eyes and couldn't join the Army. His mother and father were proud of him. His brother Davie was an electrical engineer, in a reserved occupation. Charlie had done well at school, taken five subjects in Higher instead of the usual three, but he couldn't go to university like his brother because their business had failed so he'd gone into Cedric Beynon's office to work for his articles. Mrs Jones had been keen for him to go into the Church, and was upset when he refused because he was an atheist. I remember the horror my mother put into the word. Or perhaps I'm inventing it, as I sometimes find myself doing with my parents' moral attitudes.

I was too young to go out with boys when I first knew him, and still too young for him when I started, going for walks on the Prom after Sunday chapel with Johnny Harris and Dai Mason, my first innocent Swansea boyfriends. Charlie wasn't a student, like Johnny and Dai. He worked. We only got to know each other after I went to college, in Aberystwyth, became interested in politics, and decided I was a Marxist. I went out in the vacation with old schoolfriends, Joan Roberts and Glenys Watkins, who had gone to Swansea University and were keen members of the student Socialist Society, Soc. Soc., which had members of all colours from pale pink to deepest red. They used to meet in Rabiotti's ice-cream parlour or the Kardomah, and knew Charlie, who would join us and sometimes walk home with me. I told him about a paper I was writing for the Students' Literary Society in Aber, a crude Marxist analysis of Thackeray. Charlie knew much more about Marx than I did, though he never went through my Communist phase. A man of rational passion, sensitive in ways I didn't suspect at first, he didn't experience my intense adolescent religiosity either. We were walking past the Tenby, in Walter Road, when I started to say something about the cash nexus, and his ginger eyebrows shot up.

'You don't say?' he grinned, affecting the jokey American accent he and Percy acquired from the Hollywood gangster films. It was intended to send itself up, as well as mock any hint of jargon or pretentiousness. Goaded by his rudeness, I defended myself resentfully, then started to look at him with interest. I spent the next couple of weeks refining my arguments, and re-reading *Vanity Fair*, and reading *Das Kapital* from beginning to end, discovering to my pleasure the wonderful discussion of money and *Timon of Athens*. The paper I gave was much better for my put-down by Charlie. If it was a put-down.

The *odi* became *amo*, passing through friendship to a hopeless crush on my part, which disappeared in the course of my Aberystwyth love-life. He was so much older than I was – actually only seven years, but even that seemed a lot when I was nineteen. Nothing happened for a couple of years, till I decided to do my Ph.D. thesis at Swansea instead of Aberystwyth, because it was cheaper to live at home. I started going to a discussion group which met in various people's houses. We gave papers on the poets and novelists of our day, Auden, Spender, Koestler, and Rex Warner, on town planning and post-war reconstruction, and we had play-readings. Charlie gave an impassioned talk on Lewis Mumford, but my attraction to him really revived when he read the part of the American in Shaw's *The Applecart* with the phony accent and comic abandon. Then I read Mrs A, the little woman, and he read Mr A, the little man, Auden's choric couple in *The Ascent of F6*, and things began to look promising. I had gone canvassing with him for the 1945 election but we were both seeing other people at the time. It was a slow process.

With Timmy it was quick, an accelerated case of dislike turning to attraction. I thought him brash, as perhaps he was, but charming and remarkably good-looking. He made a proposition, I laughed, he made a pass, and I felt the charm. Eventually the scales fell from my eyes and I was back with those first impressions of shallow wit and facile appeal. I never bore him – or myself – any ill-will for the misplaced desire. If I'd met him before Charlie we might even have married, but we certainly wouldn't have lasted as long.

A couple of times it was the lightning-stroke. Once at a dance in Aberystwyth I noticed a big handsome man with an odd triangular face. He was leaning against the wall, surveying the scene and I was talking to my friend Annie as we waited to be asked to dance. I asked her if she knew his name.

'That's David Smithie', she said in impressive tones. 'He's captain of the rugby team. He's English, and not a student. He works in dairy research. He's quite old.'

As she spoke and I looked, he caught my eye, detached himself from the wall, and came over to ask me to dance. He was the first Englishman I knew, studying diseases of dairy cattle in the Department of Chemical Agriculture. I was maddened by his posh accent, and casual references to maids and country houses, but he was glamorous beyond words, and our passion started with that exchange of looks across a crowded room. It never seemed like a cliché to me.

The other bolt from the blue was my passion for Mel. He also met and kept my glance. We met in the welcoming reception at the beginning of a conference, and when we went to our rooms after dinner he telephoned, inviting me to come and have a drink with him.

I can clearly hear his offhand drawl, 'It's that obnoxious American, Hammett.'

We didn't get our drink. The conference bar was closed, and we went for a walk in the empty streets of the Canadian city, empty except for big cars, its buildings near and huge. As we walked along the narrow pavements, exchanging our stories, a sudden mist came down, swirling round so that we could hardly find our way back to the university lodge.

'I think they're trying to tell us something,' Mel said. Before we got back he had kissed me, and he had told me about his wife's illness. He had a sick wife too, and had to become a house-husband for a while. He was a rehearsal for Mick. In some ways. Mel was one of those brilliant beautiful people constantly led into temptation, spoilt by getting all the lovers they want, and some they don't. He became addicted to promiscuity. He was a hopeless romantic, and very much the married man. Mick's genius was quieter, he was a realist, and not dangerously gifted with good looks. He had been a faithful husband, and was a faithful lover.

For Mick it began with a mixture of love and lust at first sight, backed by his need and decision to acquire a replacement for sick Ellen. For me it was my usual laziness, a friendly feeling, and the fantasy of undomesticated steady loving. He'd been clever to say on our third meeting, the first time we were alone, a week after the party:

'Pretend you like me.'

Pretence was a charm, a bridge from unreality to reality. I was a method actor getting into the skin of my part.

The week before, I'd gone to that party with a slight and general sense of expectancy. I glanced round, as I often did in those foot-loose fancy-free days. I was half-consciously on the look-out. But I wasn't looking at Mick, the uxorious husband, whose wife I would get to know when they came to dinner with me. I was genuinely startled when he voiced his delicately phrased proposition.

'Would it amuse you to meet me unprofessionally?'

He sounded spontaneous. He had left the suggestion to the last minute, as I was putting on my coat in the bedroom. I was making a stupid joke about Marilda's mink lying on the bed, saying I'd often thought the easiest way of getting a fur coat was to pick up the wrong one after a party. I don't know if he heard, because he immediately put his question. Some time later I asked him if he'd decided what to say in advance, and he said:

'Yes, I'm afraid I did. Is that bad?'

A week later we met and went to bed. The following weeks laid down our routines. He would telephone me early in the morning, last thing at night, and at odd times in the day, at home or at work. I would take the train to Oxford and the tube to Knightsbridge. On Saturday afternoons he would come over to Earls Court, while Ellen slept. Early on Sunday mornings we would walk with Antonio, his poodle, in the park, while Ellen slept. We would meet at Albert Gate, eager and punctual lovers. I liked to arrive early, and watch for him as he walked up William Street. We walked round the lake, up and down the paths. The ducks and pigeons were courting. Once he said no minute of the time would be lost. Once he said he would be glad when it had been going on for years.

One Friday afternoon coming into the flat I stood still and looked round. I looked hard at one of the pictures, a black and red Appel lithograph I'd bought in a little gallery in Evanston. It hung over the old brown leather Edwardian sofa from Harrods second-hand furniture department, where you could once pick up bargains. I felt happy. So happy I wondered why. Then with a mild shock I realized I was feeling happy because I was in love. I was amused by my own solemn process of tracing cause from effect. It seemed silly. But I didn't mind. Mick and I were middle-aged, but everything was new again. It was early June, nearly summer.

We gave each other our books and articles, composing cryptic, amorous inscriptions. I spent much of the night reading or rereading his books. I had read a lot of his work before, and liked it, but now I was savouring something personal, in mind and words. I tried to find the cadences and language of his speaking voice in his prose. His talk was relaxed and slangy in style, his written prose elaborate, sometimes stiff, often polysyllabic and erudite, sprinkled with words like 'congeries' and 'exfoliate'. I told him exfoliating was a term used by advertisers of cleansing cream. But now and then the style would relax, and become colloquial and slangy. It was the beloved's mannerism. Reading the books was like brooding over love-letters and love-speeches, but in public print. Perhaps he felt something similar, but I hadn't written so much, and my work was more conventional. Mick's was bolder, and though he had stopped writing poetry, his prose was a poet's. Best of all was the volume of poems, *Passages*, though I was jealous of the love-lyrics, glad they were abstract, impersonal, and metaphysical, and addressed to the passions or the gods rather than people.

He would present books to me when we met, and packages kept arriving through the post. On my birthday I got his new biography of Dickens, replacing cautious Edgar Johnson. It was lying on the hall table with parcels from my mother, Idris and Gaynor, and cards from cousins and friends. I carried them into the flat, and tore into Mick's parcel. My colleague Neil had come back with me from a staff meeting to have dinner, and as I unwrapped the book I asked him what he'd like to drink. He said he'd wait so that I could open my birthday mail. I opened Mick's present, looked at the intimate inscription in his cramped handwriting, then at the affectionate printed dedication to Ellen, put it on the mantelpiece and went into the kitchen to take the wine out of the fridge. When I came back Neil was looking at the cover of the book, in the idle curious compulsive way of a scholar. I didn't know if he'd read what Mick had written, 'O *Florence! O ma reine!*' Neil shared my republican dislike of title and I half-expected him to make a joke about the inappropriate royalist metaphor, but if he saw it he was too tactful or embarrassed to comment. He was an amusing, unmalicious gossip, and I don't know if he gossiped about Mick's inscription. He didn't say anything, just tactfully flicked through the pages, put the book down, and drank my health. I didn't care. I was to become a model of discretion but in those early weeks I didn't care.

In the notes for my novel about Mick, I thought either of having us meet on a balcony in a Manhattan party, or picking each other up in a café after visiting the Sistine Chapel. In the New York scene the lovers discussed vertigo and suicide, agreeing that they were tempted to jump from the high apartment, twenty storeys above the street. As they talked they drank martinis, ate cheese, and fell in love. In Rome they disagreed. Hot from the Michelangelo 'Creation', 'Clara' insisted that it was the uncreated Eve who was looking over God's shoulder as he fingered Adam, but Mick – or rather 'Daniel' – said it was an angel who looked like Eve because the faces were identical. Angels, prophets, young men, sibyls, Adam and Eve, they all looked alike except for God whose features were hidden by his beard. As they talked they ate garlicky drumsticks, drank fizzy mineral water and fell in love.

The sketched conversations were designed as beginnings. They were meetings loaded with premonition, vibrant with death and love. But they were useless, far too solemn, no medium for Mick's fond kidding understatement and my tender prickly caginess. I gave up. It was hopeless. I couldn't change the real beginnings, those London meetings in Bloomsbury, Knightsbridge, Hyde Park, and Earls Court. So I kept the places and most of the events and only changed the characters' names.

It was too good to reinvent. Too good to be true and far too good to be made untrue. Surprise of happiness. Meeting in April. Hopeful omen of tulips and cherry-blossom. Middle-aged love bright-eyed like young love. A promise of permanence. The unpeeling of the leaf. All that. Arrival of the dreamed-of one, friend of the family, tone-deaf wit and short-sighted funny man, midnight and dawn visitor, fellow-scholar, inspired amorist, my *semblable*, my twin.

FOUR

The Saturday Dance

It was the Easter vacation and I was working at home, rewriting my introduction to *Cousin Phillis* for the umpteenth time. Each rewrite got more feminist, which was good. I have a problem about putting my real day-by-day practical feminism into my work. I think I'm liberated as lover and mother, but I'm not explicitly committed to politics as a critic. When I was very young, between thesis and teaching, I was a crude Marxist, and when I started to think of myself as a critic, leaving Marx behind, everyone was a New Critic, rejecting the old literary historians. The only live Marxist was Arnold Kettle. We still read Christopher Caudwell, but he was more of a poetic anthropologist than a critic. After I published my first book, on Elizabeth Gaskell – whom we still called Mrs Gaskell – a man came up to me in a party and asked nastily if I only wrote about women writers. I was taken aback, then cross, but it never occurred to me to say 'Yes, of course', as I would now. I said stupidly that I'd only written one book and I was going to write about Thackeray next. Reading my early book now I see feminism implicit in it, but not spelt out.

When I was teaching at Northwestern in 1969 women students lined up outside my door to complain about the absence of women professors, tell me about the Boston Amazons, and ask about Doris Lessing, one of the few living writers they could wholeheartedly admire. I recognized the old political desire to find ideals and models in art which I felt in my student days as a socialist,

53

not a conscious feminist. A decade later I read the American and French feminists but they were too Freudian for me, even the post-Freudians. For me Freud is a maddening misogynist. And a good laugh.

Imagine dreaming up penis-envy. Imagine going to bed with someone who believes in penis-envy. There's a bit of sense, as my mother would say, in the Oedipus complex and Freudian slips, but Sophocles and Shakespeare wrote about them first. Of course that's stupid. I hated his partition of the mind, but it's hard to dispense with super-egos and ids. As Charlie said, they come in handy. Mick said it was an uphill struggle being a biographer without Freud, but reminded me that Freud had made the metaphors we grew up with. I admitted I'd been awed by Eros and Thanatos, his governors of impulse and negation, though perhaps more because of Auden than Freud. It was with Mick that I finally understood Auden's great line, 'He taught us to be enthusiastic over the night'. An urgent Freudian message for the offspring of Welsh puritans. I first read it in Charlie's *Another Time*, which he didn't take with him when we split up. Its emerald-green paper cover is falling apart.

Mick said feminists would find me too sympathetic to authors who are too sympathetic to their male characters. It's the same with my socialism. I read Marx but I was rooted in the Welsh working-class tradition, too undoctrinal to shape literary response and judgment. I read later literary Marxists like Frederic Jameson, whose writing is passionate and lucid, and as I read I'm persuaded. But when I write I'm back to text and form, in the old way. I hate forcing political correctness and it's nice to find it emerging effortlessly from concentration, which can bring out the history in things.

That April morning I made some coffee and telephoned Patsy, our super-efficient departmental secretary, to ask her about mail from other universities. Someone might want an urgent reference or a three thousand dollar lecture in Santa Barbara. It was raining and I watched the drops slide down the pane as Patsy read out a couple of routine requests for reviews and then said:

'There's one here from Oxford, Magnus College.' I knew it was

Mick. He said I'd be getting an invitation to a party.

So I said 'OK. Patsy, do you mind opening that one, please.'

She said doubtfully, 'It begins in Italian.'

'Italian? What Italian?'

She pronounced in her perfect accent, '*Cara nome*', then said 'Oh, it's just an invitation', and read it out.

Years later when I was telling Mick how I never seemed to go to the opera after I met him, he said 'Do you remember when you were '*Cara nome*?' and I saw the rainy window and heard Patsy's Italian.

I was misled about his musicality, which turned out to be non-existent, like his love of nature. I don't think he was tone-deaf so much as completely unaural. He was actually a bit deaf. He even tried a hearing-aid but found the amplified background noise impossible. Unless we sat in the front row at the theatre he invariably fell asleep. (We used to book for seats next to each other but arrive and depart separately.) During all our years together we didn't go to a single concert or play a record or hear music on radio. I have a dim memory of him once humming a snatch of some old comic song – perhaps by Schnozzle Durante, if Schnozzle Durante ever sang songs. I suppose he put the Italian because he was poised between politeness and solicitation, a bit shy, like my first boyfriend Rob Lewis, who hadn't said 'I love you' but '*Rhiw'n garu di*'. And Mick wouldn't have wanted the letter to sound routine. He'd asked me not to look in my diary to see if I was free for our first date because he didn't want it to be just any old appointment, a matter of free days and cancelled engagements. I have the letter still, the only one of his hundreds of letters which isn't a love-letter, strictly speaking. Unstrictly speaking, it is:

Cara nome,
The *fete galante* will take place on May 13, at Flat 2, 19, Hans Crescent. I'm looking forward to seeing you again, between 5 and 8 o'clock. Till then.

> Yours ever,
> Mick

I went expecting a lover of opera, and found Mick. He once gave me a record, in the early days when he would ask what I'd like for a Christmas or birthday present, and I was too polite to say I hated being asked. I said I'd like a replacement of a record I'd loved and lost, *'Bist du bei mir'*. Perhaps Charlie took it when he left. The singer Mick chose, probably after asking advice in Blackwells' music department, was Marilyn Horne, too rich and fruity and complacent for my taste. The version I'd lost, which Charlie gave me, was thinner and purer, more heartbroken. I've forgotten who the singer was. I shouldn't have asked for a sacred object to be replaced, and the new one never became a love-memory. It served me right. I once did it the other way round when I put a line from a poem I wrote for Mick, 'A longing so like prayer', in an elegy for Charlie. The words fitted remorse better than desire. I was too shy to show my first poem to Mick, because what I wrote was so different from his cool elegant meta-physical verses, so he never knew about the little betrayal. But things have a funny way of levelling out.

The Solomons' party was our second meeting. I can't remem-ber what I had on, though I know what I was wearing when we first met at the tea-party before his lecture, a wine-red and grey stripey velvet dress with a long skirt. It's in the dressing-up box. Mick opened his door and said 'Hi'. Weeks later he told me he was disconcerted because I didn't look as he remembered. I didn't bother to ask if he'd been disappointed, just said 'Too bad' and gave him a kiss. By then it didn't matter.

He showed me into their small bedroom. I took off my coat – a heavy coat, long and red, so it must have been a cold spring day – and threw it on the big bed, covered in coats, that I was to get to know so well, then followed him into the sitting-room where I'd waited after the lecture. It was full of talking people. He introduced me to Ellen.

She was sitting still and upright in a big armchair. Her full image comes from later meetings, years afterwards, but I got a first impression of dark sharp eyes behind round glasses, and a white face. I didn't notice what she was wearing, then or ever. I met her five times, in fifteen years. I remember saying I'd met

Mick after his lecture, and he'd told me about the book on
Hawthorne and how good it was. She gave a little cool surprised
but not unpleased smile and said, 'Did he really?' Then some
other people came up and I was introduced to a gushy thin woman,
also American, wearing emerald-green velvet. She was Marilda,
the interior decorator who had done their flat. I looked round
the room for the second time, wondering how you could ask
somebody else to choose your colours and furniture and stuff.

I had longer to look this time, and there was more light. There
was the little sofa, the *chaise longue*, the mahogany table, and a
few slim and shapely chairs, toning in with curtains and carpet
in shades of lime-green, dark green and grey. No cushions or
rugs, but one or two small pieces of ceramic and silver, well
spaced on mantelpiece and window-sill, and a few pictures, well
separated and perfectly lined up, on the pale walls. A small
Epsteinish bronze of a woman's smooth head. The painting of
hounds running in a landscape by the painter nobody's heard
of. The books on a bookcase, neatly ranged, as Aziz says in *A
Passage to India*, not sprawling or crammed together or shoved in
horizontally. After a bit I went into the bathroom, and there were
four or five books stacked on a shelf by the loo, a Thurber, the
Penguin Book of American Verse, a couple of *New Yorkers*, and *Pride
and Prejudice*. They stayed there for the fifteen years I was to
visit the flat. Of course it wasn't their main house, but their London *pied à terre*. When I paid my two visits to their house in
Oxford just before his death, that was inelegant and lived-in and
untidy. I was as envious of the intimate mess in the rambling
house as I was jealously turned-off by the elegance and order of
the small flat. I envied their household gods and their friends
and their parties, but I didn't want them. It wasn't quite sour
grapes.

I took a strong instant dislike to Marilda, which returned whenever Mick mentioned her, though I never saw her after the party.
That was clairvoyance. There was nothing wrong with her, or if
there was I didn't get to know her so I never found out. Later on
she simply offended me by being one of the characters in Mick's
other life, a friend of horrible Ellen's, like Sir Wallace Elliott and

his wife Elizabeth. Your lover's family friends are your enemies. But that night I had no idea he was going to be a lover. I talked to Marilda again later on, just before I left, and she told me how much she admired Mick, to which I could find no reply. I remember saying I had to go on to another party, and she said 'How very gay' in a bright artificial voice. Of course, you could still say that in the early seventies.

Ellen and I didn't meet again for many years. Once it was by accident at Logan airport. I was waiting at the gate and they paged me, because two of us had been allocated the same seat. After it was sorted out I saw Mick coming towards the desk, having heard my name. We'd met the week before at a Holiday Inn in Chicago, and knew we were coming back on the same day, but not that we would connect with the same Heathrow flight. Mick said apologetically that I'd better come over and say hullo, so I did. After take-off he joined me, in the next seat which happened to be empty. Ellen was asleep fifteen rows back. I was unnerved by her nearness as Mick and I touched. At Heathrow they had a car waiting, and went off without another encounter. It was a chain of unlikely happenings, the mistake in seating, my name on the public address system, the cancelled flight which brought Mick and Ellen to Boston, the empty seat. In a Thomas Hardy novel the linked chain would end in discovery, but our luck held. It ended in lovers meeting.

Another time it was a brief exchange at a big party, where the guests were seated at two tables, and Ellen and I were as far apart as we could be. I once saw her in the distance at the Royal Court at a production of Beckett's *Not I*, but I knew they were going so I was able to avoid a meeting. There was a brilliant hysterical performance by a terrifying Billie Whitelaw which almost took my mind off the thought of Mick and horrible Ellen in the audience. That was the time Jo and Susie saw her. They managed to get a look when buying ice-cream in the interval, and reported loyally that she wasn't very good-looking. I remember wearing a black crepe trouser-suit from Biba in which I always felt good-looking. I still have the trousers.

Ellen was good-looking enough, I thought, as I moved away

from her corner of the party. Your lover's household is bad territory. Bachelard's poetics of space leaves out stuff like that. I didn't know then that it was my lover's place. Only that the two rooms in Knightsbridge couldn't have been more different from my cluttered flat, a stone's throw away in Earls Court, crammed with vases, bowls and jugs, live and dead flowers and pot-pourri, books, magazines, typescripts, letters, bills, old teddy-bears, Noah's Ark animals and dinky toys, fans, shawls, masks, puppets and dolls from Japan and India and Turkey. Walls crowded with Susie's caricatures, torn posters I'd meant to frame, and Charlie's unframed photographs of Welsh limestone cliffs and caves and mountains, Florentine towers and arches and old shops in narrow streets. Magpie junk picked up and never thrown out. Rich unexcavated strata of marriage and family. The Solomons' flat was beautiful, in a subdued way, carefully thought-out and harmonized. The carpets were wall-to-wall softness, a dark grey-green. Our rainbow floors were our pride and joy.

Charlie and I borrowed money on an insurance policy to buy our first carpet, for two hundred pounds, a lot of money in 1950. I still have it in my sitting-room, a Persian carpet about a hundred years old, made in Agra, its colours faded but distinct, dim rose-red, lime-green and a wonderful soft sand-colour. We wanted colour and pattern for floors as well as walls, and it was our first big extravagance. We used to sit on it and trace the curves, working out the shifts of ageing weave and tone. Like everything we bought, it was a choice. We began by not being able to afford new furniture, and ended by loving old things.

When I knew Mick better I asked him why they got an interior decorator and he said Marilda was an old friend, Ellen was too sick to cope, they'd just come over from Boston and he was starting the new Oxford job.

'And learning to be a woman', he said, grinning. 'I do all those woman things now, you know.'

I supposed he meant bedpans and washing and laundry, and I shied away from the domestic detail. At that moment I was glad his wife was ill, but didn't want to think about her illness.

The Solomons' dog, a pale-brown poodle called Antonio,

bounded up to thrust his head under my skirt. I pushed him off. Mick laughed and said 'I'm afraid he's uninhibited.' Antonio was to play a prominent part in our early meetings, because Mick would bring him out for a walk when we met in the park. When Mick saw the film *A Touch of Class* he told me the story and said it was a parody of our affair, down to dog-walking and dinners. But Ellen and I weren't rival cooks. I only made one show-off meal. And Mick never forgot Antonio. Once he got in a fight with another dog, and I was impressed by Mick's control and presence of mind. I hadn't thought of him as a man of action, and there he was dealing coolly and calmly with two big snarling creatures, snapping and rising up on their hind legs. He asked me to stand back as he held and quietened Antonio, speaking to him in a reasoning voice. It was all over in two or three minutes.

I remember Mick laughing and saying, 'They looked heraldic, didn't they? The lion and the unicorn.'

When Mick and Ellen first came to live in England Antonio had to go into quarantine for six months. Mick told me how he used to visit him. I was touched, though I don't keep pets and I'm not mad about dogs.

I asked 'Did you talk to him?' and he said, 'Well, yes I did.'

I didn't talk to Antonio or fondle him, but I occasionally gave him a polite pat. It seemed wrong to forget such a peaceful and pretty creature in my novel so I changed him to a black cat called Merlin.

Mick held Antonio back from my velvet skirt, and introduced his younger daughter, Sandy, a thin fair girl carrying round a tray of vol-au-vents. Fragments of conversation float into my head. Someone said something about a *bouquet garni*, Mick praised their French, Marilda explained loudly that it's a common kitchen term. Mick's French was good in a literary way but his kitchen ignorance almost matched his ignorance of music and nature. As I gobbled the delicious Harrods titbits I reflected on the ease of giving a party where you buy all the food and mix pitchers of whisky-and-soda and that's that. I can never shed my Swansea-trained insistence that hospitality means sweating for three days over a hot stove and cooking everything yourself single-handed.

The drink was plonk in the parties Charlie and I used to give.

Mick took me over to a woman sitting on a divan. She had a round ordinary face, lit by intelligence, and looked straight at me while Mick introduced her as his editor, Clarice Blount. For a full minute I smiled and searched my mind for the nagging lost link. It came. I'd been spending a couple of days with Mel, in a hotel in New York, wondering whether I could leave Charlie and my job to get a divorce, marry Mel, and go on a honeymoon canoe trip to the Okefonokee swamp. When Mel talked about the canoeing and the alligators and the eagles and promised it would be heaven, I laughed and said, 'Well, perhaps I will then.'

Mel left me in the Berkeley for a couple of hours because Clarice was being given a farewell party by her publishers. She was about to leave America for ever, after a terrible love-affair. She and her lover – by then her ex-lover – couldn't inhabit the same city. New York was too tiny. I can taste my room-service martini, sipped as I watched a news programme with pictures of Eisenhower, then Mel came back back on the dot, with that punctuality which always seemed astonishingly out of character.

I said, 'I thought Ike was dead,' and Mel laughed, 'So he is.'

Mel told me about the party. Everyone was there, Robert Lowell and his present wife and his previous wife, Alison Lurie, James Merrill, and Mary McCarthy. Mel told Clarice he had a friend in London, somebody nice – very, very nice – and gave her my college address in case she wanted to call. But she never did and I hadn't thought of her from that evening in Manhattan to this evening in Knightsbridge.

I said I knew a friend of hers, Mel Hammett. I'd seen him just after he'd been to her leaving party in New York. She looked thoughtful and said she remembered. She was probably just remembering her party and saying goodbye to them all and to New York. I'd been saying a similar goodbye, though I didn't know it at the time. When Mick and I became lovers I hadn't forgotten Mel, who had probably forgotten me. It felt peculiar to have him brought into Mick's party. Now it seems appropriate, being off with the old love before getting off with the new, and another reason for not thinking about Mick in an amorous way at the time, even after *'Cara nome'*. I was still not quite finished with loving Mel.

Mel and I once had a party for two by a river in New Hampshire. He brought an ice-box which contained not only ice but chilled glasses. Someone had given him the typescript of an anthology, hoping he'd do an introduction. We swapped pages to and fro, reading bits aloud, laughing or solemn, agreeing and disagreeing. Then in an interval between poems we suddenly start to argue. I try to remember what it was about, but all that comes back is my anger. We're trembling on the verge of a quarrel. Mel smiles at me, refusing to be hostile. He says, 'Stop. Please stop. Hang on.' He stops the quarrel. He reasons us back into fondness. I know I'll never be angry with him again. We go back to the poems. The only one I remember is James Kirkup's poem about a surgeon performing a mitral stenosis valvulotomy. I can hear it in Mel's voice though for all I know I read it to him.

Other parties with Mel come back. One in his hotel room at a Holiday Inn, late afternoon drinks set up to charm some of my London colleagues at the conference, who didn't care for his larger-than-life-size glamour and ironic brashness. He wanted them to like him because they were my friends and he thought they disapproved of our affair. I liked sitting on the bed, all dressed up, neither guest nor host, watching Mel stir the gin. When they are all there, seated on a chair or the wide bed with martinis, he plays records of Lee Wiley. He is behaving himself, charming and quiet. He isn't showing off, but asks politely if she's known in England.

'She's wonderful. I hope you agree. Listen, right on the beat.'
Jack and Cara listen and relax.
'You do something to me
Something that simply mystifies me.'
And after that,
'I've got a crush on you, sweetie pie.'
The sun's shining and it lights the faces, Mel's straight fair hair, the ice in clear crystal, the blue plastic beaker of icy Beefeater gin and martini.

Mel was a good jazz pianist, and at the farewell party he played for us to dance, not dancing himself. The man I was dancing with said:

'I thought I'd ask the pianist's bird to dance. And see if he minded.'

I didn't mind. I felt pleased. I loved being the pianist's bird. Mel minded a bit, saying with a shrug, 'You danced with all those old men'.

But they weren't old. It was a light interlude in a heavy affair. When Mel called himself Heathcliff – an all-American, Brooks Brothers Heathcliff – that was a bad joke with a grain of truth.

I only danced in Wales. Swansea parties began as kids' parties, but I remember them becoming grown up. We didn't dance until we were students. At school, still called pupils, we were graduating in our early teens from 'Postman's Knock' to 'Hyde Park Corner' and I remember being kissed for the first time by somebody with a beery open mouth, and feeling sick. But it was a game and you had to play. And when I was invited to a sequel party, given by some of the boys but under cover of an invitation from a girl, Betty Harris, I was flattered and disappointed because I had a boring all-girls party on and couldn't go. A bit later when I was seventeen, in the Lower Sixth, I went with my friend Sheila Norman, in the Upper Sixth, to a students' farm-camp in Herefordshire. We had sing-songs and seances and a few mild necking sessions, but no orgies.

Party games were exciting, and not only when there were boys. I remember the thrill of playing 'Murder in the Dark' and 'Sardines' in Joan Roberts's big house on Knoll Avenue. Your heart beat fast with fear of hiding and waiting to be silently murdered or surprised in some dark corner. The dread was bound up with the wonder and envy of people rich enough to live in such huge rambling houses. I never had parties for my friends, first because we were too poor, then because I was too ashamed of not having an indoor lavatory and big rooms.

But our family parties made up for that. They came round every Christmas with songs and recitations and games, fruit cordials bestowed on my grandfather by one of his customers, ginger wine and one bottle of port. There was 'Man and his Object',

'How Green You Are', 'Compliments', where everyone invented
inspired insults, and 'Twenty Questions'. Even Auntie Mary liked
'Compliments' and said something nice about everybody. I loved
all the games, especially when Uncle Bert set a question. He always thought of something abstract and obscure, like 'The Last
Post', which nobody could get, and 'Family Feeling', which my
mother, archivist of such feeling, guessed, on the last guess, to
great acclaim. We played cards in winter and cricket on the beach
in summer, and there were all the times when parties burst into
spontaneous life, because aunts and uncles or cousins turned up.
The only drink was strong tea, but that was stimulant enough.
And the men could always go down the pub afterwards. The
women only drank alcoholic drinks at Christmas.

Charlie and I gave a few parties after we moved to London,
but soon they were for my friends, not his. He would say his
colleagues were too boring, or he didn't like them, or they wouldn't
mix with mine. Not that he didn't make friends with my friends,
but he talked less and less, then started to drink in order to talk
more. After a while I would take friends out to dinner rather
than bring them home, or wait till he was away. But we had
some good occasions. Charlie loved mediaeval poetry and got
on well with Maggie, my colleague who taught Middle English.
He had a good memory, and when she praised the food and
wine he quoted *Gawain*, one of my old set texts which he'd read
and loved, patiently looking up all the words I couldn't remember in the difficult technical vocabulary. Maggie was pleased when
he lifted his glass to her, and changed the personal pronoun:

'And ofte she called it a feast.'

And I remember a long argument about *Waiting for Godot*, when
it first came out, almost causing a riot in Paris and astonishing
London. Charlie insisted that Pozzo and Lucky were images of
colonial oppression, and the argument, like the play, had no end.
We sometimes had political friends round, and Charlie was at
home with them. I'd joined the Labour party by then, years after
Charlie, and enjoyed meeting lively Lena Jeger, whose husband
was our MP till he died and she succeeded him, and serious Ivor
Richards, now Lord Richards, whose benign face and thoughtful

voice on Newsnight brings back Holborn in the fifties. Charlie and I always canvassed and addressed envelopes at elections, and I minded terribly when Labour lost, but as I was sucked into academic life I stopped going to branch meetings. Our social life in London moved us apart instead of bringing us together. Coffee and cake with Percy was far away in Swansea.

I longed to give a party with Mick. My rare fantasies about our cohabitation always began with Ellen dead and buried in the cemetery outside Oxford where the train often waits, and always ended with a party. The guests were his friends I could never meet, my friends he could never meet, and the mutual friends who didn't know of our secret ménage, all drinking champagne in surprised congratulation. We were sometimes invited to the same party and when that happened I never showed up. I didn't want to be in the same room as horrible Ellen. I didn't want to see her, especially not at a party when she was with Mick. It wasn't guilt but jealousy. At a publisher's party, not long after the meeting at Logan airport, I was possessed by her presence, though she was over on the other side of the big room, in her corner. I made sure my back was always turned, and had a cool little chat with Mick, in which I refused to go and speak to her. It was a miserable party, in spite of joking with my old friend Bernard Crick about never going to Greece together, and meeting Valerie Eliot, whom I found warm and relaxed, and without a trace of side. Eliot was lucky. But I was never going through that again.

But avoiding Ellen didn't solve all problems. Party conversation is a minefield for clandestine lovers. You see your lover as others see him, as they talk behind his back before your face. They gossiped about Mick's success and his sick wife. An old colleague from Harvard said, 'Mick Solomon is a saint', and somebody raised an eyebrow. I was dumb. I wanted them to praise Mick and put down horrible Ellen. I wanted them to say it was a bad marriage. I wanted to know things Mick wouldn't tell me about Ellen. I was ashamed of my jealous curiosity, as bad as the nosy gossip. Worse, because less innocent. Sometimes it was hurtful because partly true. When they said something spiteful about a

huge advance or a lecture where he used something he'd already
published or an error or a wild surmise, I flushed with anger
and embarrassment. Once I made the mistake of stammering a
defence, regretted opening my mouth, then realized that nobody
had been suspicious.

I asked Mick to come to a party for my second Gaskell book
– the only one I managed to persuade dear frugal Alexander
to give for me. He was impressed that I was friendly with
Mick, better known than most of my academic friends and
colleagues, and took him off to give him some special malt whisky and beg him to let them have his next book. 'Fat chance,'
Mick said afterwards, on to a good thing with the wonderful
New York agent who negotiated the advance for his work in
progress, the critical biography of Thackeray which was to redo
and outdo Gordon Ray as he'd outdone Edgar Johnson and
Gordon Haight.

We talked about the party in bed afterwards, like husband and
wife. After Alexander and his lubricious Picasso drawing we got
on to Mick's jealousy, provoked whenever he saw me talking to
men, whoever they were, young or old, gay or straight, acquaintances or strangers. I was jealous of Ellen, he was jealous of other
men. He cross-questioned me about my innocent colleagues, a
couple of Alexander's other authors with whom I exchanged a
word, and one literary editor I might have fancied in another
life. I didn't dare tell him that thoughtful Dennis Masters, who
had given a reading at the university, brought me freesias. After
an hour or so I persuaded him that nobody at the party was a
past or present lover or a candidate for speculation.

Once we met unexpectedly at one of Sonia Orwell's parties.
I'd met Sonia through Bernard Crick when he was working on
his Orwell biography. It was a good party, lots of people, argument, heavenly food, David Sylvester, John Gross, Robert Lowell,
the brilliant beautiful Spenders, and Mick. I was talking nervously
to Lowell, who politely mentioned a review I'd written in the
TLS, attacking Alexandra Southey's book on Victorian women
novelists. She may be a good poet but she's a lousy critic, I thought,
but too shy to say it out loud as Lowell mused, 'A hostile review'

or 'A rather harsh piece'. I looked across the room and there was Mick coming in with Natasha Spender.

I didn't recognise him at first because he looked smaller than usual, shortened beside her, and an unexpected guest. I'd told him I was going to the party, to which he hadn't been invited, but he'd run into Natasha and Stephen, old friends of his, and came along with them. He smiled at me, my mind went blank, he came up to say hullo, and I missed my only chance of a talk with Lowell. Mick and I weren't anywhere near each other for dinner, which was a sit-down affair, and soon after he had to leave to go back to Ellen. By then she was usually too tired or ill to come to big parties. I felt embarrassed and sad, though glad I was wearing a new long blue spotted cotton dress which cost me a vast sum at Browns, bought in one of the extravagant fits Mick half enjoyed and half disapproved. I got the feeling that Ellen wasn't interested in clothes. Perhaps she was, when she was well. It was one of the questions I didn't ask. He took her to buy things at dull places like Jaeger's. Sometimes if he liked one of my expensive buys he'd want to pay for it, and sometimes I'd let him.

Sonia's party ended for me long before I left, despite its sparkle. As Mick once said, 'It's funny being with other people. Everything is phantasmagoric.'

The best party I ever went to with Mick – or rather with Mick as a fellow-guest – was in Atlanta. He was teaching at Emory for a semester and I was paying a brief visit to give a lecture. We had spent the morning in bed at my hotel, with intermissions for lox and bagels, which he adored and I think overrated. He and Ellen had been invited to the party my friends Jake and Mary were giving on the day after my lecture. Reluctant and hostile, I couldn't get out of it, and braced myself for meeting her. Mick turned up miraculously alone, coming over to give me the permitted social kiss, saying nice things about my lecture. We talked unselfconsciously, in public but together, colleagues and old acquaintances. It was like the first talk at the dinner-party in Senate House, except that we'd been lovers for years.

'Tell me a bit more about Mrs – sorry, old habits die hard – Elizabeth Gaskell and Tennyson. Did she ever meet him? I should know, I suppose. You called her 'Mrs' in your book, if I remember correctly?'

The last bit was for public hearing, since he'd read and discussed my first book with me many times. At first we were talking in a group, then the others melted away and left us alone in a corner of the big kitchen. My lecture had been on Gaskell and her allusions to English poets, which I'd worked on and written while he was away, so it was an unfaked question. He was picking up what I said about Gaskell's assimilation of Tennyson in her novels, starting with the famous episode in *Cranford* where spinster Mattie's old flame speaks with passionate admiration about the marvellous new young poet. We went on to talk about the other novels, then about George Eliot's mixed feelings for Tennyson. Scholarly conversation became a language of love.

It was familiar ground but new facts. Mick asked me if I knew George Eliot's review of 'Maud' and I'd forgotten it. We were amused by her strange mistake in *Daniel Deronda* where she attributes a bit from 'Locksley Hall' to 'In Memoriam'. We quoted from the poems, to and fro, patching each other's recall. We wondered if Tennyson guessed that George Eliot wrote the anonymous review, if some friend or acquaintance had told him, as they will.

We got on to the days of anonymous reviewing in the TLS. Someone once told me an American colleague was wounded by what he took to be a TLS review I'd written of his book; in fact I hadn't written it. The editor refused to print my letter saying I was not the author of that or any anonymous review, so I talked to Freddie Bateson, dead set against the anonymity. He wrote a paragraph about my compounded complaint in *Essays in Criticism*. Freddie published my first article, and apart from my gratitude, I loved his candour, querulous wit, pugnacity and malice-streaked gossip. He was one of the Oxford people I found totally unexclusive. Perhaps it was because his career as a teacher there had been brilliant but not conventionally rewarded, perhaps he was too rebellious to take the mould.

Once Charlie and I and the children visited Freddie and Jan in their house – was it Temple House? – in Brill. Jo and Susie were fascinated by the family portraits, like the ones in books, and the treasured collection of children's books Jan showed them. We had pheasant, and apple-pie, a delicious Sunday lunch, and went for a walk to see the Windmill.

It was one of our good family times. Charlie was relaxed, savouring Freddie's lively knowing talkativeness about law, politics, and the Civil Service, which Charlie detested for its public-school power and privilege. Charlie was more talkative than he'd been for years, telling a story about his cousin Eddie, from South Shields, who had been Lord Harrington's private secretary, and refused to be deferential. Like Charlie, he was a bright working-class grammar-school boy, good at passing exams, who had never been to university, hated titles, and loathed lords. On one occasion when Eddie dispensed as usual with the polite form of address the noble earl corrected him under his breath. Of course Eddie didn't last. Members of both houses would inherit their official private secretaries, but could kick out mere assistant principals in the twinkling of an eye.

'God, I'd hate to have to say "My lord", or even "Sir",' I reflected on the road home. 'It's barbaric.'

'Mind you,' Charlie added, 'I wouldn't like to have Eddie as my private secretary. He was a thorn in the flesh of his teachers at school, from what he used to tell me when I went up on holidays. The mind boggles. Give credit where credit is due, as Mam always says. The noble lord must have suffered. My heart bleeds for him.'

That memory of Charlie and lunch in Brill was a subtext at the Atlanta party. That day in the country only came to mind when I was on the plane going home. Since I'd recovered from the grief after Charlie's death I'd censored my marriage-memories. Mick had been hurt by my tears and long mourning. After Mick's death the memories returned in their layerings.

I hadn't told Mick the TLS story before, and we had never talked about Tennyson, so it was a real flowing conversation. Anyone could have listened and joined in. We must have talked for half an hour. The talk – all the lovely shop talk – was spontaneous and fresh, as we smiled, in the larger circle of talk, looking and sounding like the other guests but intimately linked. Our looks and words and smiles and thoughts were public and private, in the elegant kitchen with a late afternoon sun shining on the red tiles and the golden pine, the dogwood brilliant outside the window. After the first polite and public words about my talk – I'd been petrified with him smiling in the second row – it got real. I breathed the heady mix of the social and the secret, the seeming and the true. I never really minded the secrecy, except when promiscuous gossip hurt, but at the party in Atlanta secrecy was fun.

Of course I was sorry I could never take him to my friends' parties or visit his friends with him. My friend Bettina Lightfoot, who lectured in the French department, knew of his existence but not his name, and asked me if I could bring him to have dinner with her and Patrick. Of course I said no, thinking regretfully how they'd have got on, as she was working on a translation of Racine's *Phèdre*, and Mick used to translate Baudelaire for fun, saying it was the only use he could find for his defunct poetic skills. After he died I told her who he was. I told Jake, whose kitchen I revisited eagerly not long after Mick's death. I told Isabella, the only one of my friends to guess, but right at the end when she had clues, and Flora, a friend in Dublin, whose marriage pains I'd observed. I felt a compulsion to tell, and began to think I couldn't stop. After the long secrecy the story came rushing out. I didn't think Mick would have minded. But after a while I stopped talking about it.

When I told Jake, the only close friend who knew us both well, it was April again, and there actually was dogwood outside his kitchen window, which I thought might have been an embellishment of memory. It was another party. But I felt like Silas Marner going back home to find his old places gone. The room was changed in shape and size, enlarged by a big new conservatory, paid for by Riverside, Jake joked. He'd edited a couple of best-selling academic anthologies of poetry and stories. He asked me how Ellen was, if I'd seen her since Mick's death, and I had to tell him that I was the last person to ask, and why. He didn't seem too thrilled by the revelation, which I suppose changed his view of three friends. Some time later he admitted that he had wondered what he might have said to me about Mick, and to Mick about me, in his ignorance. I told him how his royalties had reshaped my remembered space, and tried to locate the spot – was it where the glass wall began, or by a pillar? – where Mick and I talked about the TLS and 'In Memoriam'.

From Tennyson and Hallam to Dido and Aeneas. The English poet's memory of an Italian poet's sad memory of good times led to a Roman poet's memory of a Greek poet's sad memory of bad times. We reconstructed Aeneas's reluctance to remember. Dido begged him to tell her about Troy. We patched together school memories of Virgil and the reply: *'Infandum, regina, iubes renovare dolorem.'*

'Infandum? So does *infans* mean speech?' Mick asked.

We managed a translation, 'Great queen, you are asking me to renew an unspeakable sorrow', but weren't satisfied with our words for dolour – sorrow, grief, pain, agony, misery; they wouldn't do.

Virgil spared us the later memories of elderly Aeneas, resting on his laurels in Rome, recalling the brief interlude in Carthage as something that happened to somebody else, forgetting the intensities – the storm and the cave and Dido weeping at his bitter history. There are worse things than sad memory of grief, or sad memory of happiness. There's a dulling of memory, retrieval without passion.

I remember the party I went on to that Saturday night after I left Mick and Ellen in Hans Crescent, more than twenty years ago. It was Maggie's party, just after she married Martin, a post-wedding party to mark a domestication and a settling-down. But Maggie never settled down. It was a fatally open marriage, a fragile construction, a house of straw that fell in the first high wind. But that night they were laughing and dancing, looking fondly at each other. It was a young party, Maggie's generation, but I was pleased to be there with younger colleagues and friends, though I didn't join the dancing. I ate and drank and talked and half-listened to the music. Some of it I liked for its vigour and clarity. I remember a Kevin Ayres song with a vigorous rhythm

and weird words. And the perennial Beatles. Of course it wasn't
my kind of music. It wasn't my kind of dancing, though I'd tried
it once or twice. I went home and played old records, 'Smoke
Gets in Your Eyes', 'These Foolish Things' and 'Our Love Affair'.

Long ago in Swansea and Aberystwyth our dances were the
quickstep, the waltz, the tango, and best of all the slow foxtrot –
slow, slow, quick-quick, slow. Even as children we used to go
once a year to the Hospital Ball, held in the Brangwen Hall of
the Civic Centre, with Frank Brangwen's flamboyant flora and
fauna all round. When I was in the Sixth I went with friends
who were students of Swansea University to the hops on Saturday afternoons in the engineer's lecture hall, dancing to 'You
Are my Sunshine', 'Yours', and 'I Don't Want to Set the World
on Fire', a song whose sentiments I despised, but whose tune I
liked. When I sang it around the house Charlie mimicked my
rendering of 'Fi – yah', which he found funny. Later on in Aberystwyth the high spot of the week and our dating rituals was
the Saturday night hop in the big stonefloored quad, with a gallery from which you could look down on the dancers. We used
to go out coatless in our party clothes to have a drink in one of
the hundred Aber pubs, or step across the Prom to watch the
waves. My digs were close to the sea, too, and every night the
last sound before sleep was the rhythmical drag of surf on shin-
gle. I remember waltzing to 'Who's Taking You Home Tonight?',
played for the last dance, and the fraught question of who was
taking you home. To be asked for the last dance meant to be
escorted home, kissed on the doorstep, and probably asked for a
date.

I remember 'Our Love Affair', one of my favourites, transferred
from Aber boyfriends to Charlie. Just after we got engaged, we
whirled round my mother's kitchen, in the family's absence. He
laughed when I said ours was one of the great loves, 'From Adam
and Eve to Scarlett and Rhett'. (Though like most of my friends,
I preferred cool elegant Leslie Howard as Ashley to crude old
Clark Gable as Rhett.) But after marriage I was shut off from the
dancing of my youth. In spite of that high-hearted private waltz,

Charlie and I didn't go dancing. I think it was my fault. Dancing seemed to belong to another time, other partners. Before we got married, he took some lessons, because he knew I loved dancing. I waltzed with him once at his office party, as well as in my mother's kitchen. I remember his hand soft and his step light. I don't know why we didn't go on dancing together. I never danced with Mick either, come to think of it, or Mel, or any of my grown-up lovers.

Mel suggested that we should dance after we had supper in our bedroom – I ate sweetbreads with black butter sauce – at the Grosvenor House in Park Lane, but my dancing years seemed remote. It was a bit like it had been with Charlie, but Mel was a dancer, a jazz man. My dancing had stopped, though. I was shy, middle-aged, afraid I'd be clumsy, that we wouldn't keep in step. So I said no. When we'd made love and it was still early, I changed my mind and said I'd try, but Mel said it was late, we'd missed the moment. He played for me to dance with other people. Mel never missed a symbol.

Once or twice I'd tried the twist and the new dancing, but not happily. I watched Maggie and Martin, not touching, but intent on each other and the music, joined in a wild glee. I didn't mind being a looker-on. I wasn't jealous. I was still elated by Mick's invitation. Had I agreed to meet him again? I went over our dialogue in the bedroom. I'd said 'I don't know', but opened my diary, and he'd said, 'No, don't. I'll call you next week.'

I was pleased to be at another party, thinking about the one I'd just left, warmed by the promise of something. I talked to people the way you do at a party, smiling idly, sometimes engaged, sometimes half-attentive, listening to scraps of other people's talk, scanning the scene. Savouring the immediate past, enjoying the party goodwill, I didn't dance but I wasn't a wallflower.

Maggie shook her straight gold hair out of her blue eyes and said how much she liked the wedding present I'd given them. It was a skull. It was there on the dark oak dresser her husband's parents gave them, in the middle of the feast, an old skull, shiny and yellow. She suggested it when I asked her what they'd like, saying she had a mediævalist's longing for a skull. I hunted everywhere, King's Road, Camden, Portobello, stopping at the shops and stalls to ask 'Have you got a skull?', a question out of Monty Python. I found it when I'd almost stopped looking, in a shop in Kensington Church Street, visible through the window on a high shelf, cheek by jowl with another whiter one. I bought it for eighteen pounds, after holding and inspecting the two skulls and choosing the one I liked best. It gave me a funny feeling, of course, to be buying a skull for a present, and a wedding present. Above all, it felt wrong to be buying somebody's skull.

Before wrapping it up in gold paper to give Maggie and Martin, I wrote a couplet, typed it on a slip of paper, and put it inside the skull to avert the omen:

Lovers, look at my bony grin
And then rejoice in flesh and skin.

Maggie died young, a couple of years before Mick, after her third bad breakdown. She and Martin split up not long after their party. She left an empty bottle of her pills and an empty bottle of whisky on the bedside table. I went to see her in the Whittington hospital, not far from Dick Whittington's cat on Highgate Hill. She was angry.

'It's not fair. Why should I have this incubus? Where does it come from? Out of the blue.'

She was twenty years younger than me. I remember her running down the aisle at her wedding in the actors' church in Covent Garden, to the rushing music of Messiaen, in a brilliant pink trouser-suit and grey silk shoes from the Chelsea Cobbler, with high thick heels.

FIVE

Going to Bed

Mick phoned from Edinburgh to say he'd be with me soon after two o'clock on Friday. He began as he had begun once before and always was to begin, even when his voice packed in, stressing, slowing, and drawling the first syllable of 'Florence'.

'Florence. My plane gets in at midday so I should be with you by two, with luck.'

The first time he had said 'Florence. I'm calling to compound the plan to meet next Friday. It will be in the afternoon. I give my talk on Thursday night, and I've got to have breakfast with Alastair, but I'll let you know more definitely when I get there. I'm not sure about the plane.'

I'd been dithering about saying I'd meet him, but he wasn't asking a question. I forgot all about my uncertainty and just said, 'That'll be fine.' I spent the week wondering what I was getting into. I couldn't make out if I was anticipating a pleasure or dreading a problem.

Joanna was working at home that week revising for her 'O' Levels. I have entries in my diary for May 1972 saying 'M.S.' for the Friday afternoon, after '7 a.m. J's Physics'. The day before it had been '9 p.m. J's History'. I wasn't a maternal martinet, far from it, but Joanna organized my testing her in history and physics. I knew about Chartism and the Hungry Forties but heat, light, and velocity were mysteries to me, and helping her was exhausting. She insisted on stopping from time to time to make sure I fully understood and wasn't the listening machine I longed to be.

75

'Don't you remember from yesterday? God, Mum, you have got a funny kind of mind, haven't you? It's so patchy. Listen. I'll explain, only please listen.'

That afternoon I put my head round her door and told her I'd be going out after lunch but I'd be back to get dinner.

'Tell Susie when she gets in, will you, darling? OK?'

Joanna and Susie didn't always ask me who I was going out with but when they did I always told them. Joanna looked up, 'Where are you going?'

'Out with an American writer I met a couple of weeks back. Mick Solomon. He's very nice.'

'What kind of a writer?'

'Mostly biography, but he has one book of poems. I'll show them to you sometime if you like. After your exams, perhaps. We're going out to tea. He'll be calling for me, but I won't interrupt you.'

Joanna hated being interrupted and that suited me on this occasion. Going out to tea seemed the best way of describing an afternoon date. I supposed it had to be afternoon because he'd be getting back to Ellen. (She hadn't yet turned into horrible Ellen.)

It was the first of hundreds of afternoons. But when I started to get ready I had no idea that it was the beginning of anything. I had no precise idea what we were going to do, though he'd made his intention plain with that word 'unprofessionally'. Would it amuse me to meet him unprofessionally? I didn't know. Perhaps he really was going to take me out to tea, in some nice quiet little place in Knightsbridge. That seemed unlikely. Americans don't have tea. The phrase sailed in from the distant past.

I met my very first American, in the flesh and off the screen, in Cwmdonkin Park. I was wandering round the paths, through the Dylan Thomasy groves, mine long before I met his hunchback in the park. I was dreaming my delicious futures, all poetry, love, and freedom. I was about thirteen. I met this American girl and we fell into conversation. She had long golden plaits, which she told me were called braids, and she was wearing a red and white cotton frock with a long full skirt and long pointed crisp collars. She looked a bit like Judy Garland, and she was also thirteen, a month older than me. Her name was Virginia, which made her seem even more American. After we decided that we were kindred spirits, both deeply read in the works of L.M. Montgomery, whose *Anne of Green Gables* and *Windy Ridge* made lavish use of that great phrase, we arranged to meet again. Friendship flourished. We would go for walks in the holiday afternoons, collaborating on an endless romantic serial about two girls who lived in a tower on the coast of Oregon, overlooking a wild bay where the rocks and stones were black. Virginia's mother came from Oregon and it shaped and coloured her fictional landscape as the grey Gower limestone formed mine. Minerals, tides, and books merged. She was also a mine of social information, teaching me the American for pavement, railway, and curtain, how to tell the time in American and how to pronounce 'tomato', which I knew already from a Fred Astaire and Ginger Rogers song, 'Let's call the whole thing off', which I sometimes sang to Mick after we'd had one of our cross-culture discussions.

Early on, when I told Virginia I had to go back to tea, she told me Americans didn't have tea. I pitied her until she explained that they had an early supper instead and I began to think not having tea was the height of glamour and sophistication.

I never had tea with Mick. I didn't expect to. But if we weren't going to have tea, what were we going to do? I didn't want the first meeting to be in my flat, with Jo working away at her history and physics. And anyway I knew he had something planned. The invitation, or proposition, whatever you called it, had sounded spontaneous but had been carefully planned, not casual. Perhaps we would have a friendly meeting, in his flat, a preliminary sortie. It was too late for lunch, too early for drinks. I entertained the image of a one-afternoon stand, though since this was our third meeting that phrase wouldn't do. An immediate rush into bed didn't seem likely. It seemed out of character. Mick had been so modest and polite.

I felt nervous and embarrassed as I put on a black lace bra and small black silk panties, just in case. I blushed as a terrible memory came back. About a year before that May date with Mick, I'd been thoughtlessly wearing a hideous old pair of red and orange floral-patterned panties which my grandfather had given me for a birthday, and which never wore out. I suppose they were the only ones that were clean on that day. I wasn't so liberated that I always prepared for adventure. I wore them under a long black and yellow fine wool dress, to a party where I met an Australian lecturer, Harry Macdonald, and went off to spend an enjoyable night with him at somebody's flat in Queens Square. We were too drunk and randy to care about the kind of knickers he pulled off and cast aside, but when I got dressed in the morning light I blushed at the passion-killers, as the big girls in Mount Zion Sunday school used to call them, sniggering in the back row of the gallery behind our younger group. As I finished dressing in last night's glad rags I knew Harry and I wouldn't be meeting again. The morning had that kind of goodbye feel to it, and the terrible panties were a part of the mistake. I didn't take any chances on that May afternoon but dressed with care, from the bottom up. I chose the black patent leather high-heeled shoes, looked in the big cheval-glass and concluded that I looked all right except for my red eyes and nose. I had a streaming cold.

The front-door bell rang, I spoke through the intercom, and asked him to come up. He gave me a social kiss on the cheek, and asked with the laugh that always ran through his speech, till it got badly slurred at the end,

'Ready? I've got the car downstairs.'

Unlike other friends, he never had parking problems in our busy street, because Ellen was entitled to a disabled person's parking sticker. I always felt guilty about that when he called, though he never did.

'Where are we going?' I asked through my snuffly nose.

He smiled and said, 'To bed, of course, my love.'

I called out goodbye to Joanna, as she listened to my taped voice reciting the ills of the rural poor in Victoria's first decade, and off we went.

I sat beside him as we drove through Earls Court Road, along the Old Brompton Road into Knightsbridge, then turned just before Harrods. All through the journey I tried to feel enthusiastic. I can't remember what we talked about, if we talked. I was going into the adventure cold. I was doing what I'd been doing, on and off, ever since I split up with Charlie, trying to be a man. Though I didn't feel any longings, I suppose I was hoping to find warmth. It wasn't just an after-the-party thing. The daylight was clear, and we were both stone-cold-sober. I looked at his profile, always his best facial presentation. The long hooked nose was Roman, the face serious, as I'd never seen it. On our first meetings he'd been smiling all the time. I didn't know it then, but it was the view I was to have so often in bed, looking at the profile when he was asleep on his back.

The full face was a bit pudgy, with a hooked nose and a slight double chin. He was balding, with some curly hair and side-whiskers, funnily rakish. I looked away as we stopped outside the house. I did quite like him. He was clever, funny, speaking a language of his own. He was also famous, in my world. I didn't think that made any difference, but it's always fun when books you know as books turn into a flesh and blood person. I'd only had three meetings with him, and two or three phone conversations. What I knew was attractive, but not madly sexy. I'd gone to his party at the beginning of a pleasant acquaintance, and as I'd gone to parties ever since I left Charlie, alone, footloose, free as air, prepared for anything. He'd written that enigmatic letter to 'Cara nome' but he'd talked so admiringly and warmly and sadly about Ellen that I hadn't thought of him as a lover. Not till I was collecting my coat at the end. It hadn't been a lightning stroke.

Liberated as I knew I was, I felt nervous and embarrassed at the prospect of going to bed in cold blood and broad daylight, with somebody for whom I didn't feel anything much. Only what Clarissa called a kind of conditional liking. I wasn't much of a Clarisssa and Mick didn't seem to be a Lovelace, though you could never tell. When the car stopped at the house I looked away. Mick touched my shoulder, grinned, said, 'Coraggio', got out, and came round to open the door. I asked him,

'Do you do this often?'

He looked surprised and said, 'I don't do it at all.'

I swung my legs out neatly, holding them together, as I'd read models did, and we went into the house, then into his flat.

'Come in here for a minute,' Mick said, leading me into the sitting-room for the third time. We faced each other for a moment. I didn't feel anything as we kissed.

'Do you like me?'

'I don't know.'

'That's what you said last week when I asked you to meet me.'

'I know. Sorry.'

'Let's pretend you do.'

'All right then.'

That first time was no good. But by the time I was dressed I was feeling affectionate and desirous. Mick didn't get in a state of fury, self-pity, or apologetics, as Timmy did once, or weep, like Mel. He was quite calm.

'Don't worry. It'll be all right. It's been a long time since I was with a woman.'

It had been about three years since he and Ellen had made love, and not a lot had happened in their bed for some time before her illness. After she'd been ill for months, he told her he felt old and impotent and she said 'Never!' I was puzzled. What did she think would happen to his sexuality? He explained that she hadn't meant that he'd be having it off with anyone else, but intended a wry tribute to his potency.

'What did she expect you to do then?'

He laughed, 'She never cared for it herself, so I don't suppose she gave it a lot of thought.' That was the only time he spoke of her resentfully. At all other times it was with admiration or pity or love. Once I asked him what he felt for her.

'Mick, do you love Ellen?'

And after a slight pause he said, 'Yes, I do. Is that bad?'

First they lapsed into a cycle of resistance, persuasion, refusal, anger, and acquiescence. Then the resistance got stronger and the acquiescence rarer. He contemplated a divorce. She suggested that he should have an affair. When he told me all this, amused and tolerant, as he could afford to be then, I disliked the thought that I was a convenience, part of her thinking, an object in her fantasy.

We didn't talk about her that afternoon. We dressed, kissed again, this time with more enthusiasm on my part, then sat down in the sitting-room and drank brandy. He drove me home and said as we stopped at my door, 'If I can annex your life to mine, it will make a great difference.'

He said 'It's so damned difficult to get away.' Then he smiled and we kissed goodbye.

I watched the car turn the corner, ran up my steps, let myself in, and felt happy.

'It's going to be fine,' he'd said while we were dressing, and I believed him. Some of my other first times had been imperfect too. It was passable but not brilliant with Charlie because he was the boy next door, hopeless with Mel because he was Heathcliff, surprisingly quick with Timmy because he always got first-night nerves. When it eventually turned out to be fine with me and Mick, he laughed at the memory of that first flop.

'Of course I knew that impotence bound you to me with hoops of steel.'

I'd felt the usual pity and respect for a partner's failed sex. But there was also the powerful aphrodisiac of deprivation. It was compounded by trying various solutions. We lay in the big bed, an unnecessary bath-towel spread hopefully across the white marital sheets. When I got home and remembered and imagined, my body started to flutter and tick.

It wasn't only what he asked, but the way he expected me to take the initiative. I was hopeless at all that. I'd been married for twenty years, on and off, and had a few lovers before, during, and after the marriage. Only a few, by the standards of the swinging sixties. I used to count them, before I married, and occasionally afterwards. I began to think the number was too small, then saw the funny side of counting like Don Giovanni. I began to compose a woman's version, basing my female seducer on Dylan Thomas's Polly Garter, a character I much admired, though I didn't want to emulate her fruitfulness.

When I was a small girl I started to fantasize about cruel men capturing me and making me pull down my knickers. The images grew more complicated and interesting, but they always depended on a detachment from real life. I could never bring people I knew into the stories I told myself. The characters had to be crude, larger than life. They must never have names. They must bear absolutely no resemblance to anyone in real life.

None of my boyfriends came into those wild nights. The real thing was always more boringly straight than the scenes and stories in my fantasy. Even in the early enjoyable years of marriage I found to my shame that I missed my lonely orgies, and from time to time, on the sly, I lapsed into fantasy again. But until I went to bed with Mick I could never bring my fantasies into bed. Charlie and I talked a lot about sex, but our attempts to put theory into practice lacked conviction or concentration. We ended up with a friendly and pleasurable routine. Like Mr Casaubon, I began to think the rumours and legends of poly-morphous passion were grossly exaggerated.

Charlie once said we were too close, too familiar. 'I should have undressed you that first night.'

When I was growing up in the thirties as a Swansea teenager – though we were called adolescents, not teenagers – girls waited for boys to ask. For everything, dates, kisses, gropes, fucks, mar-riage, and dances. The routine 'Ladies' Excuse Me' dance was thrilling because the ladies cut in and did the choosing. It was a little liberation. But when I was a student I asked boys to dance on three occasions, feeling brave, or what Nana would have called brazen. It was out of impulsive idle curiosity that I approached a small, dapper, beautifully dressed young man who was a good dancer. Martha and Annie and I used to call him 'the little boy'. He was polite, smiled constantly, said almost nothing, whirled me round in a firm, cool grasp, and left me wondering why on earth I had broken the rules.

When I asked Joe Fraser for a dance he assumed that I was asking to go to bed after the dance, and we did. Perhaps it was what I'd been asking, though I didn't think so. I had admired him from afar when he had been an undergraduate, and now he was back in London doing research, visiting Aberystwyth for the intercollegiate week festivities. About a month later, when Joe had written me several long witty letters about politics, my best friend Martha informed me, as best friends will, that he had told a friend of a friend of hers he didn't want to see me again. He was small, sexy, clever, and said he had gone straight from being a little Cockney urchin to joining the Communist party. I was toying with the idea of joining – though I never did – and that was my chief conscious reason for asking him to dance. He had political glamour.

After we'd been dancing for a few minutes I asked boldly and knowingly, 'Well, Joe, and how's the Party?' and he started to talk about Stalin, who was still an admired figure among the faithful. We went off to the room he was sharing at a local pub, *The Cross Foxes*, and when his friend knocked on the door Joe called out to him not to come in. An amused voice called out, 'Fine!' and I felt awful. I remembered that once when I was in Mick's room and a college servant knocked, got no reply, and started to open the door with his keys. Mick called out, 'Don't come in.' It was the same mixture of fear and shame, as if a stranger was looking at my naked body.

My mild brazenness was political as well as sexual. I hated having to wait to be approached, talking to your friends who were also waiting, and pretending you were talking away happily, looking surprised when invited to dance. If your friends were asked first, you hung about or gave up and went to powder your nose and hope to do better in the next dance.

Our dating rituals were dance rituals. When I was still at school, I met boys in chapel or in the youth club or even on the Prom, but in Aberystwyth students never made dates except at the hops. But it seemed to me that dancing didn't have to be dating. So why not ask, as a gesture of freedom? It was all so silly. My third politically correct but socially incorrect invitation almost lost me a friend. I was talking to Annie's boyfriend while she had gone to the cloakroom, and suddenly felt like asking him to dance. When she came back and found us slowly fox-trotting round the hall, she waited till we stopped, asked him why he hadn't waited for her and when he told her, innocently or not so innocently, that I had wanted to dance, she said angrily that I was a false friend, turned on her heel and went home. Next morning I apologized, saying I hadn't meant to make mischief, but she wouldn't listen. It had seemed silly, just standing there talking when the music was so inviting, but when I thought of saying so it sounded unconvincing. I knew she wouldn't believe me. She wouldn't speak to me for several days, till she and Tom made it up. Asking for a dance was asking for trouble. Good girls waited.

Asking three men to dance was all my pathetic initiative amounted to. It seemed to me to be a social initiative rather than a sexual one, but unfortunately open to misinterpretation. When I was a student in Aberystwyth in the forties I certainly never took a frankly sexual initiative, though films and novels and older role-models – successful attractive girls with lots of dates – encouraged us all to be flirtatious. And to accept dates even if we weren't keen. The poor boys were constantly misled by the passive, ignorant, date-hungry girls.

If someone asked you out and you didn't like them, it was hard to refuse. You occasionally said yes and didn't turn up, but that was rightly regarded as bad manners. Sometimes you went on pleasurelessly for weeks, accepting kisses and caresses until boy or girl said they didn't want to meet again or, more often, broke the date. If the boy said or did it first that was a social humiliation, to be kept from your friends if at all possible. If you liked someone, went out with them, and found them attractive, you never made the first move.

Some boys were slow, some were fast. Some of the fast boys carefully observed various limits, others tried to go as far as the girl permitted. Couples often got as far as heavy petting, but even when that was in full swing, the girl never touched first. The 'never' is what Jane Austen would call the 'never' of conversation. Of course sexual freedoms varied from person to person. One of my acquaintances, Marie, told me she didn't believe any of our lot had lost their virginity, though I knew for a fact she was wrong. But virgins, half-virgins, or ex-virgins, we were all pretty passive, I'm positive. When we talked about sex, it was always about what was done to us, not about what we did. And of course I think of myself as pretty representative, in spite of my feeble gestures of freedom.

Even after I'd been to bed with someone, I was passive. Even after I'd had two or three lovers, I was ignorant. All this was hard on the boys too, of course. And the men. Even after I was married, I thought being a good lover, or being good in bed, meant kissing in a variety of ways, caressing your partner, jigging up and down as vigorously as possible, and occasionally trying a bump and grind or a half-hearted vaginal clutch. Charlie's Uncle Gwyn, who had been to Egypt, told him about the talented women in the brothels who could pick up banknotes. I tried once and it seemed obvious that my gifts didn't lie in that direction. All I did was make Charlie laugh.

I didn't make much progress between my teens and the end of my marriage. In my teens love-making tended to be speechless, apart from the occasional 'I love you', 'darling', and 'don't'. No wonder I never made suggestions or tried out erotic talk. I was stuck in the old Swansea rut. When I read *Portnoy's Complaint* and Norman Mailer I was torn between incredulity and envy. I longed to be like Portnoy's Monkey but it never occurred to me to apply fiction's lessons in bed.

The first time I made love was quick and casual, with a short dark handsome theological student called Harry Lloyd, who reminded me a bit of my glamorous Uncle Bert, prize-winning dancer and lady-fancier who referred to attractive women as nice bits of homework. Harry wasn't at all my idea of a theological student, but when I first danced with him at a college hop in the Engineer's Room at Swansea University, and he held me close, then swung me adroitly round in circles I thought perhaps he had hidden depths. I never discovered his spiritual side, even after we got to know each other. He was going steady with a glamorous half-French girl called Marie-Claire but she was away on holiday and Harry was at a loose end. He took me home after the dance and kissed me goodnight. I was at college in Aberystwyth, home for the vacation, and also at a loose end.

Harry asked me for a date, and at our second meeting I found myself losing my virginity on a slippery sofa in Beck Hall, a woman's hall of residence at the Uplands end of Sketty Road. It may have changed its function now but the building is still there, though it now has a bilingual name, Beck Neuadd as well as Beck Hall. I've seen it thousands of times over the years, on my way to and from Sketty, Killay, and Gower, passing my memorial in different moods and seasons. Technically speaking, I'd lost my virginity years before, privately and gradually, without realising what was happening, but I'd read so many novels in which the wedding night was painful because of a callous spouse, or less painful because of a considerate one, that I was disappointed to find the crucial event so painless.

I was also amazed that it was so pleasureless. I'd done better on my own. But after fornication, as I grandly thought of our furtive quick scramble, I couldn't bring myself to say I didn't want to see Harry again. So I went out with him until Marie-Claire came back. Then he was no longer at a loose end, and didn't keep the last date we made. I felt some chagrin at being ditched by my seducer, but also relief and a certain slight disgust.

I can't remember anything we talked about on the half dozen occasions we went out. In this case going out was what we did. The first time we'd been lucky enough to find an unoccupied room with a bolt, but Beck Hall was usually busy and crowded, so we resorted to sand-dunes on Swansea Beach and the rhododendron bushes in Singleton Park. The act took a little longer each time but never lasted long. On one occasion Harry asked the famous question, 'Was it all right for you?' Instinctively – by which I mean from causes unknown – I gave the famous obligatory courteous answer. That was the one time we mentioned what we were doing. I have a vague idea that we discussed religion once. I have a faint memory of explaining that I was an atheist, but if Harry responded I've long forgotten what he said.

The first time I did it in a real bed, and for longer than five minutes, it was with Johnny, a medical student whom I met at a students' farm camp in Herefordshire. Johnny was a considerate lover and a mine of information on all subjects from monstrous births to fellatio. He was the first man I ever talked to properly about sex, and I remember our conversations more clearly than our love-making. In the novel he was the first real person I succeeded in reinventing. I needed to cut down the number of my heroine's lovers, because you couldn't see the wood for the trees. Suddenly I had the bright idea of a merger. It was surprisingly easy to combine Johnny with Timmy. I called the composite man Adrian, made him a dentist, and enjoyed the sense of power. Timmy was a mathematician and would have hated changing his job to dentistry, let alone being merged with another expert lover.

Johnny was amazed when I asked him 'What is an erection?', because he knew I'd been to bed with two or three others before him. But it so happened that I'd never seen a mature penis, and never felt one that was detumescent. At last convinced that I wasn't joking, Johnny guffawed and explained.

'An erection is what happens when a young gentleman kisses a young lady.' He added, 'Sometimes when he just holds her hand.'

Then he put on the light, threw back the bedclothes and said, 'Take a good look.' I remembered Johnny's surprise and my ignorance when Mick told me the Duchess of Windsor thought the penis had a bone in it.

'Speaks well for Edward the Eighth,' he said, and I pointed out that it spoke well for Mr Simpson too. Mick's story brought back my innocence and enlightenment.

It wasn't my mother's fault. She had promised to tell me the facts of life when I was fourteen, after I'd interrogated her about various puzzles, like old maids, virgin queens, and babies. She did tell me about menstruation, and I was absolutely furious to hear that men didn't menstruate. 'I think that's really unfair,' I burst out, and after looking surprised, my mother agreed that there was something in what I said.

We didn't call it the curse in our family. It was 'being poorly'. Some of my friends called it being unwell. Rhoda Jenkins, a clever girl with an airy and amused attitude to everything, including sex, called it 'funny times', which I still think is an excellent name for it. My posh friend from Tycoch, Sian Thomas, called it 'the curse', like people in books. I practised saying 'the curse' in private, but could never bring it off in public. By the time I was fourteen

I dreaded being told anything by my mother, and when she asked me if I'd like her to talk about sex, I hastily declined, thanking her but saying I knew all about it. I thought I did, till I met Johnny.

Johnny startled me by asking if he could see me naked. I agreed, closed my eyes, and threw back the bedclothes under which we had already made love. It felt like a big first time.

He said the right thing, 'You're lovely', then asked me to open my eyes and look at him. I did, with interest but no emotion. I was rapidly gathering experience. After a while, in a neutral tone, he listed some variations. Most of them struck me as disgusting, the rest impossible. I assumed his facts were imparted as abstract knowledge and when he proposed a demonstration. I rejected the idea violently, and Johnny good-naturedly nipped back into missionary position again.

He wasn't a bad tutor or a bad lover, and unlike Harry and others I'd dignified with the name of lover to dignify the act, he used condoms instead of the dangerous practice of being careful. Yet another first time. I stopped having nightmares about illegitimate babies, which I'd dreaded since I first heard about them at the age of nine or ten, not yet in serious danger. But the best I could do with Johnny was to exclaim with pleasure and bounce about energetically. I didn't agree to much. I never suggested anything. I never started anything.

Marriage changed that a bit, but I was still pretty passive. When I felt like making suggestions I thought they might sound like criticisms. One of my friends told me that when she was being stitched up after her baby the doctor had joked, 'Do you enjoy married life? If so, I'll do tight stitches', and I felt vaguely that I should be a more active lover. I tried, and improved a little. Charlie and I talked a lot about sex, and as I began to enjoy it more and more I felt sure that everything was perfect. Looking back I see how unimaginative and inert I was. And Charlie didn't ask me to take initiatives, but then nobody did till Mick. Not really.

Before and after marriage, I felt guilty if I ever masturbated and never mentioned the subject. One night I woke up to find Charlie masturbating in his sleep, and felt irrationally angry and revolted. What did I know? We were babes in the wood, children of the chapel. But Charlie was the only lover to concentrate on parts of my body with tenderness. He was also the only one with whom I felt so tightly bonded that for years the thought of sleeping without him was unthinkable. The idea of his death was unthinkable too. Though we were very young, I secretly hoped I'd die before him. And though Mick's death changed my life more than any other loss, it didn't tear me apart like Charlie's death.

By the time I met Mick I'd got to like sleeping alone. Once or twice I even moved into the spare room when he was staying the night, after he'd gone to sleep. He wasn't very pleased at that, so I stopped. I'd got out of the habit of sleeping in the same bed as someone else. He had not.

My infidelities – I thought of them as infidelities – were either too trivial or too tragic to promote much concern for the arts of love. Mel and Timmy were show-off lovers who had a tendency to demand applause, but I found that endearing rather than contemptible. But Mel and I were distracted by planning bitter futures – would it be life without him or life without Charlie? Timmy advanced my sexual education greatly, but I usually followed his lead. When I learnt to stop being passive, by playing at passivity, and to lead, because Mick asked me to lead, it was long after I'd got out of my marriage to live on my own.

Mel and I did a lot of weeping, both of us. I once ruined a wonderful dinner at the White Tower – duck and aubergines – by crying because we were about to part for ever. Once he cried noisily through a whole night.

The trouble was that I found it hard to have a fling. Except now and then. I couldn't be permanently promiscuous. At first even my fun and games with Timmy seemed like a possible permanence. It was my history. Each love was disguised as the entrance to the perfect relationship. All my love-affairs tried to be marriages.

Bed was the theatre for vows and promises and renunciations. During love-making I'd agree to anything – reconciliation, elopement, divorce, conception, resignation from my job, fresh starts, fidelity, anything. Then as soon as I started to dress I'd be seized with guilt or doubt. Could I really leave Charlie? Could I stay with him? The thought of choosing neither dear charmer and living on my own occasionally crossed my mind. But the thought never lingered. It shot in one side and out the other. If a fortune-teller had foreseen that I'd spend the years after my fortieth birthday living alone – not celibate, but not cohabiting – I'd have been dismayed.

I was having dinner with friends not long ago, talking about having our time over again. My voice surprised me with its confidence.

'I wouldn't marry. Or live with anyone. I'd have children, but I'd bring them up on my own.'

I couldn't ever have said that to Mick. I probably couldn't have said it at all when Mick was alive. I might have said it to Charlie.

I didn't leave Charlie for Mel or Timmy or Mick, or for any-body. Timmy and Mel were alternatives, almost substitute hus-bands, but the one affair was too casual and the other too tragic. My love for Mick was unclouded by any conflict with my mar-riage. He was never in opposition to Charlie. Loving him wasn't distracted by guilt or nostalgia. I loved Charlie too much to live with his rivals. Sometimes I disliked them because they were his rivals. Timmy objected that I was always telling Charlie every-thing about him, and when I told Charlie he thought that was funny. I could only leave Charlie for my own sake. That took years. It was hard because I'd loved him when we were very young, and for a very long time. It was hard because of the ways of that first Welsh world which made us and our marriage.

In our childhood and youth nobody ever left their husband or wife. In that close-knit, loving, warm, smelly, talkative, quarrel-some Swansea, nobody you ever met got a divorce. You heard about people who had to get married. I knew a friend of Chrissie's husband whose supposed mother turned out to be her grand-mother because her sister was actually her mother. You heard people described as rotters, fancy women, and fancy men, but until I was twenty-two I never met anyone who was divorced or separated from their married partner. It was like seeing ghosts –

you might meet people who knew people who'd split up or got divorced but you never met them yourself.

Charlie's Uncle Gwyn had a barrister friend whose wife was unwilling to divorce him, so he couldn't marry his mistress. That was the first time I'd heard of an actual woman who was somebody's mistress. Interesting word. You can't call anyone a mistress. It has to be genitively linked with a man, and he is ambiguously subject or object, owner or owned. There is no male alternative. In my youth it was interesting because it sounded glamorous. My mother described 'the lady in question' as 'very smart'. I gathered the impression of someone who wore a lot of black, hats bought in Paris, and a Persian lamb coat. Illicit love was exotic and well dressed. Miss Moy-Evans, our snobbish, dotty, vague French teacher, who described herself as well born and was always talking about nannies and nurseries, told us a joke in French. It was about the Prince of Wales going on a journey, concluding with a pun on his mistress's first name, Wallis, *'Il a sa valise'*. Illicit love was royal and foreign.

The Welsh exception proved the rule. About twenty years ago, my mother said, the minister of Mount Zion had been carrying on with the wife of Prytherch Jones, one of the deacons. They were discovered *in flagrante* – not that we learnt that phrase in our Latin class – in the vestry. I imagined them writhing amongst the baptismal robes, black for boys and white for girls. I think I got the image of writhing from a story in Bethan's *True Romance* whose fiction was always obscure, romantic, and sexy. I was about sixteen, flattered to be told the story of the adulterous minister and the deacon's wife by my mother. It was an initiation ceremony, a sign that she knew I knew the facts of life which I'd managed to avoid learning from her. It was also a confession of sexual tolerance, since she didn't condemn the guilty pair. If anything, she was sympathetic, which astonished me. She told the story in a secretive whisper, late at night, when my father had gone to bed early with a bad cold and a hot-water bottle. Auntie Mary had been asleep for hours, and Idris was out courting.

It was a dramatic story, ending with the Reverend Clement Wetherall's departure. He wasn't drummed out of Mount Zion but providentially received a call from another chapel, somewhere in Yorkshire, too far away for them to hear about a Swansea adultery. He gave a wonderful farewell sermon. 'Floss, I'll never forget his face. Or his voice.' It sounded more like a personal valediction than a sermon. He confessed to the congregation that he'd chosen the wrong vocation.

'He said he should have gone on the stage. He was utterly sincere, you could tell. He was right too, I'm sure.' My mother sighed, 'Oh, he was a brilliant speaker. And handsome. He had a head of thick black hair – raven-black – with one snow-white lock right down the middle. Mind you, Wyn was a lovely looking woman.'

Wyn Prytherch Jones was a placid-faced grandmother. Two of her children had been in Sunday School with me, and she sat in the front pew every Sunday evening, singing away in an audible fine soprano.

'Lovely voice, like a lark,' observed my tolerant mother.

Wyn kept on going to chapel. She had grey hair. I couldn't believe she was an adulteress, a scarlet woman. She didn't look like one. The one outward sign of guilt was her musquash coat. Swansea associations with ill-gotten furs must have been behind my joke about Marilda's mink on the Solomons' bed.

When Charlie and I lived in Swansea after we married, we were wrapped up in each other. After Charlie started in the Bloomsbury solicitor's, and I got my assistant lectureship at UCL, we were very much married. The first time someone made a serious pass at me I was taken aback. It wasn't so much a pass as a proposition. Paul Sandberg was the editor of a literary encyclopaedia. I did some articles for him, on authors like Elizabeth Gaskell and Thackeray, whom I knew something about, and others, like Susanna Centlivre, I'd never heard of. I discovered that the way to write encyclopaedia pieces was to collate entries from three other encyclopaedias. I also discovered that a proposition could arrive out of the blue, in the middle of a literary conversation. As a seducer, Paul seemed to skip the usual preliminaries, but I was too innocent to know there was no such thing as a free lunch.

Paul was in his early fifties, I suppose. He used to give me lunch at a restaurant near the Monument. I found him a bit creepy. It was partly his heavy body and flabby wrinkled face, partly his way of leaning across the table and asking intimate curious questions about my friends and colleagues. I found him repulsive but fascinating in his knowing talk about what seemed to be the literary world. It was Paul who told me – or flatteringly pretended I knew – that Auden was homosexual, which made me re-read the wonderful early poems with a new understanding. When I talked about it to Charlie, he told me that he'd been walking round in Russell Square one afternoon and a man had made a pass at him. I asked him if he'd been shocked or upset and was very impressed that he was not. When I asked him if he thought he might be bisexual he considered the question seriously, but concluded that he was probably not.

'But you never know. Interesting question,' he added with characteristic detachment and intellectual curiosity. Until I left Wales for London the only homosexual I'd ever heard of was Oscar Wilde.

When I told my students in a practical criticism seminar that the sleeping head in Auden's 'Lullaby' was not given a gender, and was probably a young man's, I was shocked by one man's violent rejection of the news.

'Dr Jones, you've ruined the poem for me,' he protested. Since homosexuality was illegal at the time I didn't make a point of discussing it but occasionally got impatient with somebody's inevitable reference to the poetic love-objects in Auden – or Donne – as 'his wife'.

Paul's gossip was lubricious, though I couldn't quite put my finger on what was wrong. He got a kick out of talking about sex to an ignorant girl from the provinces, but I didn't understand at the time. He talked maliciously about the love lives of writers and academics with an air of insider knowledge, assuming, or pretending, that I would know who Louis and Stephen and Jack and Rosamond were, which I didn't. I was flattered, though he made me feel even more of an outsider. I showed him a few chapters of a novel I was struggling with and he told me he'd do his best with a friend who was a publisher. I didn't entirely enjoy the prospect, or our meetings, but couldn't see a way to refuse. I was bad at saying no, to large or small requests and solicitations. Nobody in the family could give me any advice, and I was too proud to ask friends.

I consoled myself by arriving early and visiting Southwark Cathedral and St Magnus Martyr's inexplicable Ionian white and gold, which I'd first sought out with Charlie. Those lunches with Paul set up interfering associations with Magnus Martyr and my favourite St Mary Woolnoth, which Charlie said was like a ship.

Charlie was as ignorant as I was, though less excited by London culture. I was trying to write the novel, teach myself to teach, and turn my thesis into a book, but I found time for some wandering round London. We were living in a small flat in Bedford Place, one big Georgian room made into two bedsitters, and we used to look at the river and the city churches at weekends, when the streets were quiet and empty. I remember a corner of old St Paul's churchyard where we once took a walk and in a purely hypothetical way discussed the possibility of separation. Charlie upbraided me because I started to speculate about one of my friends as a suitable person for him to have an affair with.

'Kindly refrain from arranging my future life, Florence,' he said. 'Stick to arranging your own, if you can.' I was taken aback. I had no serious expectation of any rift, and it was my first experience of finding abstraction turn particular and hurtful. Charlie was growing up more quickly than I was, and felt the perils of airy brittle jokes about marriage and divorce.

But that was some time after Paul looked up from skilfully boning his Dover sole, smiled intimately, and suddenly said he was going to Italy in the summer. Would I like to go with him? He was going for about three months, mostly spending time in Umbria and Tuscany.

'Three months?' I gasped spontaneously, then recovered. 'I couldn't possibly.'

I felt gauche and impolite. Some explanation seemed necessary, so I added awkwardly, 'I'm sorry but I love my husband.' It sounded silly, as if I were apologizing for love, not unwillingness to have him as a lover. I felt very provincial. I almost wished I could say yes, since saying no was so embarrassing.

When I got home I felt amused, then suddenly angry. I decided he must have heard on the grapevine that Charlie was an obscure solicitor, a Swansea boy, a fish out of water in London life. He had never asked me anything about him. Mixed with my indignation was a certain guilt at having accepted the frequent invitations and listened with an encouraging complicity. I was learning.

I was shocked to find myself speculating about what it would have been like to go away with Paul, whom I found repulsive. Why did I want to toy with the idea? It was the first time I'd been provoked into imagining sexual freedom. Paul wasn't proposing marriage or a weekend in Brighton, but a sexual adventure. My curiosity was roused. And so was a vague resentment that that my sexuality wasn't my own business, that I was married and didn't possess myself.

When I first started sleeping around – though that sounds misleadingly far-ranging – it was a deliberate carelessness, a loosening of the bonds. I was making a protest against chastity and permanence, perhaps against love too. I felt something like this before Charlie, when I went out with boys I didn't care about at all, out of curiosity and convention and idleness, though I usually didn't end up in bed. When marriage started to stale, that old carelessness came back. Unless my carelessness allowed it to stale. With Mick I decided to take great care.

Mick decided from the start that ours would be the perfect relationship. He didn't put it like that because 'relationship' was one of his banned words, like 'empathy'. I said I'd ban them too if Mick promised never to write 'commence' again. But I didn't tell him not to say 'toilet' and 'pardon me' because they were signs of his cultural difference. I teased him about saying 'prehaps' and he first denied it, then listened and laughed. He was better-tempered than I was about criticism, but when I said his style verged on the mandarin he winced. Criticizing each other's writing was fun, though I was touchy too, especially when he chopped up my long sentences. The first time I gave him an article I was dismayed to find it totally rewritten but gradually got used to wholesale criticism and revision. We often rewrote each other's writing, unwrote the rewriting, and got back to the first version. He objected to my liking for starting articles and lectures with quotations, insisting that you should begin with your own words, and I saw the point and changed my ways.

Once he accidentally gave Ellen a chapter of his Thackeray which I'd copiously annotated, and she said she found his editor's remarks interesting. I didn't see many of her comments on his stuff, only the odd underlining or correction. He tactfully kept our commentaries apart. We must have been alike in some ways, much as I resisted the idea. When I read her book on Hawthorne I found it irritatingly congenial. I also recognized Mick's compressed and witty style everywhere, which I didn't enjoy.

A fastidious stylist had to find a word for our love.

'What can we call this creature that we make? Affair won't do. No, not relationship. Could we call it an attachment?'

We agreed on our attachment. There remained the problem of how to describe me. Mick was my lover. In the seventies lovers could be plural, but a lover had to be a singular male, never a singular female. Girlfriend was ridiculous, partner too domestic. Mistresses lived in Maida Vale, before the Great War.

I burst out laughing when he looked up from his pillow, as I was pulling on my tights, and solemnly asked:

'Florence, are you my mistress?'

I said he reminded me of one of the children's baby books about a chick who fell out of the nest and went round asking dogs and cats and fork-lift trucks, 'Are you my mother?'

He wanted it to be permanent and faithful. I accepted the terms, making my secret reservation. It became the perfect love-affair, guaranteeing the lineaments of gratified desire. I began to behave like a sexual equal. What he asked, I agreed to, but he asked me to ask. It took a year or two but we had time. The creature we made together grew healthy and thriving.

As we busied ourselves, we got to know each other's story. There were the unknown histories of our Rumanian and Celtic and Polish ancestors, the better documented Midwest and Swansea cultures, our only slightly less than perfect marriages, my love-affairs, our children, books, honours, and careers. Higgledy-piggledy memoirs were punctuated by our experiments in love. We read the beloved's texts. We annexed each other's lives, as Mick first hoped we would.

One of the first nights in bed with Mel, lying beside him struck by desire and warm from the Canadian sun, I thought out loud:

'You think you're going to have a little fling, an *amour de voyage*, then you find yourself in the middle of somebody's life.'

He'd been telling me about his dying father, getting up one midnight in agony and running into the ocean to cool his pains. I was in his father's life too. And his wife's, as she recovered and exercised and was afraid. And his children's, about whom he talked incessantly, saying 'They're matchless.'

I didn't come as close to Mick's father. He didn't talk much about him, and never spoke about his parents or children with emotion. I once asked him if he cared for them and he was astonished that I might think otherwise. It was simply a reserved style.

His father used to give him his cast-off cars, big Cadillacs and Studebakers, which made the other students think he was rich. Joseph Solomon was a well-to-do lawyer but Mick said vaguely the four brothers hadn't got much when the estate was divided. When we first met, his mother was very much alive, living in Florida, and he visited her two or three times a year, coming back tanned from the Fort Lauderdale sun. He sent her his reviews which she pasted in a scrapbook. She died when we'd been together for about ten years, but he said very little about it.

His parents hadn't been keen on him marrying Ellen. I immediately loved them and hoped her character defects would emerge. But they didn't. It was just because she was a gentile. I said hopefully that I was a quarter Jewish, but it was the wrong line of descent, through my father, so they'd have disapproved of me too.

We kept rewriting our lifestories. There were points in our lives when we could make imaginary joins.

'I might have met you in London in the fifties,' I said. We had both been working in the British Museum. Mick was doing research for his Dickens biography as I was rewriting my thesis. We must have brushed shoulders at the catalogues, taken out the same books. We rebuked our ghosts for blindness but we agreed they couldn't have met. They would have had to fall in love, as elective affinities, but at the time they would have been too timid and too faithful.

'Tell me the story of your life,' I asked, sitting on the green sofa in his room, after making love, drinking wine or whisky. He began at once, with a biographer's compliance and neatness, with his birth in Chicago. He was the same age as Charlie, fifty-four. Our listening wasn't cosy. I wanted to know everything about him, to possess his story, but I resented his narrative of well-to-do family and education, cushioned against poverty and class-envy, and of love and marrying which had nothing to do with me. He recognized my sense of exclusion, saying he'd always dreamed of the unknown mistress; he and Ellen had never had anything like our passion. He wasn't too keen on some aspects of my story. He would say how wise I'd been to insist on having a job. He cherished my independence, past and present, and towards the end, in the future, without him. In a way he accepted Charlie. But he was jealous of my lovers. And of course I was jealous of his wife.

Mick's story made our story plain, even while it was beginning. We were only there on the green sofa because Ellen was ill, and incapacitated for love. He wouldn't have started an affair with anybody if she had still been well. Once when I said that to him, years later, he disagreed and said if we'd met before her illness he would have thought about divorce. I'm not sure that he would. He hated the casual sex in my past and my taste for solitude in the present.

My mother had a cottage in Rhossilli, which she inherited from my grandparents, a holiday house for the family. Mick assumed that I used it as a love-nest. When I went there with Susie and her boyfriend during our first summer he could understand. That was a family holiday. But when I went there for a long weekend on my own, soon after we met, he asked me who I was going to see. At first he couldn't fathom my answer.

'Nobody. Nobody at all. Really. I'll call in on my mother in

Swansea, and see Idris and his family, who live in the next village, but I go to the cottage to be on my own. London is the place where I teach and write and see people and go to dinner-parties and all that. Sometimes I have to stop and be on my own.'

He really couldn't understand that I liked walking on my own, that I liked cliffs and hills and limestone caves and sea. He'd never stood looking at the waves coming in and going out, or listening to the surf. He was obtuse about nature. I described Rhossilli Heights and Llanmadoc Down, our dunes and woods and salt-marsh, and he knew from literature that people loved nature, but he had no feelings for it. All his sensuousness went into sex and language. He could just about tell a daisy from a rose. I came to find that funny.

Once when I told him I was going to the cottage for a week-end I said idly that if he really didn't believe I was going because it was so beautiful he could come and see. There wouldn't be any of the family there.

'Perhaps I will come,' he said lightly. I didn't give the conversation another thought.

On my second evening I'd gone to bed early, having spent the day walking along the six-mile stretch of sand to Burry Holms, my favourite tidal island, and back again. I was reading, and enjoying my tiredness. It was about half-past eight, and when I heard the knock on the door I knew it was Mick. I flew downstairs in the old blue velvet dressing-gown somebody had left behind and everybody wore, opened the door and there he was standing on my doorstep, laughing and saying he knew I hadn't thought he'd come. In five minutes we were in bed. He had to leave at dawn, and said we'd go out to dinner. I said first he had to see the beach and the sea and the headland. We got up and walked quickly through the village to the cliffs beyond the car-park, halfway to the coastguard station.

It was still light. We stood and looked down at the long curved bay, the serpentine blunt-headed Worm at one end and hat-shaped Burry Holms at the other. There was a wind blowing off the sea, as there always is at Rhossilli, and Mick admired and shivered at the same time. We turned back and had dinner at the Worms

Head restaurant, eating gammon steak and chips and Black Forest gateau before going back to bed. Next morning I gave him breakfast, pointed out the minute ancient austere church, went with him in the car as far as Reynoldston, kissed him goodbye, and walked back by the road along the common to Rhossilli.

He'd come to make love, to see my territory, to please me. It was a gesture of sharing, an appreciation he thought he should feel, a metonymy. It was like our first love-feast, the bouillabaisse. He wouldn't come again. But I was glad he'd made the journey.

And after he died I was glad he'd been there. It wasn't somewhere without a trace of him, like so many of my places, including the whole of Swansea. But there were no romantic associations with the natural scene. I knew exactly why he came, and it was not to affect or attempt a response. And when he died nature was no consolation. One of my friends wrote to say she hoped I wasn't too unhappy, there were times when rocks and hills and sea were only rocks and hills and sea. That's true, though it was different after Charlie's death. When I looked at something he had loved, like a Tree of Heaven, or a skein of flying geese, I was looking for two. With Mick that affinity was missing, but it didn't matter. We grew into a compatibility.

Once in a seminar we were discussing the way Jane Austen makes Marianne Dashwood fall in love with Brandon after their marriage, which shocked one of the students. In a way it's what happened to me with Mick. He wasn't dull and rheumatic and flannel-padded, and it didn't take long for me to feel desire, but I wasn't immediately attracted through the flesh. I went to bed with him because of liking and politeness and admiration and hope, and it turned out to be lucky true love.

During our two or three unsuccessful times I would murmur 'I love you' in the usual way, and so did he. Once we were sitting on his green sofa. After my first visit, Mick wrote of his incredulity, said he was dreaming of being visited by nymphs, on that green sofa. It became a green bank, for the afternoon of amorous fauns. It was an old post-war utility sofa, but the little geometrical pattern was unfamiliar to him, and anyway he was short-sighted. We were sprawled there drinking, naked amongst the books. They were piled on the shelves, loose on the floor, and stacked in boxes, still unpacked after the move.

I remembered my sudden thought that I was so happy I must be in love. I told him, expecting him to be delighted. But he put his glass down, looked away, and said morosely that I'd been saying I loved him from the first afternoon in Hans Crescent, so what did that mean? Why had I said that then if I didn't mean it till now? Why did I sound as if I were still teetering on the brink?

'I don't know,' I said weakly, 'I suppose I often do . . . did say it.'

Mick looked cross, 'So what are you saying now?'

It was true, I said 'I love you' automatically, because it seemed only polite to say it, like 'Thank you for having me' after a childhood party. I always found it banal and boring when people made a big deal out of not saying 'I love you'. Too much melodrama. The phrase has a conveniently vast range. When you're over forty-five and have been in and out of marriage it doesn't seem worth making a fuss about saying 'I love you'. You can usually tell what people mean. By the time I told Mick I was on the brink of love, I was out of bed, not in the throes of desire. It was more than a formula. And after a bit he knew what I meant.

We said 'I love you' to each other a thousand times, meaning a thousand different things within the real thing.

We could switch off tenderness and fondness, as you can't always. But we could always return. That agility came with the games we learnt to play.

Standing in a bookshop by the World's End, I looked through a book telling you all the things you ever wanted to know about sex. It took the form of answers to worried seekers after perfect sex. There was a sad woman whose husband wanted her to beat him, and did her personal laundry, and though she was willing she said it made her feel silly. There was another woman who liked to take initiatives but whose husband wanted her to wait for him to make the approach. I don't remember the answers but reflected on my good luck with Mick.

We never actually asked each other to do anything which made either feel silly. We had complementary tastes, and though I suppose I could have adjusted if Mick had insisted on playing laundrymaid I can't imagine resisting the temptation to joke about the convenience of that kinky genre. And I find humour unaphrodisiac.

The only breach came with Charlie's illness and death. Otherwise I always wanted what Mick wanted, often before he said he wanted it. We were almost telepathic about sex. It wasn't telepathy, but tastes that fitted. And a shared determination to advance the science of pleasure.

We were apart a lot, when Mick went back to teach in the States or when I went off somewhere on a lecture trip, so we had the incentive of separation, and a long serial correspondence. When I look at those letters now, or remember them without looking, I love their collage of personal porn, love lyric, literary criticism, gossip and quotidian story. During the absences we would hatch new sexual schemes. If I hoped he'd suggest this or that when he came back, nine times out of ten he did. And vice versa. Occasionally our thoughts would make me feel nervous or squeamish, but fantasizing together would lead to desire, and desire to doing.

Lawrence is wrong about sex in the head. Of course it mustn't stay in the head but the head's important. The descent from head to lower body is part of the fun. I remember once saying to Mick, as we moved from concept to desire and desire to act, that I supposed it was what happens to sex maniacs, except that they can't return to the everyday life. I remember a Japanese sex film, too pornographic for art and too artistic for porn, in which the lovers have done absolutely everything and through doing it get to the point of wanting to kill each other. I hated the film but had to admit that it wasn't entirely alien or incomprehensible. When I tried to explain that to Mick, he was not turned on by the idea of death. The lovers in the film spent their entire time in sex, but we had a life to come round to after the tantrums and delirium. After abandoning ourselves to each other for a time, in Mick's phrase, we would sleep and wake to gossip and worry and plan, about kids, friends, colleagues, students, exams, parties, books, reviews, partings and meetings. Wretched sex-maniacs lack that bonding in the ordinary world. They cross into forbidden territory, while average sensual lovers only imagine deadly transgression.

I'd never been very interested in pornography. Minnie, a colleague of mine at Royal Holloway who specialized in modern fiction and wrote her thesis on D. H. Lawrence and Henry Miller, used to give occasional advice to the Director of Public Prosecutions. She kindly passed on what I thought of as the superior dirty books she read, like *I Am Jan Cremer* and *Last Exit from Brooklyn*. I went to hear the case against Calder and Boyars for publishing *Last Exit*, and heard Minnie nervously speaking up in the Old Bailey for its literary merit, with Eric Mottram and Alvarez. She said afterwards that she was terrified, never having been in a lawcourt before, astonished to find her heart hammering like mad, her composure overcome with awe and guilt.

Once I was taken to the Small Claims Court, because of a neighbour whose washing-machine flooded my flat, but who wouldn't pay all the plumber's bill. I went there fully prepared, with documents showing my neighbour's admissions and silly apologies. I was full of injured innocence, but once addressed by the county judge, I felt so guilty I'd have confessed to bashing down my ceiling myself. We felt envious of Minnie for getting the books, the fees, and her picture in the papers, but after I'd been to court, even though I won, I knew exactly how she felt. When I got a letter calling me up for jury service it only took the court's letterhead to strike me with guilt. It was guilt Minnie and I were interested in, and talked about, not pornography.

Apart from the novels she passed on, which contained a few details that made me throw up, I'd read *Fanny Hill* and enjoyed its elegance. *The Story of O* was passed round the Senior Common Room and once I was reading it on the train to Swansea. Next to me was a nice woman like my mother, who talked nonstop about her husband, children, grandchildren, dogs and cats then looked at the book on my lap and asked me what I was reading. I blushed, though my blushing days were over. I said it was a new novel, put it in my bag, and read the *Guardian* instead.

Somebody says man – let's include woman – is never more innocently occupied than when reading pornography. I always thought
of it as strictly for the solitary, the unsatisfied, the sick and the
sad, not for true lovers.

I found porn tedious because I'd been in the habit of making
up my own sexy stories, from the age of seven or eight. The
scenarios developed as I did. The habit started long before I had
boyfriends, and wasn't anything to do with relationships or at-
tachments. Later on sexual fantasy came in handy for spaces
between lovers. It was strictly private and detached from reali-
ties. I was startled when Mick told me he'd used porn a lot,
because it was associated with the backstreets and men in mack-
intoshes. He hadn't intended to tell me but it slipped out as he
was recounting the story of his marriage, which like most stories
of other people's marriages made me wonder why Charlie and I
had split up. Ours hadn't been so bad, I thought. It was marriage, not our marriage, which I didn't want.

'So it soon became clear', Mick said, 'that she didn't like sex
nearly as much as I did. Evidently I wasn't going to get enough.'

He'd told me he'd never been unfaithful to Ellen, so I asked,
'What did you do? Masturbate?'

After a pause he said 'Yes. Yes, I did. Was that bad?'

I started to cheer him up with my childhood fantasies, which
I'd never mentioned to anyone before. He was amused and impressed, and disagreed when I suggested that fantasy may have
damaged my sex-life. We decided that the trouble was keeping
pornography private, and not sharing it. The pornographer was
necessary. So was the secret sharer, alter ego and double. I was
socially dominant, bossy, talkative, showing-off, blowing my own
trumpet. My anti-self had to be humiliated. I hated admitting
my bossiness, and didn't until my mother, in her outspoken nine-
ties, developed a stream of consciousness to utter the home-truths
we think and don't say out loud.

In my childhood she'd often quote Burns, one of her favourites, because she'd had a Scottish boyfriend, Johnnie Steele, and
because she and my father loved Burns's radicalism. Her favourite
quotations were 'The goud is but the guinea's stamp! A man's a

man for a' that' and 'Oh wad the gift the Giftie gee us! To see ousel as ithers see us'. The latter was declaimed with meaningful glances at her husband and children, and heavily ironic intonations. At some point in her old age she decided to make me the recipient of the Giftie's gift.

It was always difficult making her tea just as she liked it, as bad as having Jane Grigson to dinner. Though I usually managed to get it right, after sixty years of practice, I slipped up from time to time. If I did, she might say, *sotto voce*, but not all that *sotto*, 'Oh, what a horrible cup of tea.' The home-truth was accompanied by her sweetest smile, and 'Thank you, Floss, darling, that was lovely.' The worst candid comment came after I'd complained she hadn't put on the clean stockings I'd left by her bed: 'Our Floss is very domineering. She should be a prison governor.'

That was when I began to see why I was so passive and compliant, in bed and in fantasy. The passive one was my shadow. Mick was a gentle creature, so his shadow was a brute. His texts were fantasies of oppression. He hadn't invented them, but went to the classic sources, like Sade. He would bring texts to read in bed, but we began to discard them for narrative collaboration. Mick turned from reader into writer and got more inventive. We didn't resort regularly to fantasy till near the end, when, as he told the neurologist, his sexual drive and competence had diminished. Our do-it-yourself bedtime stories, which had settled into texts with patterns of repetition and routines of theme and character, came in handy then.

'Does it help?' I asked on one of our last times. I meant the embrace and the orgasm. Some nerves and muscles still worked. When he said 'Yes', I could smile, as I didn't do very often those days. I tried not to be tearful, but I often was.

'Come on, Florence darling,' he'd mutter incoherently, 'everybody's got to die, you know.'

I'd try to laugh and say something silly, 'All right, as long as you promise to haunt me.'

Judged by the standards of a sexual gymnast like Timmy our antics may not have been physically impressive, but they were blissful. Everything we had was brought into play – presence, absence, dreams, waking up, reading, writing, eating, drinking, liking, and fighting. Even trust and jealousy.

'So what did you do with Timmy that was so great?'

I'd been idly recalling the past, too sleepy for tact.

'With Timmy it was nothing but sex. Just sex.'

I was putting down my on-and-off fling with Timmy but innocently arousing Mick's curiosity.

'What did he do that was so great?'

I had to think. I evaded the question.

'Well, he used to talk about this girl who was very agile, very gymnastic. I remember he said we were good together but it couldn't be what it was like with her because she was so athletic.' I hadn't found her rivalry threatening or aphrodisiac. I was far too lazy.

'So what did they do?'

'Oh, Mick, I can't remember. Let me think. Well, they did it in every imaginable and unimaginable position.'

Obviously that wasn't precise enough. 'But exactly *what* did she do?'

If I'd ever known, I had forgotten. 'Somersaults? But I don't think even Timmy could manage a somersault and keep in position.' I went off into a fit of giggles, but sex could make Mick temporarily lose humour, and he insisted.

'What sort of things did he do?'

I really had forgotten. I tried again. 'Oh, yes. I remember now. He had this obsession about not disengaging. While you were changing position. Yes, that's right. He was quite good at that.'

Just in time I stopped myself from saying I'd never known anyone else who cared about that. Mick managed to be sexually curious and jealous at the same time, so I had to take care not to make my references too plural. It was fun steering between Scylla and Charybdis, because we weren't just amusing ourselves. We were in love as well.

Mick was irritated by the last piece of information about Timmy's high standards and expertise, especially when we tried not disengaging and didn't always manage it. 'Christ, I don't see how anyone could manage this.'

Mick was interested in other men's bodies. Once he asked, 'What was Timmy's prick like?'

'Uncircumcised.'

'What else? Big?'

'I think so. Well, no. Sort of medium. Oh Mick, I really don't know. I've never cared much about that. It's only men who think size is so important.'

But I was goaded or inspired to tell him that Mel's prick had been uncomfortably large, or perhaps the wrong shape for me. Of course he was most interested in Charlie's genital details, while I was least willing to discuss my marriage. One day I gave in and revealed that Charlie's penis, as I respectfully called it, had a little brown mole on it. More than these disappointingly unspecific memories I couldn't manage, not being a visually observant person, especially in bed where I've always concentrated on touch and taste. Probably because of my inhibited youth, when I always closed my eyes and didn't dare look, even at a kissing face.

I certainly had no interest in Ellen's body. The first time we went to bed Mick stared at my belly, and explained that Ellen had three Caesareans, so a woman's smooth unscarred flesh looked strange. He had an appendix-scar and his puckered belly looked odd to me. I wondered if her rejection of labour had something to do with her frigidity. A reluctant vagina. Or cervix. But frigidity is not woman's word, any more than nymphomania. They're man's invention, as Mrs Gamp said of the steam-engine. I expect Mick and Ellen had incompatible fantasy-lives. It's all a matter of luck. Or some deep intuition that gets clever as you grow up.

Sometimes he would turn up, taking his fair-to-middling wine out of the briefcase, and make an immediate announcement.

'I've been having kinky thoughts.'

In the early days he might add, 'Is that bad?', but after he realized that I invariably replied 'Oh good', he stopped apologizing. All that started after our first long separation, when he went to America for his son's graduation, and I went on holiday to Provence. We wrote every day, starting with an express letter he sent from Heathrow. Every morning I walked through an olive-grove, to the mail-box on a wooden post. Our letters got more erotic, the eroticism got more inventive, and we elaborated a detailed scenario for our reunion. Everything came off delight-fully, exactly according to plan. It was the oddest meeting I had known, new and strange. A funny homecoming, first of many. We went straight into sex, then back to friendly fondness. Look-ing-glass love. After the passion came affection.

'Darling, it's lovely to have you back. I've missed you.'

And 'I'll miss you', I said, after one of the very last embraces. That was when I asked him to haunt me.

Sometimes I dream we're back in bed again, and everything's easy. I wish there were ghosts, solid enough to grasp and stroke. But dreams can seem substantial. Saying 'pinch me' doesn't work, dream's touch mimics waking. And since sooner or later the body is bound to disappoint, I make the most of dream-stuff. I wel-come illusion. Like Hamlet I want it to stay, its flesh and blood hard and tangible, even though its solidity is quick to soften. My passion with Mick lasted a good long time, and it was solid. Like the delights so rapturously harmonised by our hymn-sing-ing in Mount Zion chapel on a Sunday:

Solid joys and lasting pleasures
None but Zion's children know.

SIX

Foolish Things

I always lost weight when I fell in love. After I worked out that
I must be in love with Mick because of feeling happy, the bathroom scales recorded a loss of half a stone, and the matter was
settled. Not only did I look better, because I always lost weight
in the right places, hips and spare tyre, not breast and face, but I
could go off and do what we all like to do, buy new clothes for
a new lover. All your old clothes are new to them but of course
it's to celebrate, like champagne, which always makes me feel
there is something to celebrate just by its ice-coldness and biscuity
taste and bubbles.

When I met Mel I didn't eat for three weeks. The pounds fell
off as we spent our days arguing about English teaching in universities, and our nights in love and talk. We were in an unimaginable region, the Rockies. In my adolescence there was a popular
song which began 'When it's Springtime in the Rockies/In the
Rockies far away'. I never knew anyone who'd been there, and
in my wildest dreams of fame and travel and the wide wicked
world beyond Swansea I never got as far as those white heights
and green glaciers. Charlie told me our ancient mountains were
the thing, not those young crags, but the Rockies were thrilling.
Like Mel.

I met Mel in the fall at a marvellous conference which shifted
from Calgary to Banff, where we climbed the glacier and walked
by Lake Louise. I could take in the scenery, but not the meals. It
was love at first sight. I lived on black coffee, orange juice, and

dry martinis. Mel bought me a pair of pale yellow beaded moccasins and a lump of green soapstone like a squashed face, from a horrible gift shop in Toronto, its centrepiece an obscene construction of bone and fish-skin claiming to be a mermaid. It was like being in Mr Venus's shop. I still have the presents. And a recollection of amorous euphoria, and a life without food. I never felt better. I was high on love and cold pure air. I just didn't want any solids, except for Mel.

When I was slowly agreeing to marry Charlie, against my principles, my mother got very worried, saying my clothes were hanging off me. Music to my ears.

I still have some of the clothes I bought to look beautiful for Mick. To begin with, it was summer, and family tradition decreed that you bought new clothes to be fine in the fine weather. Even in the Depression we had new clothes for Whitsun, and paraded round the Uplands, and Sketty, and Tycoch to collect praise and threepenny bits from the relations. I remember a heavy white silk sailor-suit with a square collar, a cream panama with a wide brim, and a pink organdy in which I felt I could outshine Shirley Temple. Forty years later I bought for my new May love a butcher-blue linen trouser suit, thick and knobbly with pockets and a belt from a shop in glamorous Beauchamp Place, a green Liberty-print dress with a long full skirt from Harrods, a three-quarter white coat with huge lapels from Harvey Nichols, black jeans, six black bras and black silk pants from the Kings Road, brown thick leather sandals from Shoesissima, an Italian shoeshop in Knightsbridge, and a pair of ridiculous black shoes bought in Florence with five-inch heels that raised me to Mick's nose level. I saw them tottering elegantly past, on sheer shaved legs, reflected in the shiny wall of the bank on my way to Hans Crescent, week after week, shoes chosen to look good, kick off, and slip on again. A shot from a film, realler than faces and bodies in the mirror, reassuring part that stood for the whole, love speeding on its way.

I had my hair done every week, took a course of exercises at Elizabeth Arden, and had my first pedicure. Mick looked at me attentively, but I don't think he was very interested in clothes.

Perhaps he was always in a hurry to take them off. He usually said, 'You look good to me.'

Timmy always said 'You look charming.' Charlie was good on clothes, sometimes sharply critical. We went back to days of rationing when wardrobes were empty and you made the most of every garment. I remember an emerald-green cotton suit that looked like slub silk, a grey coat, and a grey blouse made of men's shirt material, so dreadful to iron that I threw the iron across the room after smoothing in vain for an hour. And of course my shapeless heavy wedding costume. When I came to London I called costumes suits, and even met one well-born English woman who called them coats and skirts. I remember all Charlie's shirts, giving him one for Christmas and writing a poem about it. And Mick's bizarre shirts and gaudy ties. They're all in the patchwork of past garments, along with a wine-coloured winter coat made out of some bristly stuff, a dog's-tooth tweed suit my mother bought me for college with her coupons, a party dress of blue silk with gold spots I wore to the Hospital Ball, Auntie Mary standing back and saying I was a little princess.

And all the clothes I bought for Mel, who adored clothes. There was a white shirtwaist dress made of soft woollen stuff which he said I must keep for when we went to Florida in December, a blue-and-green suit with a mini-skirt when mini-skirts first came in, and lovely things from Biba, a sand-coloured floppy velour dress, a black crepe trouser-suit, and a tight-fitting petrol-blue woollen dress I grew too fat for years ago but only gave to Oxfam last summer. There was a brown and red paisley dress, like the ocean islands you see as you fly over Newfoundland. I had flown that way just before we met, coming from Heathrow to Boston for a holiday with friends in Massachusetts before the conference. I described the islands lit up below, my first sight of America, and Mel turned them into an image for that dress. There was a heavy blue and black check coat from Aquascutum, brought unnecessarily for the late summer trip. As I was packing to go home on the last evening of the conference, weather changed, leaves falling, farewells in progress, Mel lay on my bed, head raised to watch me bundle things into my case, and asked me to put it on so he would know what I looked like in London, in the winter.

I still have a big black sweater I remember wearing when I went for the first time to a meeting of the Council of Roselands, a Church of England Training college in East Putney. Auntie Mary made it for me, from thick oily wool used for fishermens' jerseys, and I love it. The other governors all seemed to be clergymen or beautifully coiffed and dressed ladies, one of whom, Lady Something, leant over to me and said with great sweetness,

'Now I shall remember you. I'll think, Dr Jones, black sweater.'

'But I won't always be wearing it,' I replied, deliberately misunderstanding.

When Mick and I went to Paris in August 1984, for three glorious days I felt obliged to buy new glamorous black underwear, and he loved that. But I don't think he really liked the floppy pale blue cotton trouser suit that looked like pyjamas, which I bought in a shop in the Kings Road. When I once wore it in Swansea, and asked my mother if she wanted me to collect her pension from the Post Office, she asked me if it was pyjamas I was wearing, and if I was going out in them.

'Dear, dear, Floss, are you really? People will wear anything these days.'

What Mick liked was the garment I'm most ashamed of, the fur coat that lurks in many women's cupboards, replacing the skeletons. It's hard to get rid of, like the cheese in *Three Men in a Boat* or perhaps on the *Bummel*. I once asked a woman in Portobello if she'd buy a five-year-old Harrods lynx, and she looked doubtful, surrounded by minks. Greatly daring, I asked the girl in the Earls Court Road Oxfam if they accepted furs, and she looked disgusted and said 'Certainly not!'

I was once asked by a militant vegetarian if it was real, and as I hesitated, to choose a form of lying, he saved me the trouble by apologizing for the thought. 'Of course it's not. I'm so sorry.'

But Mick admired my dash and daring in buying it. He asked me how much it cost, and when I told him turned pale. I think he had intended to pay for it, but changed his mind when he heard the price. Once I wrote to him ecstatically about going to an exhibition of Morandi etchings, and he sent me a cheque for a hundred and fifty pounds. Embarrassed, I had to explain that they cost thousands and saying I'd love to have one on the wall had been a metaphor. It was the sort of thing Charlie and I would say, meaning that a picture could live in our domestic space. That came of using the wrong language. I haven't got a Morandi, but I have a small pale brown Wilson Steer bought with money Mick gave me for a colour television. He had bought two, one for their house and one for the London flat, and felt he should in fairness buy one for me too. But I didn't want it. The small fifty-pound black and white set I'd bought for the girls was still going.

Mick and Ellen spent a lot of time watching television, sometimes stuff that would make you die of boredom, like Torville and Dean. I asked him rudely, 'How can you watch that?' and he said irritatedly that it was skill and grace. I gave up. There were a few gaps in taste like that between us, and I would occasionally wonder if they never became an issue because we didn't live together. He liked some pretty terrible films, too, and he and Ellen loved all the authentic glossy expensive English BBC colour versions of Evelyn Waugh and Paul Scott.

He had occasional small unpredictable failures in extravagance. Perhaps they only seemed like failures because I couldn't help comparing him with Charlie. Mick had so much money – inheritance, salary, royalties, huge lecture fees – and Charlie never had a penny but would give you everything he possessed and more. And there was the invisible line between family and not-family that's present in most affairs. Mick would give me hundreds, not thousands. He wouldn't leave me a legacy. His wife and children would get all the money and the royalties. Once I told him Susie was nagging me for a washing-machine and he kept planning to buy her one. And not long before he died he sent me the cheque for two thousand pounds, and I sent it back, because we'd just quarrelled and I didn't like money to be used for making up.

He often gave me money to buy clothes, but not fur coats – a warm Harrods dressing-gown, a dark green velvet top with small roses, which I still possess. He never chose clothes for me but once came with me to buy a nightie. With three black silk specimens over my arm, I let him follow me into the changing-room in Harrods, the saleswoman protesting as loudly as she thought proper. Mick followed almost innocently, and was too deaf to hear her calling 'But sir!'. It was a new game, trying on things with Mick in a shop, with the stern woman hovering outside but too discreet to come in and throw us out. We only played it the once.

We lingered as long as I dared, or a bit longer. I blush at the memory. I felt so embarrassed as we were paying that I couldn't look the saleswoman in the eye. Mick enjoyed the occasion greatly, and as we bought a very expensive garment, nobody said anything. I discouraged a repeat performance. Mick was surprised when I said we'd been guilty of a grave breach of Harrods decorum, and pointed out that they don't put up notices forbidding men to accompany their wives. And you can't keep dashing out to show the man the nightie.

Sometimes he would take me to help him buy things, usually in Harrods sales, where I turned into a wife fondly advising her husband. On one occasion we had bought a beautiful soft grey tweed jacket, after much discussion and appraisal. We were crossing Sloane Street when he said: 'I've got a confession to make. You won't like it. I shouldn't really have asked you to come with me today. The coat is Ellen's present to me ... for our anniversary.'

Of course I wasn't thrilled at the thought of being the mistress choosing the wife's present. I thought she would be even less thrilled if she knew that I'd helped. But the refinement of apologizing because it was an anniversary present was a straining at a gnat after a camel if ever there was one. I wanted to say spitefully that horrible Ellen wasn't an earner, and got all her money from Mick, so it was really his present to himself, but the feminist in me is glad I didn't. Mick's uncharacteristic apology showed he could see some cause for my jealousy of his wife, which he usually protested was unnecessary since I was so healthy and she was so sick. And I was in a good mood and the sun was shining, so I smiled and said not to worry.

But the incident started one of our rare detached conversations about jealousy. It was very brief but it cleared the air. Jealousy was the passion Mick felt so crazily, and expected me not to feel at all. His real or pretended assumption that I couldn't feel jealous because of my advantages had the advantage of making it hard for me to express my jealousy. But after the anniversary jacket, I felt free to raise the forbidden subject. With the utmost good temper, as we lay on our backs side by side after making love, I reasoned.

'Mick, supposing you were in my position. Supposing you lived alone, and I lived with my husband, spent most of the time with him, looked after him physically and socially, cooked for him, helped him to dress and undress, and went on holidays and lecture-trips with him, always keeping you the darkest of dark secrets? And if you were faithful, never going out with anyone except platonically or professionally, but I got madly jealous if you mentioned another woman's name? Wouldn't you feel you had a right – not a right exactly, but you know what I mean – wouldn't you be jealous of my husband, and not feel any less jealous because he was an invalid with whom I never had sex?'

After a long silence Mick admitted, 'There is something in what you say.' He didn't understand my jealousy because it wasn't sexual jealousy, like his. Of course his jealousy was perfectly understandable too. I was free, and I lived alone, travelled a lot, and I had told him too much about Timmy and Mel and other lovers. When I first went down to stay in Rhossili in the family cottage, in July, after term ended, he thought I must be seeing some man, though I had explained that I went there for family and walking and sea and hills. His obtuseness to nature made that seem odd, almost incredible. I told him about an old friend who had come over to the cottage, and how we'd drunk lots of wine and got sentimental playing records of Gershwin, Cole Porter, and Al Boley, well into the night. When I mentioned 'Smoke Gets in Your Eyes', 'These Foolish Things' and 'Our Love Affair' he got in a rage. I couldn't make it out, and it took me a good twenty minutes to realize that he had misheard the name of my friend, Joan Roberts, as 'John', and thought I was playing records with an old Swansea flame.

I was careless with things. I didn't dare tell Mick when I lost
the first present he gave me, not long after he gave it. It was a
gold and pearl brooch, a bunch of grapes, very elegant though
not exactly my style. After a couple of weeks I realized I hadn't
seen it for a while. Perversely, I never went back to the restaurant in Charlotte Street where I thought I might have lost it.
When Mick eventually asked me why I never wore it, I admitted
it had got lost, and of course he was offended and thought I
didn't value it. Perhaps that was why he never gave me anything quite so expensive again, except towards the end, and that
was something else I lost, though I didn't tell him. I was too sad
about it myself. It was a ring, a twisted ring of three kinds of
gold, pale, and bright, and dark. It fitted tightly on my finger, so
it must have been fallen through a crack in the floor or dropped
to be swallowed by the Hoover. The lost brooch was his first
present, and the ring his last. He asked me if I still had it, and I
lied and said it was in my jewel-box. I have the little empty vel-
vet-lined box it came in, and it's joined the ghostly group of lost
love-things.

There's the silver and cornelian bracelet Charlie gave me, with
oblong stones like dark orange toffees, which I loved, and lost
on a plane. And the silver money-clip Mel sent me one Christmas from Tiffanys. I gave Charlie one like it, in an impulse of
sentimental bad faith, but I never saw him use it. He was careless with things too, unlike Mick. Timmy gave me a heavy pale
jade bangle, and an unset cameo brooch. He said the cameo's
face was a lovely one, and I was to choose the setting. We split
up soon after, and I left as it was, not caring much about it.
Years later I felt sorry for it, took it to a jeweller's shop in Kensington
Church Street, and chose a fine gold frame, but they lost it. After
acrimonious argument, they gave me another one in exchange,
but I felt for the loss, not so much for Timmy's sake as for the
lovely face.

I've got lots of things Mick gave me, dozens of books, a long
silver chain so delicate it gets tangled, a chunky bracelet from
Sweden, with topaz jewels which look like cubes of transparent
gum, a mother-of-pearl and amethyst brooch he was afraid might

offend me by its cruciform pattern, and a moonstone ring, which I always wear. All good magic. But it's good magic to lose some things. To admit human imperfection, like the mistake in the carpet. Or for fear of tempting providence, like the ring thrown into the sea. I lost things so that they wouldn't become too sacred.

Clandestine presents are at special risk. I gave Mick a little ivory box, and he told me with some embarrassment that his daughter Maria had seen it and asked him if she could have it. He hadn't been able to say no, and I was hurt. Once I sent Mel a Chinese pigeon, a fragment of carved ivory, with a poem in which dove rhymed with love. When I visited his office I looked round and asked where it was. Shamefaced, he told a story about finding it broken after the office had been cleaned, its thin brittle delicate feet twisted and torn. He didn't say what had happened to the remains and I was offended, and decided he hadn't known its material or amorous value. I suppose that's how Mick felt about the pearl brooch. Poor old things.

There are all our lost toys, broken dolls, missing teddy bears, pencils worn to stumps, a doll's house Uncle Bert made with white walls, a red roof, and a green door, the jigsaws of the British Isles and 'When Did You Last See Your Father?' with their missing pieces. I wasn't a great doll-lover, aspiring after a boy's cricket bats, Hornby trains and Meccano, but I remember a big blonde doll with a blue frilled dress and curls which I ruined by giving her a trim in a fit of ambitious hairdressing. My mother talked to us so much about her wooden Dutch doll, Annie Katie, with painted black hair and face, who was chopped up by her naughty brother Jackie (a real little devil) that I forget I never saw her. I still have a doll my parents brought me back from a holiday in London, a brown velvet doll called Bella Bambina, but always regarded by me as a boy. He was cuddled and hugged, first by me, and then by Joanna, who clutched, adored, and took him to bed as her fetish, called him 'Baby', and kissed his face till it wore away. My father, who had clever hands, made him a new head of curly hair, sewed on a new face, and painted his lips till they shone like new. He lives in my bedroom chest-of-drawers, a beautiful Regency tallboy Charlie and I bought forty-two years

ago for fifty pounds in a shop on the corner of the Old Brompton
and Earls Court Roads. It was next to a wonderful poulterer-
and-fishmonger, Appleyards, who delivered our first hare, with
its little accessory tin of blood. We were out so they left it with
our downstairs neighbour, an opera singer with a large bust and
a dazzling smile. She arrived on our doorstep with the hare in a
big white dish, like John the Baptist's head, saying as we apologized that it was no trouble, 'I love them!'

The language of things has its own pathos, and power. Some
things require fidelity. It's hard to invent things, as well as people.
Or revise and reinvent them. There were so many objects I felt
superstitious about putting into fiction, but I did use a grandfather clock made by Daniel Jordan, bought as a birthday present
for Joanna to quieten my troubled conscience on the eve of a trip
to Australia. I pressed it into symbolic service, making it strike
the hours all through the night, in a way my family could never
tolerate in real life, to punctuate an overwrought scene in which
Clara sheds insomniac tears for dead Daniel. The chapter never
got finished but when I hear my clock strike I sometimes laugh
or feel guilty.

Of course you can make new things, like new people, by changing a few details in the real ones. I wouldn't use my round din-
ing-table for a dinner-party I needed in the novel, but by turning
the mahogany to oak, I could fit it into Elizabeth's sitting-room,
as I began to find her sympathetic, and it served its purpose. As
I reluctantly furnished the house in Dorchester where she and
Daniel lived I felt jealous of their things, suddenly minding that
Mick and I never shared any furniture.

I hit on the idea of furnishing my imaginary rooms with stuff
Charlie and I saw and liked but didn't buy, usually because it
was too dear. I could use them with without a pang. I remembered a shop window in the Kings Road over thirty years ago. It
had nothing in it except a small roomy yellow velvet armchair,
which cost seventy pounds, and I put it in the sitting-room I
furnished for Clara in Barfield Gardens, overlooking a garden
which is a cross between Stanley Gardens and Nevern Square. I
filled her flat with borrowed bits and pieces, a big golden Afghan

from Idris's house in Porteynon, a black leather sofa like one in my cousin Chrissie's drawing-room, my grandmother's glass vase with painted flowers, a copper kettle shone by my mother's friend Olwen in Rhossilli, my mother's brass candlesticks, and a blue and yellow Wilson Steer of Dover Beach I saw in Christie's and couldn't afford to bid for. I like it better than the one Mick gave me, which was cheaper. These were all familiar things but easy-going, not too sacred, neutral enough to be lifted and used again.

I thought of using some of the lost things too. That didn't seem inconsistent or treacherous because I would be finding them again, memorializing them and restoring them. I might have used the cornelian bracelet and the ring with the three golds, if I'd finished the novel. There was an Indian shawl Timmy gave me in our early days, which I left in a cab, that would have done nicely for Clara to wear with a little black dress to Maggie's wedding party. When Maggie turned into Sally, the skull became an old Spanish painting of a dead face, and she didn't kill herself, but was run over by a couple of joy-riders.

I let Clara and Daniel look at their reflected embrace in the gift-framed oval looking-glass Charlie and I bought. But only in a draft of a book I never finished. The mirror used to be in the bedroom, but now it's hanging in the hall. If I'm in the mood and I look hard enough I have a choice of faces to put next to mine.

SEVEN

Shortening Bread

'How pleasant to have been Mr Jones,' Mick sipped the white wine he'd brought and watched me shell the prawns. 'Did Charlie enjoy your cooking?'

'Yes,' I said, after a minute. I had scrubbed and rinsed my hands carefully before starting and I was making sure every scrap of shell was picked off the prawns. Mick had looked curiously round the kitchen, occasionally commenting on the paintings and shells and stones and bits of driftwood, and observing the lack of counters and gadgets and microwave. He picked up the bowl of *rouille* and sniffed it with a smile. I was admitting him to my domestic space, wondering why it felt more of an initiation than going to bed. I resisted the urge to ask him not to watch my fingers, and went on carefully till the prawns were all finished. I held the colander under the tap. I was making bouillabaisse, and doing the prawns to put in at the last moment, with chopped parsley and rocket. He said he'd been brought up not to eat shrimp, but had got to like it, though he never touched pork. I explained that they were prawns not shrimp, that in England we didn't say shrimp but shrimps, that our shrimps were like prawns only smaller, and that at home we caught them in the rock pools, though they weren't as good as our cockles and mussels. You had to watch out for a red tide but we got wonderful small meaty mussels in Broughton and Whitford.

There used to be cockle-beds there too, which seem to have vanished. Charlie's grandfather had once been 'musseled', according to his mother's thrilling narrative, so the Joneses never touched shellfish, but Charlie was persuaded to share my family's taste for it, encouraged at a tender age when my brother Idris and I went shrimping with green penny-nets on bamboo sticks in the pools of Bracelet Bay and Caswell.

I was brought up to love rich food. Some of the children at school were small and skinny from malnutrition, but even a fairly poor Swansea family in the thirties had plenty to eat, putting food before clothes and never having holidays or spending money improving the house or buying labour-saving machines. My mother swept and scrubbed, never had a Hoover in her life, and acquired a Ewbank carpet-sweeper as a kind cast-off from a sister-in-law, but she never stinted in the kitchen. Eating was one of life's big pleasures. Cockles and mussels, always separated, except by Molly Malone in the song, were feasts, hot or cold. There was Welsh lamb stuffed with thyme and breadcrumb stuffing, cawl with best end of neck and every root vegetable ever thought of, tasty if overdone beef and underdone Yorkshire pudding, undercut steak and thick dark-brown onion gravy, crispy belly-pork, faggots, thick slices of fat salty Welsh bacon fried with mashed potatoes and cabbage, which I called bubble-and squeak in London, Madeira cake, welsh-cakes hot from the bakestone, jelly and trifle and tinned pears and mandarin slices with Carnation evaporated milk. All the cakes were home-made, but we had Woolworths biscuits and the shortbread our Scotch cousin brought my mother every Christmas, which she loved. It came in a big rectangular tartan box, had little fork-pricks all over, and tasted of rich butter. Of all those delights, it's the only one that didn't change or disappear over the years, and my mother ate it even in her extreme old age when she couldn't chew.

Though we had shellfish from our own nets, stuffed hake, plaice and sole in crisp batter, and later on bass and dabs from Idris's rod, we never had fish stew. Once when I made it, using freshly caught eel and flounder from Rhossilli, and local shellfish, my mother turned up her nose and refused with a shudder. It was a London dish, tasted in Paris. I remember when I first saw bouillabaisse on the menu in a restaurant near the rue de Buci. It was the most exotic dish I'd ever contemplated. I pronounced its name slowly and carefully in my Sixth Form accent, but stumbled over *rouille*, which I'd never heard of and failed to find in Mrs Beeton. I was making the great soup for Mick, with saffron, green cardamom, star anise, tomatoes, carrots, onions and garlic, olive oil I'd brought back from Provence and several kinds of fish from the North End Road barrow.

It was the first time he had come to lunch and I was regretting my decision to cook such an elaborate meal. It was beginning to seem too grand. In a comparable scene in my novel the heroine just made an omelette, and the lovers ate it quickly and dashed off to bed. I wasn't always sure if I was improving on experience or cutting out particulars that didn't fit the form. The novel turned on a contrast between the two women, the domestic wife and the liberated girlfriend, hence the quick omelette. I began to wish I was more like Clara.

Mick had arrived all smiles, as he was to do for fifteen years, and presented his bottle of Muscadet. I was glad it wasn't Frascati, which Charlie and I used to drink. Charlie christened it 'Florence's ruin', because of one festive occasion when I drank nearly two bottles and passed out on the carpet. Mick's taste in wine wasn't up to Charlie's. He wasn't really interested, and never pretended to be. I shouldn't have made comparisons, but I was so aware of preferring him as a partner to Charlie – or anyone else, come to that, but they didn't matter – that I kept searching for Charlie's good points to put on the other side of the balance-sheet. As soon as I spotted myself keeping a balance-sheet I tried to stop, but didn't always succeed.

Charlie had started on beer, like all Welsh boys of his generation. He wasn't one of the huge men, like his friend Killa Hughes, who could swill ten pints without passing out, but he could manage six or seven. When I was at college I was sufficiently brainwashed by the drink-and-rugby-and-sex culture not to voice my secret opinion that beer-boasting was obnoxious and maudlin morning-after self-reproach a bore. Charlie wasn't one of the beefy boasters like one or two Aberystwyth students I went out with, but he did a lot of beer-drinking while he was working for his articles.

Once he'd been on holiday in Burgundy he turned his attention to wine, though he was never a wine snob. Beer suited him better than wine. He never drank so much of it, and he got too fond of wine. I'd never had what you call a palate, only the ability to tell a vintage Burgundy or claret from the acid plonk which gave us so much pleasure and so many hangovers in our early days.

Mick sometimes brought champagne for a birthday or Christmas, or when either of us had published an article or a book. Once or twice he produced a bottle of wonderful vintage port from the Magnus cellars. I think it was about thirty-five years old. Once I took a bottle home. I told my parents that my boyfriend had given it to me, and how old it was.

'What's his name?' my mother asked, and I reluctantly said, 'Daniel'. Daniel was his second name, the one he used when he left a message for me, at college or when I was staying in Swansea. Not with Jo and Susie, who had met him right at the start. The first time I got a message from Daniel and discovered it was from Mick I was furious and made a speech about the indignity of using a false name. He looked astonished, and protested in his beautifully innocent way.

'But darling, it is my name. It's my real second name. Don't you remember? I told you. When I told you the story of my life, and you told me yours.'

I accepted the alias but never liked saying it, and it seemed daft not to use his real name to my mother and father, unlikely to bump into his friends or family. Even though Daniel was his real name there seemed something wrong in using it. Changing names is a funny thing. When I tried to turn our story into a novel I called him Daniel, but often found myself typing Mick. I found it hard to choose names for the character who represented myself and kept changing my mind until I finally settled on Clara. I never got as far as rechristening Charlie. After my early attempts, I tried to keep him out of the novel, but from time to time he would appear and need to be exorcized.

My mother sipped Mick's port slowly, then fixed me with her light blue eyes.

'Well, well. Yes. Well, dull as I am, I can tell that's the real McCoy. No, I never tasted anything like that. No, no, no, Flora, no, I couldn't drink any more. Dear me, it's strong. Thank you, dear. Thank your friend from us. That was an experience, wasn't it, Harry?'

My father drank, nodded, and eventually had a second glass.

More enthusiastic than pretentious, Timmy fancied himself as a wine-buff, rhapsodizing about the taste of raspberry or blackberry or chocolate or banana, which I could never discern, try as I might. I had once or twice paid academic visits to Dijon, probably the first university to have a department of oenology, so Timmy expected me to have a palate and lots of wine knowledge, and was disappointed when I couldn't tell claret from burgundy. Charlie didn't take it so seriously, though he always bought good wine, even when he couldn't afford it. When I buy a cheap South African Cape, just under two pounds, I reflect that Charlie would warn me of getting a splitting headache, and Mick would enjoy it because it was a bargain.

Mick had the saving grace of laughing at his own careful ways with money. He told me that once in Paris he'd picked up a centime from the pavement, and the woman he was with laughed and said, '*Tu es juif aux bouts des doigts.*' I said that was antisemitic, but he said he hadn't minded. Of course I was jealous of his frank French friend. He was proud of his Jewishness, and pleased I had a Jewish grandfather. He could be touchy about anti-semitism but surprisingly tolerant if there was a joke to be seen, as in the coin on the street.

He wasn't extravagant but he was generous. He bought me hundreds of bottles of wine, champagne, and whisky, always the Famous Grouse. He would order baskets of gleaming fruit from Harrods, especially when we quarrelled, then arrive eagerly asking if there was any left for him. He loved food though he was hopeless at spotting the ingredients. He could usually tell onion from garlic but it was a toss-up between orange or lemon, brandy or rum, thyme or sage, cumin or cardamom. He was like the man in the street judging art, he didn't know anything about it but he knew what he liked. We had hundreds of heavenly picnics,

lox and bagels, croissants and smoked eel or salmon, gorgeous
pasta, Indian take-aways from Earls Court Road, taramasalata
when that came in, the cream of delicatessen. Sometimes I would
go to Gerrard Street and buy the Saturday Chinese dinner for
Mick and Ellen – dumplings and crispy duck – so that Mick could
spend Saturday afternoon with me instead of doing the shopping. He would tell me to buy something for myself and the
girls if they were there, and I didn't mind doing that.

He loved it when I cooked but I'd had enough playing house
with other lovers. That first bouillabaisse was a ritual gesture, a
part that stood for the whole, a recognition that we were em-
barking on a kind of marriage. That was why I was so self-conscious about cooking and serving it, and wished it wasn't so
delicious. I should have left out the scallops and *rouille*. I should
have made a simpler salad, and not heated the bread. I should
have served it on trays in the bedroom, as I always did in later
days, instead of laying the dining-room table for two, with silver
and shining glass and white linen napkins. At least I didn't make
a pudding – dessert, in Mick's language – refraining out of pride
or modesty. I wasn't going to show off my qualifications as the
perfect wife, or the perfect mistress. But with its display and re-
serve, the meal was an acquiescence and a ceremony. By the time
we'd finished it and went off to bed, it stood for all the dinners
we never ate together at a shared table in a house of our own,
together or with friends and relations.

As our affair developed its routines, we never wanted to spend
time on long complicated meals, so I tended to cook something
quick, eggs or grilled chicken. But even simple dishes could be
competitive. Ellen's kitchen, like Ellen's bed, shadowed mine. I
remember him looking up from an omelette and saying, 'This is
good. My family likes them drier than this,' and another time
telling me they had bought a poached salmon-trout from Harrods.
I built up a profile of Ellen's cuisine. I was sometimes critical of
her for not liking to cook, regarding it as part of a general sensuous
failure, like not liking to fuck. Sometimes I admired her freedom
from domestic pride, which was one of my weaknesses. My mother
certainly hadn't forced me into domesticity, because she had a

fierce ambition for her children. I used to blame my housepride on early rivalry with Charlie's mother, but it's a relic of a whole nurture which has made me, like most women of my generation and some later ones, feel a need to do everything. Job, creativity, social life, sex, homemaking, child-rearing, cooking: we have to excel all round.

So I didn't show off, after the beginning, but leaned over backwards to show I didn't aspire to be Mick's Elizabeth David as well as his Mata Hari and his Elizabeth Barrett. Occasionally I succeeded in failing. Once I made cheese and chutney sandwiches which he found disgusting. Once I gave him some homemade ice-cream which he found too gritty. Eventually I lowered my standards of hospitality and would ask him to bring something because I didn't have time to cook.

We had arguments about choosing wine to go with poultry and game.

'Only Yanks drink white wine with chicken,' I said. 'And with duck. Or pheasant. Pheasant!'

He would laugh and ask me how you cooked pheasant, or say mildly, 'You may be right. I thought everyone drank white wine with poultry.' I would calm down and laugh and cook pheasant next time.

He was amused at my habit of using my bedroom cupboard as a cellar. My bedroom is on a corner of the house and two outside walls, a north-east aspect, and my taste for the cold night air, make it ideal for keeping wine. My heating arrangements made Mick regard me as a good housekeeper with a fatal flaw, which made me feel less of an aspirant angel in the house. When I saw *The Crucible* I felt guilty as the frigid wife says she kept a cold house, though I didn't think my liking for low temperatures had any sexual significance.

'My god!' he would lament, his teeth chattering, as he leaped into the cold bed, keeping on his unaphrodisiac vest and pants, or T-shirt and shorts, as he called them. 'How can you live without central heating?'

If he'd been more stoical I might have apologized, but I leaped to the defence of my gas fires, in a spirit of patriotism, marital nostalgia, and working-class snobbery. 'I can't sleep in hot rooms.

I spent the first eighteen years of my life in ice-cold bedrooms. No fire anywhere in the house except in the kitchen. That was the living-room.'

'What about the bathroom?'

'There was no bathroom.'

'Where did you bath?'

'In a zinc tub by the fire.'

'Wasn't that too small for your parents?

It occurred to me for the first time that my grandparents, and for a long time my parents too, did without baths. They didn't have bathrooms, or privacy, or hot running water. I don't remember anybody except children using that small tub, in which we soaked the week's wash. Eventually my parents had a proper bathroom put in. I couldn't remember my grandparents using it, when they came to stay. My mother didn't bathe for the last three or four years of her life, and was furious when she went to hospital and the nurses insisted on baths every other day.

My Welsh working-class deprivation wasn't acute. I was always clothed and well fed. But my upbringing cast Mick's Midwest, middle-class, well-off, centrally heated boyhood into a socially shameful shade. How could he call himself a liberal with left-wing leanings, as he'd mildly boasted on our first meeting, with a background like that? He'd never gone to bed in a cold bedroom, or used a chamber-pot because there was no inside lavatory, or pretended to have gone to Tenby for a summer holiday, or been ashamed of his parents' clothes or his auntie's aitches.

I was irritated by an article in a learned journal about Victorian women's hygiene and the use of cut-up Turkish towelling before sanitary towels were invented. The author wrote as if it was history, as if no living First World woman ever used such primitive protection. I'd used towels for four years, before I went to university, and nasty rough things they were, rubbing the tender skin of the thighs. Sanitary towels were expensive, and my mother gave me the towels she had used. I raged against constant hot water in tiled white bathrooms and Florida and Cadillacs and central heating, then saw his quizzical grin at my boasts of social disadvantage. I caught myself in the act of humourless superior self-pity. I was a political prig, as bad as my dear dead South African friend, Gillmore Lee, who concluded one discussion by abusing his London friends because none of us had been to prison for our anti-racist beliefs. It was a party and he was comfortably drinking whisky and wearing evening-dress at the time, but nobody's perfect. Gillmore used to drink a pint of milk or a couple of spoonfuls of olive oil so that he could drink as much whisky as he liked without hurting his stomach lining.

Sometimes Mick and I would meet in Harrods food department on Saturday morning, as he did the weekend shopping, on a modest scale because they only stayed for the weekend, and often ate out with friends on Saturday night. I would buy something that was cheap even in Harrods, rabbit or sprats or kippers, and enjoy myself comparing what Mick paid for cheese and ham and butter and fruit with what I paid in the North End Road market. But I loved the food hall with its great rondeaux of sole and lobster and navy-blue mussels, and the mobiles of hanging ham and smoked meats. When I fantasized about living with Mick, my plans for food never went beyond the first dinner party. We were going to have sucking-pig, which I once ate at a Hungarian restaurant but only ever saw uncooked in Harrods. I never decided what the other courses would be, and the guest-list changed frequently.

Mick would walk off to eat the Harrods delicatessen or the Chinatown take-away with Ellen in Hans Crescent and I would go back on the tube to Earls Court, to have lunch and then go to bed, waiting for him to come and spend the afternoon. Clean sheets and flowers. Then he would go back to have dinner somewhere near their flat and come back at dawn on Sunday. Sometimes Ellen would sleep and never know he'd gone out, but his alibi was taking the dog for a walk, then after Antonio died, jogging in Hyde Park. In our early days I used to get up at seven and meet him by Albert Gate, but as the years went by we gave up walking by the water for Sunday morning bed. I don't know if that was laziness or lust. I gave him a set of keys, telling him solemnly and truthfully that he was the first man to be so honoured.

I would wake to hear the distant sound of the house door opening down below, or his key already in the flat door, and he would
arrive with a beaming smile and all the Sunday papers.

'It's the paper boy.'

After he'd gone I'd make myself coffee and spend the morning reading the papers and listening to the Archers and Desert
Island Discs, alone or with the children.

In the novel I had a chapter in which the Mick character, the
dead poet Daniel, was the guest on Desert Island Discs, in the
good old Roy Plomley days. The records he chose were my favourites and Charlie's, Mozart and Bach and Gershwin and Jerome
Kern and Britten, and singers like Deller and Lee Wiley and Ella
Fitzgerald and a Swedish tenor called Schiotz – or something
like that – who sang one of Charlie's favourite Dowland songs,
'Shall I sue? Shall I seek for grace?' We used to laugh because he
sang the first line as 'Shall I shoe?', but that didn't mute the
melancholy of the words and air, brimful of love-longing. I put
in 'Our Love Affair' for old times' sake. But I never finished that
chapter. Transforming Mick into musical Daniel was too much
of an effort, and I felt treacherous about endowing him with
Charlie's tastes.

I left Charlie out but gave Daniel his second name, Jacob, as a
surname with an added 's', and awarded him school prizes in
Latin and Ancient History, like Charlie. He wasn't American, but
born in South Shields, like Charlie's uncle by marriage and his
cousins Eddie and Hilda. The novel was going to be called *The
Conversation of Widows*. There were two narrators, the wife Elizabeth,
and the girlfriend Clara. I had finished working out the girlfriend's
story and was developing the wife when Mick told me about the
diagnosis. I stopped writing the novel. Its widows, lovers, and
dead authors had been overtaken by life. Its plot would soon be
stale news.

Elizabeth was an English wife and mother who couldn't liber-
ate herself till her famous husband died and she started to write
his biography. She never knew about her husband's affair with
Clara, the other woman, in spite of clues in his later poems. I
transferred my identification from Clara to Elizabeth, but perhaps

she was too much a creature of the imagination, too invented for me to handle. She was the woman I'd have been if I'd stayed in Swansea. She wasn't Ellen, though Clara's jealousy was my jealousy of Ellen. She had been just a wife and mother, while Ellen had always been a writer. She was healthy and strong while Ellen was an invalid. She was like Ellen in surviving her husband.

Ellen only came to London at weekends. In the week I would go on a day return to Oxford or Mick would come to London. Sometimes I would meet him at Paddington. We would go to his flat or mine. He preferred mine, but though the girls got used to him being there I preferred the privacy of his flat. We would have our picnic, brought by Mick or bought in Sloane Street by me, and drink brandy, partly because there was always some around. We would get slightly drunk, and sometimes he would leave me there, drowsy with love and drink, to get up and make the bed and go home in my own good time. I learnt to make the bed their way, with sheets drawn tight under the pillows. Once we had more time than usual and while Mick was sleeping, I read the paper and idly went on drinking brandy, not noticing how the level was going down. I got up and went to the bathroom, where I gently passed out on the floor, to be found by a terrified Mick.

'I thought you were dead. Or stricken. Once I found Ellen after she'd fainted. I don't think that was anything to do with her illness, but it happened just before the symptoms started. I thought yours was the second woman's body on my floor.'

As I got up he began to relax, and put his arm round me.

'And were you worried about disposing of the body?' I was post-coitally or post-alcoholically grumpy.

'No, of course not. What would I do without you?'

'Find another clever and literary sex-maniac, understanding enough. And old enough.'

On one of our early meetings he'd explained that as well as wanting to go out with me he'd decided that I'd be understanding enough, and old enough, to accept the situation.

'I'm afraid it's an unalterable situation,' he said.

'Don't worry,' I said.

It was like being asked if you'd stopped beating your wife. I couldn't say, 'I don't mind because I don't want to get married again.' I couldn't tell him it would be better because he couldn't move in. I didn't want to get married again but I did mind.

I minded not being able to eat out with Mick without him looking round the restaurant to see if there was someone who knew him. The first time we ate out in London together was in an Italian restaurant in Knightsbridge, where he fidgeted and rushed through the meal until I asked him if something was the matter, and he told me. But there were some meals far away from everyone who knew us, like a dinner in Copenhagen, where we had managed to get invited on the same lecture programme and arrived the day before, to have nearly a day to ourselves. Someone had told Mick about this restaurant, and what to order. I've forgotten what we ate, but not the feeling of being relaxed and private. He didn't look round to see if there was anyone who recognized us, as he did in London and outside Oxford. After we finished we went to see the statue of the Little Mermaid, that heroine of love.

I remember one disappointing meal on a lovely trip, the crumple in a roseleaf. It was the only time we went to Paris, in a restaurant I'd gone to with Susie, when the food seemed wonderful. Mick had suggested somewhere else, but I'd insisted, and gone on about the wonderful grilled Camembert. Somehow it wasn't as good that second time, though Mick ate with enjoyment, and said, 'This place is something of a find.' But I could tell he was being kind.

None of the old Paris memories came back to spoil that time. Once before they overwhelmed me. I was in Paris, waiting for Mel. I had come from Dijon, he was on his way to Switzerland, and we had planned to spend a day and two nights together. Arriving with an afternoon to spare, I wandered by the river, guessed at a short-cut back to the hotel, and suddenly found myself at a meeting of three twisting streets. On one corner stood a brasserie, *Aux Trois Portes*, where Charlie and I used to eat on our first trip abroad, newly married. We hadn't quite grasped the difference between café and restaurant and ate in some odd places, including a hotel called the Luxor, which had the toughest steak I've ever struggled with. The *Trois Portes* became a favourite, and after going to the theatre or the cinema we would have supper there, always ham and delicious cold potatoes with lemon on them. It was the first time we tasted lovely tangy Dijon mustard.

And we had picnics by the Seine, buying stuff from a little shop in the rue de Buci where we stayed in the Jeanne d'Arc and listened every morning to a bird singing in its cage outside. It was winter, but we used to picnic at noon by the Seine, watching the running water, the poplars, and the boats on the river. *Quiche Lorraine* was an unfamiliar name, not yet a heavy steady in every pub and buffet party, and we savoured it for the first time, soft and warm and creamy, with baguettes and olives.

When I stood at that corner, before going to meet Mel, I found my eyes stinging with tears. Charlie had ousted my new lover. He only did that to Mick when he died. The time in Paris was unclouded, right from the moment Mick telephoned me at my mother's house, to say he had to go to Paris and would I like to come. I told my mother and she remembered her friend Dora Pugh going with the Llanmadoc Senior Citizens a few years ago.

'Dora had a lovely time, though she said they couldn't get a decent cup of tea. But that won't worry you, Floss. You were never a tea-drinker. I'd like to have seen the bright lights of Paris. But I'll always remember that lovely holiday in Holland. The best holiday I had in my life.'

That holiday was a spur-of-the-minute idea, suggested by Susie's school project on Holland. I'd come back from a Dijon trip with some spare money and a restless feeling. Charlie and I weren't talking much, but when the spring turned out warm and sunny I thought of taking my mother for a family holiday. We couldn't get a bed-and-breakfast place in Amsterdam but were offered one in Utrecht. My mother loved it all, crossing the North Sea and seeing the oil installation sticking out of the waves, the Van Goghs and the Rembrandts, the cherry brandy, the chips with mayonnaise, and the tea. She and our landlady, a small round woman, talked nineteen to the dozen in their own languages, smiling and nodding and pointing and kissing goodbye. The children couldn't eat all the big breakfasts, and Charlie and I used to finish off the huge slices of thin underdone bacon welded to overdone eggs with lacy whites so as not to hurt the landlady's feelings.

My mother was enthusiastic about the tea. This astonished us because she was terribly fussy about her tea. Making the perfect cup of tea for Grannie Thomas was a family trial and rite. Charlie, the children, and all relations, friends and visitors in their turn, were given a rigorous course, in heating the pot, measuring the quantity of leaf and getting the right kind, pouring on the water when it was really bubbling, leaving it for exactly three minutes, and putting in just enough milk – 'No, no, Charlie, our family doesn't like a lot of milk like yours. Just a drop, please' – and not too little sugar – 'Two level spoonfuls please, Josie, love' – and that was the trickiest bit because actually she liked three spoonfuls but would never admit it. Innocent callers who offered to make her a cup were discreetly warned off. No wonder I hated tea.

On the last morning when she was saying how lovely the breakfasts had been, she asked what kind of tea it was. She was instructed, in Dutch but with visual aids and a demonstration, that it was made in the big brown pot with tea-bags. Mother exclaimed, incredulous but admiring, then said with the convert's zeal that in future she would always use tea-bags. And so she did. Charlie and I kept straight faces till we got upstairs and collapsed on the bed laughing. Just like old times. Mother loved that holiday with her daughter and her daughter's husband and children. It was our last trip. Three or four months later Charlie and I split up.

Two years after Mick, Mother died slowly and peacefully of a gentle self-starvation. She smelt fragrant, because of all those compulsory baths she swore would kill her. And perhaps they did.

'All those baths, they're no good to me. Lovely when I'm in, of course, but they'll give me pneumonia.'

Her only other hospital grievance was the tea, which was weak and very milky, because they were trying to get her to take some nourishment. We tempted her appetite with offers of sponge-cake and lamb broth but she was adamant. She wouldn't touch anything except a drop of sherry and drinks of soda-water. Looking back I wish I'd insisted on making her tea, but I felt nervous and helpless, and didn't like to interfere. I just watched while they offered it to her and she shook her head. Ever since I remember, she'd lived on tea, drinking a cup at three-hourly intervals with immense relish. In the war she gave most of her meat rations to us, and when she was very old her toothlessness made eating difficult, but until the end there was always a nice cup of tea.

My mother was full of surprises. When I left to go back to London and pack for Paris, she said she hoped I'd enjoy myself. 'And I hope it's somebody nice you're going with, Floss. Is it Daniel?'

It was a weekend snatched from routine. Everything we ate and drank was fun, even the disappointing meal. We went to the Pompidou to see a gorgeous Bonnard show and all the sunlit red-checked breakfast tables were ours. Mick had two short meetings with his French translator, and the rest of the time was ours. We went to a bizarre Parisian imitation of an English pub, where we drank thin beer, then to the café where Joyce used to drink his favourite white wine – was it Fendant de Sion? There Mick told me two rabbi jokes, and I told him about a conference in San Francisco my friend Madge had attended. It was on the politics of sexuality, with one paper on the political incorrectness of heterosexual fantasy, and another interrogating the correctness of lesbian sado-masochism. We giggled, but were fascinated as well as frivolous. We talked as we always did, joking and gratefully serious, teasing without a scratch, handing thoughts over in friendship, drinking the Joycean wine. Mick was one of the few people I knew who read *Finnegans Wake* for pure pleasure. He loved Joyce, he said, because he was like Thackeray.

On the third day we had lunch in the sun, before catching the plane. I kept Mick waiting in the restaurant while I went to the market to buy my favourite *Tôme aux raisins* and *Bleu d'Auvergne*, not easy to get at home, and at first when I joined him he seemed edgy, as he tended to be when anticipating departures. After we'd been away together he was no longer driven by desire, and relapsed into worry and guilt. When I sat down he frowned, then suddenly relaxed and smiled. He unfolded the huge linen napkin for me, poured out the golden wine, and asked me if I'd enjoyed our stay. He had an omelette and I had oysters. It was a perfect love-feast.

There were many. Perhaps the best came as a surprise in Mick's room at Magnus. Sometimes when he was lecturing he'd leave the door open and I'd wait for him, wandering round, and looking at books. One summer morning I arrived, took off my coat, opened the window and looked out into the quiet street. As I leaned over, I noticed plums under the sill, full and yellow, though not quite ripe, with a green tinge. When Mick came in he leaned out too, picked them, and gave them to me. We ate them with his wine, I wrote a poem about it, and showed it to him, as I hardly ever did. He said cautiously that he thought he was right in thinking it was good.

I showed him another poem I wrote about making love in the middle of all his books, on shelves and tables and the floor and in boxes, packed and unpacked. He said he liked it but he didn't say he thought it was good, and I don't think it was. He was a poet and I wasn't, but once or twice we wrote poems just out of love, offering them as presents, like flowers and wine. I showed him bits of fiction too. When I was trying to write about Daniel, the Mick character who was a thirties poet, he liked the obituary, and wrote a pastiche of Auden to be included as one of Daniel's pieces of light verse. It's somewhere amongst his letters. I've forgotten what it was about. It was one of the few poems he wrote for me. Another was the verse in couplets about meeting in Hyde Park, in which Albert's Gate rhymed with 'interanimate'.

'Not much good,' he apologized, 'but at least it shows attentiveness.'

In the summer we would have a day in the Cotswolds, usually buying a picnic in Oxford Covered Market, sometimes going to a pub or restaurant. It became a tradition, my treat, an outing in the country. I remember one hotel, a converted country house. The bar was at the end of a huge drawing-room, with a chatty barman who said he only had bar-snacks but they were very upmarket bar-snacks. After we feasted on them we walked in the sunny walled rose-garden, by a stream.

The first time we went for our country drive we went to an old pub in Thame, where Mick astonished me, as I was slowly scanning the menu and wondering whether to have lamb or duck, by summoning the waiter and saying we'd have the steak.

'How do you like it?' He gave me his innocent smile.

'Mick? Please, darling. You're telling me what to have?'

He looked amazed at my amazement. It dawned on me that he was used to choosing for Ellen, though the impression I got from his talk was not of a weak woman. I didn't ask if he'd always done it or if it was since she'd been ill. Perhaps it was an act of love, just for me. I didn't go into the motives. He apologized and we ordered our different dishes. And at the end I had the grace to laugh.

There was a time when I did ask him to choose for me. We were having a Chinese meal in one of those small plain restaurants with wooden tables in Gerrard Street. I had seen my first explicit sex programme and I was recovering.

The first shock was to find myself the only woman in the cinema full of the men in macks. The man at the ticket-desk told us invitingly that it was 'explicit'. Mick made a joke about the high price, and the cashier, or manager, or whatever he was, repeated the word with emphasis. It was most explicit. I think we had both expected to be excited, but we were left cold. The only thing I can remember about the several short films we saw is an episode where a woman knocks on the door of a room where a couple is having sex. When the man opens it she announces that she is 'The Supervisor', and proceeds to supervise and criticize and help, like a bossy school inspector. She took the man's requests, or perhaps gave him the menu. I've forgotten all the other details. What I should have expected but hadn't was the abysmal quality of the acting.

I was shocked by something you don't experience with pornographic books, where the body's image, not the actual body, is degraded. I don't mean to suggest that such imagery is harmless, but that it strikes from a distance. In these abjectly terrible blue films there were the poor awful actors. It was the worst acting you could imagine. But unlike the character-dummies in the books, the actors were all individuals, with real bodies, and worse still, real faces. They looked out of real eyes. It was horrible to see faces so expressionless, but in a way I was glad that they were.

I had asked Mick to take me, and when we sat down in the restaurant, I looked at him, and laughed weakly. I said he could choose for me on this occasion, not because I was stimulated into docility but because I was feeling negative. I certainly didn't care what I ate. I was also feeling turned off sex and Mick agreed that he was too though that only lasted a couple of hours. We remembered the supervisor, who became part of our mythology.

After he found me on the bathroom floor Mick said, 'I think we'd better give up brandy and stick to wine.' And we did, always sharing a bottle, till he began to get ill, when he would just take a sip and leave the rest to me. But he could always eat, while I still saw him. We went on having picnics right to the end.

Mick was always a fast greedy eater, but I never minded until the last months. I was startled and ashamed to find myself feeling squeamish as he stuffed food into his mouth and gobbled it up. Once or twice I looked away, or made some excuse about getting the salt. That was the only physical distaste I felt, as he got worse. He got weaker, and couldn't manage stairs. His walking got very slow and hesitant. He looked all right dressed, but when he was naked I could see his limbs getting skinnier, and his skin flabby. The droop of his head got worse but lying down in bed and resting on the pillow, he looked the same as usual, with his Roman profile. Of course he was less energetic, but over the years I'd grown less passive. Our routines and stories helped. Love-making was briefer, but went on. His muscles didn't feel feeble when he held me. The moods of love were much the same.

There was one new thing. There was a very faint smell, at first almost imperceptible. When my mother was dying, two years after Mick, her softening breath was as pure as a baby's. Perhaps I noticed it because Mick's was not. There was a taint of staleness or sourness on what had been a sweet breath. But my first distaste turned to tasting. I was almost eager. After all the jealousies, I'd won. I wouldn't get a seat at the deathbed, but only a lover could get so close to his dying, and his death. I could embrace it and breathe it and kiss it. Like nobody else. Too intimate to mention, it came and went in those last months, a halitosis of the grave, in my nostrils and on my tongue.

EIGHT

Kiss and Tell

We came after the Beatles and before Aids. That was a good time even for middle-aged lovers. Mick felt a liberation.

'The world is sexualized,' he kept saying.

I'd tried a personal permissiveness, long before the swinging sixties, but Mick had not. He had held back. He knew much more about sex in his youth than I did but lacked the advantage of those aphrodisiac Welsh repressions which led to my first flings in Swansea and Aberystwyth. For better and worse. I was very ignorant, but I had made a start. Mick had been in the army, but he stayed a virgin for a long time because he was afraid of syphilis. I suppose I might have been too, but it never occurred to me. One of my friends told me a story of a boyfriend who had asked a girl he went to bed with why she wasn't afraid of getting VD, and that was the only time I heard the subject mentioned. Some public lavatories had notices about clinics, but for me and my friends it wasn't a matter of public fear as it was for Mick and his brother. They had visited brothels, but only to drink and watch. They didn't dare do anything. I was impressed and just a bit disgusted.

Mick had the bad luck or bad judgement to marry a woman who was wonderful in every other way – clever, witty, creative – but not keen on bed, or on his bed. So when we became happy lovers it was something new for him. For one thing, he enjoyed being a good lover, as he hadn't been before. Ellen's lack of enthusiasm may have been cause or effect or a bit of both.

After the first few tries, we saw the lineaments of affection if not of gratified desire. Mick said he couldn't bear to think it wouldn't last. I said there was no reason why it shouldn't. I had offended him by saying I had two or three lovers scattered over the globe. I thought I was just making it clear that I was free, not committed to a steady lover down the road, but he took it as a declaration of promiscuity. Eventually he relaxed, believed that I loved him, and joked about my global connections.

Mick used to say our love-affair was fun because it was old-fashioned monogamy. I suppose there was something in that. It was monogamy, more or less. Rather more than less. Mick had been faithful to Ellen till she got too ill to have sex and he couldn't bear the thought of never having it again. I had a theory that her illness was the perfect excuse not to have sex, but I never said so to him. Although he hadn't had a sexy marriage, he believed in fidelity, and had practised it. I thought I probably had a much better marriage, but I had not been faithful. I met him after a phase of liberating myself for the second time, renewing adolescence, having fun, living alone, not wanting love-affairs to be marriages. Now I was prepared to settle down, to some extent, drawn by the idea of a steady lover.

I said to Mick that I didn't believe in monogamy or fidelity but since he wanted it, we would have it. Not out of submission, though I did tease him and say monogamy was the kinkiest thing out, his ideal of permanence a playful humiliation. But on the principle of doing as you would be done by. We promised to do anything and everything the other wanted. Charlie and I had been within a hair's breadth of making marriage work, but we hadn't – perhaps I hadn't – thought hard enough about what the other one wanted. I was going to do better this time. But I didn't want to spell everything out.

There were better reasons than the promise to say yes to everything. Our attachment was better than anything. We were clever together. It couldn't stale. There'd never be a three-year or a five-year or a seven-year itch. I knew that after one year, and after fifteen. Why would I want anyone else?

But everything is political. I understand women being ideologically lesbian. I'd say I was ideologically unfaithful if it didn't

sound ludicrously solemn and probably self-deceiving. Some sacrifice. I remember Mel once drowning his sorrows in a bout of
promiscuity and expecting pity, so I was wary of making big
claims for lust and laxity. But as I swore fidelity, I truly believed
the vow was politically incorrect, though I laughed at my high-
mindedness as I made a private reservation, a secret trust, an
unwritten liberty clause. If and when it seemed convenient, and
only in circumstances when Mick couldn't possibly know, I might
allow myself to sleep with someone else.

There I was, still using the old language. Fidelity and infidel-
ity. The rhetoric of property and patriarchy. My friend Marge,
who was securely and happily married, but liking to have her
cake and eat it with romantic icing on top, protested when I talked
about being unfaithful. It's the lexis I grew up with and I was
stuck with it. When I tried to unlearn it I couldn't. Perhaps I
didn't try hard enough. In some deep fold of the heart I felt it
would be only fair to Charlie if I was unfaithful to Mick. But I
did one thing for Mick I didn't do for Charlie. I held my tongue.
I didn't fuck and tell. I was still young enough to love, but also
old enough to know.

I was unfaithful three times in the fifteen years. The first time
was after a drunken party in Dublin, the second after a college
dinner in Royal Holloway, the third after a small dinner-party
with friends in Highgate. All one-night stands, by mutual desire.
Each time I was a bit drunk.

The first one was an Irish actor, a small tough stringy man
who'd played the son in Yeats's terrifying play *Purgatory*. It is a
purgatory of horror, a terror-struck vision of sex after death and
murder after death. Everyone is dirty with hate. The sex is
pleasureless and drunken and unloving.

Something of the nastiness of the play rubbed off, on him and
me and on our going to bed. I didn't mean to go to bed with
him. It never entered my head. That secret trust was in existence
but this was really nothing to do with independence and the
liberty clause. It was just whisky and fatigue. After the play we'd
all been drinking and telling stories and singing in the hotel lounge.
After a bit when I was talking to this actor, he said it was too

late for him to go back to his lodging and asked if he could sleep in my room in the hotel. On the floor. I was too taken aback to refuse. I took him along. Of course he didn't sleep on the floor. To let him into the room was to let him into my bed, and into me. I was shocked to find myself liking it. But when he tried one of Mick's bed-tricks I pushed him away. I was nearly asleep, knocked out by Black Bush, disgusted and thrilled by my body's liveliness and the bodies decaying in the play, but I had to mark a threshold. It was a long way from Knightsbridge, and Oxford, and Swansea. The hard love-making was angry, like the harsh wild play with its taint of the grave. I had to fight him off. I've forgotten his name. When I was thinking about putting this episode in the novel I christened him Declan and changed the play to *The Dreaming of the Bones*. That was a sweeter haunting.

Like a couple of other middle-aged womanizers I've known, the professor of politics from Edinburgh said apologetically that he went to bed with lots of girls, told me a politically incorrect joke about an airline hostess to whom he'd said, 'You're very articulate' and she'd said 'Come again?' and joked about the way he shouted in a Glasgow accent when he came. He told me his first marriage had failed because his wife was a mood-swinger. We had eyed each other over the dinner-table, drunk lots of wine, and come back to his flat in Kensington Square in a taxi. He was an awful sexist, but I rather liked him.

Neither of us got in touch again. Neither did the poet – Jacob – who told me about his mad wife and I told him about my dead husband. We both had friends who sympathized with us too much for having a mad wife and a dead husband, instead of sympathizing with the mad wife and the dead husband. We agreed that friends were terrible, and I said I'd have to go home early because I had a madly jealous lover who always phoned me early, sometimes at five or six. We'd met at a friend's dinner-party, and gone home together in his account taxi, instructed not to tip the driver. Jacob had tipped the driver, asked me in for a drink, and told me enthusiastically and candidly how much he liked women. The morning after the night after the college dinner I had to pretend to Mick, who did phone early and wonder where

I was, that I had stayed the night with friends. I thought I'd better not push my luck and use the same story twice so I did leave early, refusing Jacob's sleepy offer of breakfast or coffee. I walked home from West Kensington to Earls Court in the summer dawn and got back in time for Mick's dawn song, 'Florence'.

I felt rather unfaithful, a bit mean, but defiantly free. I had that secret licence, though I wouldn't say the one-night stands had been sacrifices in the interests of sexual politics and feminism. I'd found Jacob attractive and amusing, and his flattened nose reminded me of Thackeray's. I liked his poetry. I had a good time with all three though I didn't particularly want to see them again. Each time was the end of a party, a digestif. Once was enough for my token liberty. I was sorry but not eaten up with guilt. I think I know what I was doing, but I'm not boasting. What do I know? At least I didn't tell Mick.

One night he picked me up from the flat very late, and we drove in the night to a hotel outside Cambridge, where he was giving a lecture next day, and we were staying for the weekend. Somewhere along the road we got lost, and kept going round in circles, Mick map-reading and driving as he always did. Neither he nor Charlie minded getting lost on the road. I would navigate for Charlie, and sometimes get us spectacularly lost – once we found ourselves in Keighley on the way to the Lake District, and made a surprise visit to the Brontë country. But Mick never asked me to read the map. He had been driving since childhood, like all Americans, and would delight me by saying with a grin, 'What a driver!' about himself, not all the others.

Suddenly as we encountered a roundabout we'd circled before, he asked me if I'd ever been unfaithful to him.

Sometimes in bed he would talk about things he'd done with a woman called Theresa, whom he knew in Harvard, and with Beatrice, the wife of a colleague in Oxford, but I knew he was lying, just playing games. Their names were dummies, objects in our fantasy. He never said he fancied anyone else, out of bed. He told me about another woman, a rich woman fan, who fancied him, he thought. When he thought she seemed to be coming on strong, as he put it, I said he should tell her he had me, and he said he had. I felt wildly jealous.

I wished I hadn't enjoyed those three one-night stands. Telling Mick about them would make them too important, as actual men. As it was, if I didn't tell, they could stay in the place I'd designed for them. They were gestures, political signs.

Mick kept on, as he looked for the turning to our hotel.

'I just think I'd like to know. It won't make any difference.'

I kept saying 'no', but he kept asking. He kept saying he wouldn't mind, he'd forgive me. I said I had always been faithful to him.

'I've never gone to bed with anyone else, since I met you.'

Then he asked me if I'd swear that I hadn't been to bed with anyone else. So I did.

'I swear it, Mick.'

He was elated, smiling and laughing, so overjoyed that I felt hatefully false but glad I'd sworn, or been forsworn. I'd learnt to lie but I didn't feel too thrilled about having lied to him. If he came back as a ghost I fancy he'd forgive me. He might even smile and say he'd guessed. I don't think he did.

We had a lovely weekend, and I enjoyed the lunch I ate on my own, while Mick was being entertained by his Cambridge hosts after the lecture.

'There's a pool,' Mick said, telling me we were going on an advertised weekend break for two, 'Bring your swim-suit.'

I spent the morning swimming round and round in a small warm turquoise kidney-shaped pool, which I had all to myself, then lounging in the sauna. I booked it again for the afternoon when Mick would be back. Glowing after the swimming and the heat I found him reading the paper disconsolately, having come back early. He'd got out of lunch and hadn't known where I was. When I told him I'd booked the sauna for two hours and waved the key, he cheered up and said it was like being asked to play when you thought you'd been left out of the other children's games.

'See, you're never too old for another first time.' We sweated happily together on the baking boards, with the smell of hot pine, real or simulated, then went to bed till dinner-time.

That night he said. 'If I die – when I die, don't tell anyone our things?' He wasn't expecting to die at the time. When he was ill he never asked me to do or not do anything after he died.

I hated making promises but I could willingly make this one. I promised.

'OK. I won't', I said, and I kissed him.

'If you ever get back with Timmy, don't talk to him about us.'

Mick had a thing about Timmy, whom he'd never met. He was better disposed towards Mel, whom he had known in New York, though I'd adored Mel and never taken Timmy very seriously. Perhaps it was that tactless remark I once made about it being pure sex with Timmy. Perhaps in some obscure corner of his jealous fantasy Mick thought Mel was more my kind of person.

'Of course I won't go back to Timmy. Or anyone. I won't want anyone.' That was true.

Then I said, 'But Mick, if I die, you get somebody else. You need it so much. So do I, of course, but now just because of you. I could do without it better than you could.' That was true too.

In our early days I marvelled at his enthusiasm. Sex made him so visibly happy. Perhaps because his youth was restrained by fear and his marriage-bed was one of straw. Perhaps he just had lots of libido. My friend Mattie says wryly that her husband is a goat, but that isn't the image I'd choose for Mick. It suggests crude bucking lust, and Mick's insatiable desire was always delighted and happy.

I was impressed and amused.

'I never met anyone else with such a will for sex. You love it so. It's like some people's will to power. Only healthier, of course.'

And he said, 'What else is there?'

Of course he knew perfectly well that there were books to read and write, as well as sex. He would say the bed of down was good for writing. We were euphoric with gratified desire, and that was fruitful for work, he said. Besides, talking about our books gave us something to do in between embraces.

Sometimes we would be exhausted after a night of loving, but when we woke up, or if we were still awake when it was getting light, he would always say, 'I think we might manage one more time.' He never waited till desire woke, or woke again, as my other lovers did. It was a remarkable determination. He sometimes said I was too rich a mixture for him, but that wasn't so. I never wanted to refuse him, except when Charlie died and I was distraught.

There was one other time, late at night in Oxford. I was there for a conference, and for once we were out walking there together, with Antonio on the lead. The streets were almost empty, and we heard all the clocks of the city strike twelve, as we were talking about Auden, who had died that day. Mick knew him, but I did not, and he'd been nervous and rather rude the only time I met him. He was always the great companionable poet for me, speaking my language, his times my times, his books punctuating my life. Mick felt a personal sadness too. We were sharing a loss.

We went back to Mick's room and he told Antonio to stay quietly in a corner. He didn't make a sound. I don't think it was the dog, or the death, but I had to hide a reluctance. It didn't last long. Afterwards I said it had been lovely, and it had. Then I admitted my disinclination: 'Though I didn't really feel like it.'

Mick frowned. 'You should have told me.'

'I thought it would be all right, and it was.'

'Don't be a wife,' he said.

'No fear,' I said.

Another time I said, 'You couldn't do without it, could you?'

Once when I told him to find somebody if I died, and once when I predicted he would find somebody if I left, he quoted Pound. The first time I didn't recognize the quotation. I like Pound's fooling, wit, and generosity. I pity his silliness and tragic end. But I don't enjoy the poetry. Mick wasn't crazy about the *Cantos* but loved 'Mauberley' and twice said what he meant in one of Pound's best lines. Mick always said you should begin and end with your own words but he wasn't too proud to speak through another voice now and then:

'I will not stain my sheath with lesser brightness.' I like the reversed sexual symbol almost as much as the sentiment.

NINE

Hospital Blues

I've been in hospital three times, twice when my children were born, and once when I had a kidney stone a couple of years ago.

The maternity ward was fun, once all the pains were over, and the children turned out to have the right number of toes and fingers, one crying all the time and the other sleeping all the time, both healthy. The only sad person I met was Marie, in the bed next to mine the first time I was in, for Joanna's birth. She was a single parent. They were much rarer then than they are now, thirty-five years later. Most of us were struggling to get the babies to suck, under the professional care of the improbably named Lactation Officer, who would have been a character out of Kafka if she hadn't been the kind and chatty mother-in-law of one of my students. Marie was the only one who wasn't breast-feeding. Advised that even a week or two was better than nothing, she told me she didn't want to start, because she'd have to stop as soon as she went out, and that would be upsetting. She didn't cry or sound sorry for herself as she explained. She would have to go back to work as soon as possible, and make some arrangement for the baby. She didn't say anything about the baby's father. Every night before visiting-time when we combed our hair and put on all the stuff we used to put on our faces then, even in hospital – foundation, powder, lipstick, and eye-shadow – she took out her mirror and made up her face too. For the ten days we were there – much longer than they keep you now – he never turned up. As the rest of us were greeted and embraced, smothered with flowers and stuffed with fruit and chocolates, she held her baby and gave him the bottle.

The second time, with Susie, no one was sad, and I got copies of Iris Murdoch's *The Sandcastle*, from two of my women friends, Annie and Bettina. There was a lot of palaver about test-weighing after every feed, and I had cystitis, but the maternity ward in University College Hospital was bright with love and hope. I decided it was within sound of Bow bells, though I never heard them. My children were lucky little Cockneys, born in Bloomsbury, after natural childbirth classes which, as far as I could tell, didn't seem to make any difference. They were born in the usual struggling pain, welcomed with great joy, brought up by fond parents and daily nannies in Earls Court, adored by Swansea grannies and grandpas.

A few years ago I was staying with my mother in Rhossilli, and woke up in the night with a feeling of nausea and a stabbing pain down on the left of my abdomen. Something I'd eaten? I got up and tried to be sick, but nothing came up. The pain subsided and I went to sleep again, then woke to find it still nagging. I got dressed, took mother breakfast, kissed her goodbye, and caught the early bus to Swansea.

On the London train the pain came back. I asked the ticket inspector with piteous restraint if there was some little rest room where people could lie down if they didn't feel well. He shook his head, saying no they didn't have anything like that, but I was quite right and they ought to, and would I like to be put out at Swindon. I declined, suppressing the nightmare of being in hospital as a stranger in Swindon, where I had never been and didn't know a soul. When he went away my heart sank, but after ten minutes he came back to rescue me from the half-term children laughing and shrieking and running up and down the aisles, and their anxious loving parents yelling and whispering and scooping them up, and trying to amuse and punish and bribe them. He had found me a seat in first class. I told him he would get a first-class place in heaven for that, and he said I was very welcome. I contemplated my pain and prospects in quiet and a comfortable seat for the rest of the journey, and decided that instead of telephoning Susie to scare her with an undiagnosed pain, I'd go to the nearest casualty department.

At Paddington I found a First Aid Post and they told me to go round the corner to St Mary's. It was quieter there than in my favourite television programme, *Casualty*. There were notices saying people who didn't have life-threatening conditions might have to wait up to two hours. I told the receptionist, whom I was delighted to speak to, that I had a severe pain, and where it was, gave her my particulars, then settled down with *Romola*, which I was rereading as I do every five years or so, in the hope of liking it better. It is not a novel to read when you're in pain and I wished I'd brought some more gripping favourite like *Nairn's London* or *The Loneliness of the Long Distance Runner*. I was bored by George Eliot's Savanorola, even when he was contemplating walking through fire and suffering terrible pain. I looked at my watch. Perhaps another hour to go. How did they know what was life-threatening? I wasn't bleeding to death and I hadn't passed out. Worse luck. How bad was pain before you fainted? It was worse than labour pains because old Dame Kind cleverly rewards fertility with little rests in between pangs, at least in the first stage. And in the second there's all the urging on and activity. Not to mention the result to look forward to and your knowledge of what's the matter. Perhaps it was appendicitis. Perhaps it was peritonitis, and ghastly things were happening inside my large or small intestine. I wished I was better informed about my body. The pain got so bad that I thought I must be going to die, then it got worse and I didn't mind the thought of dying. Then the receptionist called my name and I staggered over.

The doctor would see me. He introduced himself as Dr Cole, an assistant registrar. After prodding me and asking some questions about urination he said it was almost certainly a kidney-stone.

'Is it the worst pain you have had in your life?'

I nodded. 'Could I possibly have something for the pain?' He said I could but that I would have to have a staining injection before the X-ray, and then the X-ray. I thanked him for the explanations.

The X-ray table was hell. I had to lie on my back and not

move, and all you want to do when you have a pain in your side is move from side to side in case it's better on one side than on the other. When a nurse came, I asked if I could move; she said I could, so for another ten minutes I happily writhed and tried to yell quietly. After the blood-test and the injection and an X-ray, they put me back in the cubicle and I called out and a nurse came and I said I was sorry but the pain was severe. She said the doctor was with an urgent case but would be with me very soon. At last he came to say it was definitely a kidney stone and I'd have to go into hospital, there if possible. When I passed the stone, as they hoped I would, they might be able to tell what had caused it. I didn't care, I was longing for my painkillers. Angelic Dr Cole gave me an injection and said the pain would go in twenty minutes. That was tactful and clever, because it went in fifteen. I timed it.

I took a solemn vow not to grumble or complain, however awful it might be in hospital, as long as pain could be kept at bay. I lay in the cubicle, yawning over *Romola*. I was bad at re-membering theorists like Derrida and De Man, but I had a vague recollection of somebody – was it Barthes? – discussing language that was null, which he called *écriture blanche*. Bleached. A great word for George Eliot's Romolan non-language, invented for another time and another country. I wished I'd talked to Mick about it. Good. I was thinking about something that wasn't my pain. I cheered up.

They tried to find me a bed at St Mary's, but couldn't. They said they'd send me to St Charles's, Ladbroke Grove. It was a famous night of delays in the London Ambulance service, failure on the telephone exchange, I think, and I waited for three or four hours. I tried to telephone Susie on a mobile phone but she was out. In the end I was taken to Ladbroke Grove by an ironic taxi-driver who told me I was in for a culture-shock. He said he did a lot of work for the hospitals because he was cheaper than an ambulance. I felt cheerful because I was well enough to travel by taxi, and not in pain. It was midnight when I arrived, clutch-ing the sheet of paper I'd been given.

The porter at reception tried to send me to another department but I'd been told to say they were expecting me in Ward G, and it turned out that they were. Along came a big cheery nurse who introduced herself as Rosa. Rosa asked me if I had a nightie, and when I said no, I'd come straight off the train, laughed loudly. It was my lucky night as it was a mixed ward and I could sleep starkers. She got me a yellow nylon nightie with a slit torn up the back, and I wondered if that was for easy examination by the doctor or easy access to the bedpan. I wasn't sure if they still had bedpans. Rosa put me to bed, took my particulars, and I heard a man's soft foreign voice come from the cubicle on my left. I had thought it was a joke about the mixed ward. What a pity Mick was dead, I thought, we could have had jokes about him being jealous of my male companions. He probably would have been jealous.

I kept my promise and wasn't cross about the wait, the late hour, the reception clerk, or the nightie. The taxi-man was a friendly guide, though I hadn't felt a culture-shock yet. Rosa was a merry angel. Having men around in hospital was something new. Thinking sleepily that perhaps that was the culture-shock, and hoping he hadn't meant a racist comment, I fell asleep, and slept till morning. I woke to a ward full of cries and shouts and laughs.

I was only in for three days but I was happy in the world without my pain. Susie and several friends came to see me, but I was like a child at school, concentrated on my peer-group. My fellow-patients were good companions. It was indeed a mixed ward, and everyone seemed to like it that way. The gender-mix was for ease and economy, I supposed, but it was great for morale and recovery. The best of therapies. The patients grumbled about the noise, about each other, about the nurses, about the doctors, about the food, about the television, about the shared telephone, about the zealous cleaners who tidied your newspaper into the rubbish if you looked away for a second, but I never heard anyone, man or woman, complain about it being a mixed ward. The mix made for sociability and better grooming. I know I asked Susie to bring me a dressing-gown and black silk pyjamas to put on instead of the yellow nylon nightie, and I'm not sure I'd have bothered if Jan, the soft-voiced Pole, hadn't been in the next bed, glimpsed through the curtains that didn't quite meet. We were all ages, mostly fifty-something and over, several in their seventies, but there was the glad buzz of sex in the hospital ward.

I got to know the people in the beds near me. Jan, my left-hand neighbour, introduced himself as a former officer in the Free Polish Air Force in England, living in a hostel in Hammersmith. He was in his middle seventies, with a handsome well-cut face flawed by a slightly swollen reddish nose, and a charming smile and voice. He wore a dark blue silk dressing-gown and was one of the two or three patients who didn't have to be chased into the bathroom. When I took a bath I was aware of his presence through the partition, having seen him go in. In the evening he asked me if I was going to watch the television news, and we got out of our beds, with an odd intimacy, and walked down to the far end of the ward. Earlier on the signature tune of *Neighbours* had summoned its fans and I had dreaded a loud telly, on all day and all night, but it wasn't too near. It was easy to renew my vow not to feel aggrieved about anything, especially after the second dose of lovely pain-killer. Jan and I watched the news with a silent smiling woman with beautifully permed hair and a red velvet dressing-gown. The hospital seemed festive.

Jan was in for an ulcer on his foot that wouldn't heal. I listened to his doctor making discreet disappointed noises and giving evasive answers to Jan's questions through the curtain. When I left to go home I asked Jan if I might leave him my freesias and roses, and he thanked me like Anton Walbrook playing a count. He didn't kiss my hand but he smiled when I asked him if he liked flowers. He said he did, as he enjoyed all the good things of life.

On the second day, Jan told me about the most enigmatic of our fellow-patients, the man in the bed opposite him, the only one of our little group whose name I never heard. He was a very tall man who was blind, always led down to the lavatories and washrooms by a nurse, or occasionally by Brian the policeman, his neighbour in the next bed.

'I was friendly to him at the beginning,' Jan confided. 'He seemed lonely and never had any visitors. I couldn't hear his voice clearly from over here, but I could tell the nurses had to speak slowly. And he looked foreign. Another foreigner amongst all these English. So of course I went over to speak to him. But that was the only time. Do you know what he is? He's German. Do you know what he was? A member of the SS.'

Jan's soft voice was disgusted. He had not spoken to the blind man again. I didn't either, though I felt slightly guilty about it.

The other patient I talked to was my right-hand neighbour, a West Indian woman called Moira. She was wonderfully aggrieved about everything except her illness. She wore an attractive blue and yellow cloth round her head and I didn't know if this was for adornment or if she'd been having chemotherapy and lost her hair. She had a narrow face and bright eyes. She told me she had been ill for some time. She was much better, but they'd found a new, small tumour in her neck. She was going home in the afternoon. Her friend was coming for her. She complained constantly about being in hospital, moaning that she wanted to go home. Her lamentation was poetry. I had vowed not to feel irritated and anxious in hospital, to enjoy my lack of pain as a positive pleasure, and now I was surprised by expressive rhythms.

'I want to go home,' she chanted, repeating and varying the phrase in a deep musical voice. 'I want to go home. To go home. Yes, I really want to go home. I want to go home.'

Her chant moved from gloomy monotone to fresh surprise and combativeness. I recognized her as our singer and spokesperson. She was strong and melancholy as she spoke the common longing: 'I want to go home. Yes, I do. Everyone wants to go home. Of course everyone wants to go home. Yes, everyone wants to go home. Everyone in hospital wants to go home.'

She was interrupted by a loud Cockney voice.'No, they don't. I don't. I don't want to go home. I want to stay here. I like it here. I don't want to go home. It's great here. The food's great, and the service is great, and the nurses are great.'

It was the voice of Brian, the policeman, our male star, over six foot, with broad shoulders, a pale handsome bruiser's face, a slightly bashed nose, curly red hair and cirrhosis of the liver. After his revisionary contribution Moira was silent for a few minutes then sang out a new chorus blending incredulity and sympathy with reaffirmed longing. Sometimes she stressed the wanting, sometimes the going, sometimes the home:

'I want to go home. Yes, I want to go home. But some people don't want to go home. No, some people in hospital don't want to go home. Some don't. But I do. I do, I do, I want to go home.'

Brian would saunter down the ward, towel slung over his shoulder, bare to the waist, a fine sight. I heard most of the discussion between him, his well-dressed, mellow-tongued consultant, and half a dozen nervous-sounding students. Brian sat nonchalantly on the edge of the bed, obviously enjoying his own history, as Miss Brown rehearsed it in response to the doctor's command. I strained to hear as she recited the symptoms, expressionlessly muttering something about an enlarged liver, then saying something I couldn't catch in reply to the consultant's loud question about the patient's drinking habits. The patient wasn't a passive listener, and confirmed in his loud clear cheerful voice that he drank twenty cans of lager a day. The confident doctor on his ward-round was a thirty-five-year-old English public-schoolboy, dominant and well groomed, and his patient, about the same age, was a match for him in self-possession, good looks, and articulate voice.

I had trouble getting sense out of my doctor, a registrar, a reticent, vague man who said little beyond asking me if it was the worst pain I'd ever had in my life. When I asked, he said they hadn't found a stone. Since one of the nurses had confided that they'd accidentally not recorded – which I assumed meant thrown away – one of my carefully strained and jugged specimens, I wasn't too surprised. I was most interested in my pain. I wanted to know how they knew if it was still there, and how they'd know when it went, since I was being given the wonderful pain-killer at regular intervals, and felt nothing. The doctor looked surprised at my question, thought for a minute, then said I should leave it slightly more than twenty-four hours this time, wait for the pain, then ask for the injection. This struck me as an heroic prospect. But I took his advice, a twinge eventually spurred me into urgent demand, then on the third day no pain struck with the hour. The stone never turned up. I was disappointed never to see it in the small tea-strainer I gazed at several times a day. When I tried to imagine it, it was sometimes a grain of sand, sometimes a golfball.

Painless, after what they said was the worst pain in your life, and promised a short stay, I spent the three days concentrating on the rich human scene. Moira was my favourite, almost my friend. She was hard on the doctors, spitting with venom. They had promised she could go home on the morning of my first day, then they suddenly said she couldn't have her breakfast. She was going for more tests and mustn't eat. She was hungry. She called out to every nurse and doctor who passed to ask when she was going home and complain that she was starving. She protested in anguished tones that she hadn't even had a cup of tea, and when a very young doctor with a sense of humour said he hadn't either, he'd been so busy, she turned her choric complaint on to him:

'And the doctors! First they starve you, then they mock at you. That doctor, he mocked at me. When I told him they hadn't given me breakfast, he mocked at me. He laughed.' She repeated her complaints to a faithful friend who visited her twice a day and listened with sympathetic murmurs.

Her finest hour came after a new patient made a noisy entrance in the middle of my second night. She was a terrible loud-voiced bossy woman called Alison, whose life-story we had to listen to at three in the morning. She spent the next day, from dawn to dusk, fussing about the whereabouts of our elusive mobile phone because she had to cancel the man who was coming to mend her washing-machine which had been playing up. You could feel the ward bonding in antagonism. She was everyone's bad neighbour. That evening a man who had been brought in after an operation had screamed on and off in his separate cubicle at the end of the ward, and we had pitied and feared his pains. But when Alison's clear English voice recited her history of heart trouble, first and second heart attack, diet, weight, weight-loss, keys, kitchen, and washing-machine man, we were united in callous hostility.

She abused one of the nurses so obscenely that a staff nurse was called in and said if she didn't behave she'd be reported to Matron. I don't know if there was a matron or if she was a figure of speech. We never saw her, but the threat quietened Alison for a few minutes. Then she told May in the next bed that she knew all about it, she'd been an SRN, and knew her rights as a patient. Moira turned on her when she demanded the phone for the umpteenth time, got out of bed, and unhooked it from Moira's bedside.

'Get out of my space, you!', Moira chanted in a deep and rhythmical diatribe, 'We never got our sleep because of you. Coming in here in the middle of the night with your loud old voice. You woke us all up with your big "Bo, Bo, Bo". You only think of yourself. We don't want to know about you. So you get out of my space and you shut up your old "Bo, Bo, Bo".'

Jan and I exchanged delighted smiles through the space in the inadequate curtain. 'She speaks for everyone,' he said.

Alison's neighbour May, in the bed opposite mine, listened patiently. She was a thin, frail, pale brown woman with visitors of all ages and all colours. Friends, children, brothers, sisters, and a great many grandchildren, in jeans and leather, constantly crowded in, carrying crash helmets, fruit, bunches of flowers, and boxes of chocolates, rushing to give her a hug and leaving with waves and loving farewells. There was always a throng round her bed. She was probably younger than Jan, but she looked ancient and wrinkled and powerful, always the centre of her assembly, very much the grandmother. She was determined not to exert herself, and I admired her bland refusal to get up, or practise walking, or go to the lavatory or the washroom. She never raised her voice, and was always sweet and explanatory with the nurses and doctors, especially when they said she should start getting a bit of exercise. She would smile, shaking her head regretfully, and explain that she was too tired.

'No, dear,' she would beam at the nurse or young doctor or physiotherapist, 'I just don't feel up to it,' Or sometimes, for a change, 'No, dear, I would, but I'm expecting my friend, or son, or granddaughter, so I'd better stay put.'

Moira would join in sympathetically across the ward, 'Yes, you have your rest. I want to rest, too. If I'm too ill to have a piece of toast or a cup of tea then I'm too ill to have a wash.'

I spoke to one of May's friends in the washroom, as she was rinsing a garment or a jar or a cup, and said, 'May looks very ill.'

'Yes,' said the friend, 'she's very ill indeed. But she'll be all right. She'll be fine. She has many friends and many people to look after her when she comes home.' I didn't like to ask what she was in for and never found out. Her friends and family saved the nurses and cleaners a lot of work, as they were always cheerfully helping her on and off the commode, making cups of tea, washing and washing up, and carrying off her rubbish to be emptied.

I went home after three days, saying goodbye to everybody except the SS man and Alison. I went back for my check-up twice. The first time I had to wait so long that I gave up, made another appointment and went home, meanly breaking my vows of patience and good temper. They were all hopelessly over-worked, especially the nurses. The second time I saw a consultant I hadn't met before, who asked, 'Is it the worst pain you have felt in your life?' He told me, when questioned, that they had no idea what might have caused the stone since it had never been found. Asked what might have happened to it, he said it had probably disintegrated, so I said goodbye, thanked him, and decided to nip into Ward G. I hovered for a minute, looking down the two rows of beds, in their groups of six. All my old mates had gone except Jan, so I went and greeted him. He looked sleepy, and his leg was still bandaged. When I spoke he looked at me vaguely.

'It's Florence Jones,' I said, regretting the impulse to come back, 'I was in the next bed.' He nodded and smiled, and told me when I asked that the leg wasn't quite healed yet. I thought we'd had an *amitié amoureuse*, hospital style. After we'd watched the news twice, he asked me if I lived alone, and I told him about my children, who'd left home but were often with me. 'It's not good to live alone,' he had said. Now I was fully dressed, in my scarlet duffle-coat and Liberty scarf, carrying a briefcase, in from the real world, I wasn't sure he recognized me. His polite smile turned to a broader one of relief when I said goodbye. Everything had been there, politics and family, courage and lamentation, bad behaviour and kindness, agape and eros, meeting and parting, self-contained, in close quarters.

When I told my mother, she was horrified.

'Oh, no, Florence dear, oh dear, how dreadful. Mrs Davies told me she's read something in the paper about the mixed wards but I told her they'll make up anything for sensation. Dear me! How did you manage?'

It was no good explaining that it had been nice, so I said it was all right, people were mostly too ill to care. I didn't tell her about Jan from the next bed, but amused her with the quarrels of Alison and Moira, and May's devoted family. She nodded absently, then asked in a whisper:

'What happened when anyone wanted to . . . do something? You know . . . ask for a bedpan, or . . . one of those bottles?' She'd never been in hospital but had done her share of visiting. I laughed and told her they'd called out to the nurses, 'Nurse!' or 'Bedpan, please!' She smiled sympathetically, shook her head, and went off to take the walnut cake out of the oven. I was getting a special tea because I'd been in hospital, too far away and for too short a time for my mother to come and visit. When Charlie was in hospital for the last time, she'd been there, taking welsh-cakes he couldn't eat and giving them to the man in the next bed.

The first time he went to hospital, it was St Mary Abbots (now closed down) after a minor car accident. He had broken his collar-bone and a couple of ribs. That was quite a jolly time, at least for the visitors. Charlie was in the bed between a rag-and-bone man on one side and on the other a boy who ran round the ward and swung on the curtain-rails. Charlie was pleased to be alive and not smashed up. He enjoyed surreptitiously reading his notes, which in those days were hung supposedly out of the patient's reach at the top of the bed. I remember they described his state of consciousness on arrival as poor. We liked that. We used to eat the grapes and chocolate and look forward to his homecoming.

The other time I visited him in hospital was not such fun. It was eight years after we'd split up, four after he'd married Jean. It was late October, and the girls were spending half-term in Swansea, half a week with each grandmother. I'd just come back from giving a lecture at a teachers' centre in East Acton, on *The Return of the Native*. Short talk, good discussion, a drink with the old friend who was an adviser to teachers, in the days before the Tories did away with that job, then home.

As soon as I got in the phone began to ring, as if it had been waiting for me. It was Joanna, phoning from Swansea.

'Mum, it's Dad. He's been taken ill, and he's in hospital. I've been trying to get you for hours. They said at college that you were giving a lecture somewhere but it didn't give the address in your diary. Jean wants you to ring her.'

'Jean?' I'd never spoken to her, only knew a little about her from Joanna and Susie, who had met her. There was no reason why she would want to meet me, the first wife, and I wasn't keen on meeting her.

'Why? How is he? What's the matter?'

Joanna was controlling tears. 'Sorry, Mum, but they say he's too ill for us to see him. Anyway Grannie Thomas thinks we should wait a bit. But Jean wants to speak to you, because he is asking for you. Would you like to speak to Grannie?'

My mother was a great provoker of storms in teacups but fine in real turbulence. Her voice was tense but calm.

'Florence dear, I let Jo ring because I thought if I spoke first you'd think there was something the matter with one of them. Charlie was taken into hospital this afternoon, and he is a bit confused, and he's been asking for you, dear. The doctors say it is something called a sub-arachnoid haemorrhage. I'll spell it.' She did. 'He has been speaking to them but he seems to have gone back a few years. He gave them your name and address, and said you were his wife. Of course it's terrible for Jean. So she wants you to phone her. If you don't mind, dear. She's in the hospital, all the time. With Sarah, of course.'

'How are Jo and Susie?'

'Fine, don't worry, dear. They're good girls, wonderful, but they'll be better when you come. Can you come?'

'Yes, yes, of course. But I'll telephone the hospital. I mean, I'll telephone her, Jean, and then let you know. I'll probably come first thing tomorrow. I'll ring you again. Can you give me the number?'

I talked to Susie, then I got a chair, and sat down to ring the hospital. They told me Charlie was a bit restless and confused, but satisfactory, and they'd get Mrs Jones from the day-room. At least I was Professor Jones, I thought, not talking to an exact sound-alike. Her voice was more Welsh than I expected. My heart was hammering so loud I thought she'd hear. I sounded apologetic and flustered in my own ears, my voice too loud, but she was very calm. She had a more pronounced Welsh accent than I did. I certainly never tried to lose mine but somehow through the years of lecturing in London, it had diminished. When I first started I said 'Dullan Thomas', but one day I found myself saying 'Dillon' without being aware of having changed.

'Florence. Sorry, but I can't very well call you Professor Jones, can I? I hope you can come. He is very confused. The doctors say they do quite often lose a few years, and he seems to be back with you. Thinks he's in London. He thanked his mother for coming all the way to see him. I'm afraid he doesn't know me. He's very bad. I think he'd like to see the girls. He's said their names once or twice. But I thought it would be best if they waited for you. It will be upsetting for them, I'm afraid, and better if you're there. If you don't mind coming. Will you be able to come down?'

I didn't know what to say. I felt apologetic, but what could I apologize for? I collected my wits and said I'd be there sometime tomorrow, at midday or a bit later. I'd see Charlie first then think about whether to bring the girls. I said I hoped she didn't mind and she said briskly of course not, how could she? I asked her what had happened and she said she'd found him on the bathroom floor when she came in from school, at lunch-time. She taught the reception class at a primary school. She explained that her school was so near she sometimes popped back at between morning and afternoon school. He'd been fine when she left him after breakfast, but apparently he hadn't been in to the office so he must have been taken ill in the morning, soon after she left.

'Don't ring off, please, Jean. Hang on. Is he very bad? I don't know exactly what it is – is it a stroke – is it – is it very bad?'

'Oh God, you know what the doctors are like. They're so bloody cagey. But my cousin Bet's married to a doctor – Haydn Lewis – and I spoke to him, and he says some patients walk out of hospital after a sub-arachnoid haemorrhage. And some don't. He seems almost normal, in snatches. For instance he gave your Earls Court address and said you were a university lecturer. He rambles a lot. Says the girls' names and yours. He's terribly restless. He will keep trying to pull his tubes out. They've had to bandage his hands. But he looks all right.'

We said goodbye, and I went through the necessary phone calls to colleagues about covering classes and cancelling tutorials in case I wasn't back on Monday. Then I phoned Mick. He had been coming up as usual on the Saturday, for their usual weekend, and for our Saturday afternoon and Sunday dawn.

After saying how sorry he was, he said, 'Look, we'll come up earlier, first thing in the morning. Can I see you? Perhaps you can go on a later train?'

I hesitated, and then agreed, saying reluctantly, 'Well, all right, but I really must catch the one o'clock. I can't be later. I'll have to leave soon after twelve.'

When he arrived next morning I took him into the sitting-room instead of the bedroom and told him everything Joanna and my mother and Jean had said. After I'd finished he said how sorry he was again, and then came over to my chair, holding out his hand to me.

'Come on darling. We can comfort each other a little, can't we?'

I was aghast. The idea was monstrous. I pulled away and got up. I asked him how he could possibly suppose I could want to make love when Charlie might be dying. I burst out crying. He put his arms round me, but I pulled away. He was aghast too, but I saw it and didn't care. I was furious. He was all right. He was healthy and randy, but I was shocked and repelled. Then I sat down and didn't say anything in case I attacked him.

'All right, darling, all right.' He kissed my cheek, gave me his handkerchief, and stood looking down at me, a space between us.

'All right, darling, I'll go. I've got a lot to do today anyway. Call me from there, will you?'

I felt nothing but outrage and old loyal love for Charlie. I got my bag, locked the door, ran to the tube station, caught the Edgware Road train to Paddington and left for Swansea.

It was awful seeing the children at my mother's house, frightened and sad, not knowing what to say. It was awful to meet my ex-mother-in-law, at the hospital, trying to stop crying and introducing me to Jean. It was awful to meet Jean, in the sunny day-room, polite and grateful-sounding and trying to reassure me. I couldn't take her in. Grief took me back to Charlie, so who was this other woman? She was smaller and prettier than I'd gathered from the children's descriptions. She was neat, smartly dressed in a suit, provincially smart, with carefully shaped curly hair. I felt superior, more appropriately dressed in my sweater and jeans, then petty, jealous, hostile, guilty at feeling hostile, furious at feeling jealous, even more guilty because Charlie didn't know her, and as she seemed to keep on saying, had been asking for me.

It was awful seeing Charlie, in his bed, tubed and bandaged, muttering angrily and tossing from side to side. Jean said of course I must go in on my own, and I did. I sat by the bed, and took his hand. He quietened down at once.

'Charlie, it's Florence. Do you know me?'

He didn't say anything but looked at me, and squeezed my hand. Then he muttered something I couldn't hear. He started to toss and turn again. I got up and asked a nurse if that was all right, as he seemed so violent in his movements. She came back, took a look, and said yes, that was how he'd been since he came in, with a few lucid intervals. I just sat there for half an hour, holding his hand, trying to calm him down, talking about the children, saying I was so sorry he was ill, telling him various old friends in London would be sorry to hear about it, anything that came into my head. I gave myself an hour, then I kissed his cheek, said goodbye and went out.

Jean was sitting in the day-room, holding a book. The other Mrs Jones was sitting in front of the television. I heard myself say, I thought I should go now and did Jean think I could bring the children in the morning. She nodded, and I phoned for a taxi and went home. All the way I couldn't stop crying. I didn't try to stop. I couldn't cry in front of Jean and my ex-mother-in-law. Or Charlie. Or the children, when I got to my mother's house. But I didn't mind the taxi-driver seeing me cry, because I didn't know him and it must be what they're used to when they pick up people from the hospital, who've been with the sick and the dying. I remembered I'd meant to ask if I could speak to the doctor but I'd forgotten. Probably it would have been an intrusion. Probably I should leave all that to Jean. A terrible etiquette was imposing itself. We had to pick up its rules as we went along. I didn't really care. All I felt now was a possessive tender solicitude for him, an awkward sisterly sympathy for her, and a sort of pity for us all.

It lasted for ten days, with the children and me visiting him every day, his breathing getting worse, fluid thickening in the bronchial tubes and lungs, the attempts to clear them not too successful, his restlessness getting worse, his muttering wilder, till the last day when he died.

The girls and I had been sitting with him, and the nurse asked us to leave for a bit while they shaved him. It seemed ghastly to shave a man who was scarcely conscious, but they did it every day. This time the staff nurse came where we were sitting in the day-room with Jean. She always appeared much more composed than I was, though hollow-cheeked, and with great violet smudges under her eyes. I think she stayed there all the time, and she was with him except when I visited. My mother told me afterwards that they'd found a bed for her. She always looked neat and clean and pale. She was always lightly made up, with powder and a little lipstick. Sometimes she wore glasses, big round ones with gold rims, and I noticed she always took them off as she went into the ward to sit by Charlie.

By that time he didn't seem to know anyone, but we held his hand and spoke to him just in case. I remember trying to calm him down, holding his hands wrapped in bandages to stop him tearing the tubes out. I remember the man in the bed on the right saying, 'Poor bugger. With all those tubes, even in his private parts!', and the man in the bed on the left, who was very old, and unvisited, telling the two nurses who were sitting on his bed that they were angels, real angels. I remember the staff nurse coming into the day-room and facing the five of us, all Joneses, a mother, two wives and two children, with a sad look. She was very, very sorry. He had passed away when the physiotherapists were with him. Would we like a cup of tea?

My brother took the girls to the funeral, but I didn't go. I stayed at home with my mother. I thought that was Jean's show, and I didn't grudge it to her. I didn't want to see her again and I'm positive she didn't want to see me.

All that time I phoned Mick several times, and he phoned me, and we had brief but friendly conversations. I said darling when he said darling. He didn't say his ritual sentence, 'I kiss your lips', but he said my name like an endearment, as he always did.

When I got back I couldn't sleep with him. At first I tried to, but it was no good. I wept and turned away. He was angry and I got angry and I told him to rape me, and he nearly did. I fought him, tooth and claw, and beat him off, violent, disgusted, and determined. The bedroom games turned nasty. Sometimes I apologized afterwards, saying I hadn't meant it or couldn't help it. I told him more than once to go away, and stay away, that I was beside myself, that I was fond of him, that I supposed I still loved him, but it was no good, there was no desire in me. Sometimes I was callous and hurtful. I showed him a condolence letter from Henri Basch, an old Dijon friend, who wrote warmly about Charlie's wit and bad-taste humour, and invited me to come over and eat and drink and talk with him and his wife Sophie.

When Mick handed it back without a word, I said, 'Yes, Charlie was funny. Actually his humour was a bit like yours, only he didn't tell so many jokes. He loved terrible puns. I suppose you are alike, in some ways.'

Mick said I'd told him that several times already. Once or twice when I told him to go if he didn't like what was happening, he said he would take me at my word and call it a day, but he always phoned within twenty-four hours. When he did I was glad, and said so. When he wasn't asking me to go to bed, it was all right. We talked, we read each other's work, we ate and drank. But our affair had always been so sexual, our meetings never without sex. It was terribly strange, even for me. It was like a truce, but we weren't enemies. We were passing the time, waiting for something. I was possessed by Charlie.

Night and day I went over all our early times, climbing Tryfan and Snowdon, looking at Bronzino and Della Robbia in Florence, and the pictures of the languid saint and the married couple bathing in San Gimignano where we thought we might have conceived and christened the foetus Little Cisterna after the town fountain and the hotel, listening to Bach and Britten and Dowland, Peter Pears and Deller, reading Auden aloud, feeling close to MacNeice's 'Sunlight in the Garden', and *Autumn Journal*, like him and his wife sleeping in linen, as soon as we could afford it, and cooking with wine. One rainy night in the small flat in Bedford Place we read 'London Rain', and said it was our poem. I felt guilty because I'd gone off MacNeice and started to read him again. I went to the Tate and looked at all the sculpture and painting we'd found together, before Mel and Mick: Vuillard, Valadon, the Epsteins, beloved Picasso. Charlie's death bereaved me not so much of his existence, from which I'd been cut off for years, but of our past. I hadn't wanted to look back before, tearing off chunks of the calendar. Now my grief was half-unreal, romantic, out of proportion to the visible occasion, but not all illusion. And sentimental grief feels real enough.

Bereavement started longings for what I'd abandoned. Of course guilt came in too, sentimental guilt for which you can't be required to pay. There was a lot to cry for, our youth, our love, our fun, our loss, my guilt, perhaps his. I didn't know. I cried a lot, mostly in private. I didn't bother not to cry in front of Mick, and perhaps in a way that was a show of loving, though it felt like aggression.

He tried to console me, but he was the last person to dry my tears. He was on my side, like all my loving friends, and their reassurance fell on deaf guilty ears. I wanted people who would feed my remorse, Charlie's mourners, not mine. I sought out Portia, a woman I hadn't seen for years, an old colleague of Charlie's and his friend rather than mine. She could be guaranteed to say I'd been unfaithful and selfish. She was a help as she rehearsed the story of my marriage, casting me for the villain's role. On one or two occasions when Joanna and Susie blamed me for the break-up and the pointless mourning, their bitter words quenched my thirst. Nothing they could say was as sharp as my self-reproach, and I was proud of them when they understood and shut up.

I knew the poison to dip my needle in. I could feel contemptuous with myself for using the knowledge. Nothing was right, even remorse, stupidly idle and indulgent. The only time I behaved well was when I stayed away from the funeral and left him to Jean and the children.

I cried for weeks on end, then on and off for those three years. The tears tasted sweet though not to Mick. Then suddenly, after months, my frigidity thawed. One afternoon I said I'd try going to bed with him again. As we were lying together, I tried to be passive, to find myself going through the old motions. It was like pretending that I liked him, right at the start. Affectionate experiment turned to pleasure, and it was all right again. I still wept and mourned, but not in front of Mick.

Mick said he'd read some classic text on bereavement – was it Freud? – and had been terribly depressed to know it could last for years. It did, but I could usually control the symptoms and it stopped crippling desire. During those three years I hid the bereavement from Mick, and my love for him came back. Now it existed side by side with my love for Charlie, apparently there to stay; but it didn't have to be put to the tests of marriage and friendship and I wasn't proud of it.

Mick and I were back together, almost as good as new. Charlie's death married me to Mick. It had something to do with feeling that my marriage with Charlie was over at last, because he was dead and because Jean was his widow. But most of all it was sharing something outside desire, as you do in marriage. We had weathered a domestic crisis, as couples do with children and mortgages and illnesses.

Mick felt it too. In the Cambridge hotel where we shared the sauna, made love, had dinner, and made love again, we started to quarrel in the middle of the night. Mick said he'd like to leave early in the morning though we had planned to stay till the afternoon. I knew he was thinking of getting back to Ellen. Desire was gratified, and conscience pricked.

I knew the pattern, and it displeased me. I would leave early too, even earlier, there and then, before dawn. I'd phone the desk for a taxi and wait at the station for the first train to London. I started to get out of bed.

He reached over, and pulled me back: 'Oh come on darling. Calm down. You know I'm your pal. Think of all the fun we've had. All the other things. All we've been through together. Your husband's death. All that.'

But I hadn't realized that married feeling would disappear when I became a friend of the family.

I only paid two visits to their house. The first time he invited me I refused. He asked me to walk back with him from the Randolph to his house, because he wasn't walking steadily any more. It was the first time he took my arm in public, in Oxford. I thought illness was making him careless, so I asked if it was all right. Wasn't he afraid of someone seeing us? When he stopped, held on to me, and turned his dropping head to say it was all right, I realized that my scruples were out of date. I was supporting a frail sick old man, not linking arms with a lover. He'd told Ellen and Sandy that he was going to have coffee with me, so I could come in and have a drink with them all. I said no, I was too cowardly. I would meet the family, but not just yet. I stood outside while he rang the bell, then walked off quickly as I heard someone open the door. I knew that sooner or later I'd have to go into his house, because he wouldn't be able to make it to the hotel.

He made it one more time before I paid my first visit. He had invited me for drinks, at about half-past five. He could still walk very slowly and with difficulty. We spent the afternoon in bed, in a long narrow room in the Randolph. When we left and I shut the door behind us I knew it for a last time. But that was pushed to the back of my mind. I was wasting emotion. I was feeling apprehensive about meeting the family. I was going to have drinks with horrible Ellen and then she wouldn't be horrible Ellen ever again.

I walked back with Mick, then left him at his door. I was to return in an hour. I walked round St Giles and Little Clarendon Street. Mick told me there was a new shop that sold rather good Indian jewellery and I should go and choose something from him. His daughters had told him about it. I went and looked and thought it was all pretty dreadful. I tried to like something, to please him, but I couldn't. I looked at my watch. Time to pay my call.

I couldn't remember what Ellen looked like. I'd have to look into her face, right at her. I remember standing outside, lifting my hand to the bell, taking it off, looking at the blue front door of their house, wanting to go back to the hotel. But by the end of the hour – I timed myself – I was horrified to find myself almost bending to kiss her as I left.

I have no idea what we talked about, except that Mick went out of the room to mix the drinks and she said he was going to allow himself a martini, to help him with 'his troubles'. We had a couple of dips with our martinis. She was much better-looking than I had recalled or imagined, and very sharp and amusing. She seemed much worse than I was at deciphering his speech, and he kept using a clever little machine which printed his words on thin strips of paper. I was shy of asking him to repeat things in front of other people, and shy at understanding him when they didn't. Other friends turned up, including a couple I'd met in Dublin, so we had some Irish literary gossip and conversation wasn't a problem. I kept my eye on the time, left as soon as I decently could, and was enormously relieved to be out of the house. I was becoming a friend of the family and I hated it. I expected to hate it because of seeing Ellen, but it turned out that I hated most of all being a visitor.

The second time I was to go early, to help him with the wording of some notes, and stay for supper. That was the one time I stayed in the hotel alone, without him coming round. His walking wasn't up to it. This time ringing the bell wasn't too bad. He let me in, and I greeted Ellen, and that wasn't too bad either. Then he asked me if I'd like a ride, and I rode up to his study after him on the stair-lift they'd had installed. He watched from the top and laughed.

When we passed a bedroom and went into his study, I felt terrible. I was afraid he'd want me to go to bed with him. I didn't know if he really wanted me to help with the notes, or if that was his story. I'd always said I'd do anything he wanted and except for the period after Charlie's death I always had. I would not be able to do anything in his house, with Ellen underneath in the sitting-room. I would not be able to refuse him anything. It might be the last time. It was, though I didn't know for sure. So I was petrified, afraid of Mick, sick at the idea of being afraid of Mick.

I went in after him, and left the door open. I needn't have worried. He embraced and stroked my face, touched my breast, said how much he wished we were naked and could go to bed. Then he took his hands away, and asked me to look at some queries on a typescript. We worked and talked for over an hour. It was all right, we were working as we had worked in my flat, hundreds of times.

I'd forgotten his family when his son Leo appeared at the door, saying jokingly, 'And what are you two doing?'

He said an old student of Mick's had called, but Ellen hadn't liked to disturb us. Then I remembered hearing the bell. We went down, I made a joke about the lift, and the four of us had an early family supper. Ellen had made a meat-loaf and said it wasn't very interesting. It was rather dry, and didn't have much taste. Mick was sitting at the other end of the table. He smiled at me and said he expected I made a good meat-loaf. The remark seemed terribly intimate. Ellen asked me what I put in mine. I said with an effort that I put sage or marjoram, bread-crumbs and egg. I can't recall anything else we'd talked about at the meal. I met Leo at a party in Atlanta, a year or two after Mick died, but I had to remind him who I was when we met.

The sitting-room was also the dining-room. It seemed full of furniture and full of people. We moved into a smaller room to watch the film about Auden to which Mick had contributed. He was interviewed briefly, after Spender and several other people, and spoke about meeting Auden in New York at a party after a reading, and also about when Auden came back to Christchurch to live in the small sixteenth-century cottage once used as the college brewery. He didn't speak about Auden's isolation and apparent despondency in Oxford, as he had to me, but only of the great pleasure he felt at their chance meetings, praising the total originality of the personality and the poetry. It was his old relaxed smiling chat, his voice drawling pleasantries in the way I first loved. The film was made just before the Canadian trip when his voice began to be a nuisance. He said he was a Victorian scholar, who never wrote about modern writers, but he had a tremendous admiration for Auden's voice and craft and passion, and would have liked to be his biographer. Too bad the timing was wrong. I remembered the day Auden died, when we mourned him together.

The film was soon over, and we were all talking about its clever hotchpotch of reminiscence, opinion, poetry and music, and all thinking about Mick's lost voice, when horrible Sir Wallace's wife Elizabeth turned up. We were introduced. I was incapable of talking amiably to Sir Wallace's wife, but I didn't have to try because Mick's daughter Sandy and her four-year-old daughter Rachel arrived. They created a welcome diversion, and we got up to move back into the bigger room. It was a good time for me to go. As I said goodbye to her, the child said politely, 'Come again.' I kissed Mick, somehow, then kissed Ellen on the cheek, promising to come again in a week or two and bring a picnic lunch.

Before I became a visitor and casual acquaintance of the family, and after the diagnosis had been made, but he wasn't too ill, there were good times. I went to see him in his private hospital in Stepney Green, looking forward to being the sole caller, as his daughters were looking after Ellen in Oxford. I was. I wasn't a visitor then, but his lover. He was my darling invalid, in my territory.

He was trying everything, second, third and fourth opinions, Chinese herbal medicine, acupuncture, and now this new place where a new consultant had referred him for new tests. He had decided they would be the last and clinching ones. I stopped off at Whitechapel and bought salt beef sandwiches at Blooms, but when I arrived Mick had already eaten, so I sat on his bed and ate. He told me in his slow slurred speech that he'd had a wonderful lunch, but they hadn't brought the bottle of champagne he'd been promised on arrival. When a nurse looked in to take his temperature he asked her for the champagne, but she laughed and thought he was joking. He said it had been on the publicity brochure about the hospital, and he'd come there for the champagne. She laughed even more uncertainly and said she'd go and ask but she didn't think they had any champagne. She explained unnecessarily that they were still working on the building, and having growing-pains.

I think everyone there was new. They were still building. Mick's wing was finished and smelt of fresh paint, and the reception hall had been only half-floored. I visited him three times in the two days he was there and the banging and drilling went on all the time, making conversation even more difficult than it was already, with Mick's poor enunciation and throat-clearing.

I'd been told how to find his room. He was sitting up in bed, propped on pillows, and reading his typescript. We kissed enthusiastically. Sitting in the chair beside him I saw that his arm was skinny, and his long hands wasted.

I asked him about the first test. He hadn't had any result yet. He said he'd told the nurse who wheeled him down to the room where they did the test that he was relying on them to find he had some new unlife-threatening illness, and the man grinned and said they'd do their best. When I came back next day they had told him the results would be sent to his doctor. I saw he had read no news as bad news. That was when I decided I'd have to visit him at home, feeling sick at the prospect. But meanwhile I had him to myself. He had tasted the boiled beef sandwich on the first day, and the Belgian white chocolates from Harrods on the second. I sat close, and I fondled him. Food and sex, like old times.

'I'm enjoying being in this hospital,' he said.

'Is this fun?'

'Yes, it is. You're a very good sick-visitor.'

He hadn't come up to London for several weeks, but I was still going down to stay in the Randolph every week or ten days, and he could still get there, walking slowly from his house in St Giles. I remember meeting him in the hotel lounge once when we only had an hour and thought we'd have tea there, and just talk. I came down the big staircase, and saw him sitting by the door, looking at the paper. I saw him suddenly, without him seeing me, and as a stranger. He looked old and very tired, his head drooping on his chest, like a wrynecked chick's. But that evening when he was lying down beside me, his head on the pillow, he looked as he'd always done, only thinner. His shoulders and arms frightened me.

Each time I thought it might be the last, till I knew it was the last. I suppose if I'd tried harder to be the family friend I might have been able to visit at the end, but then I would have had to face his family as well as grieve. I don't feel bad about not doing all that. He had other things to think about in those last days. We had talked about everything that might happen, except the detail of not being able to hold his hand on the deathbed. When I held my mother's, on hers, I felt deprived of Mick's death, but only for a minute.

Once I had been sternly rebuking him for greed, priggishly and enviously, when he was talking eagerly about money, which I didn't like. As usual he was trying to get his agent to screw a larger advance from his publisher. He said jokingly, to quieten my anti-materialist sermon, that ever since Ellen had her first symptoms he thought he should accumulate money for nursing. He didn't need much. When he was given his diagnosis, he had enquired about the likely ways of dying. They had withheld the diagnosis for months, and when at last they told him he was angry, protesting that he had a book to finish. Dates were important.

They explained that some patients became wretchedly demoralized on hearing that there was no remedy and no hope. But he was never angry when he talked about the process of the disease.

I had come back from seeing *Ghosts*, at the Pit in the Barbican, with Joanna. When Mick phoned just before midnight, I was full of the production and the acting, which I'd especially loved because I had once played Regina in a production by the college dramatic society. Mick asked a question or two, then said he'd seen the doctor that day and now had a diagnosis. I realized he'd been listening to me patiently. They had told him what it was, and he told me. It was motor neurone disease. His doctor had spotted it right at the start. He had asked them how long he had, and they said probably a year or a bit more, perhaps less. There were always some cases that surprised the doctors. It might be longer.

'Right,' I said. 'Let's talk about longer.'

About two months later, another sufferer who had heard about Mick's course of Chinese medicine came to see him; he had had the disease for about twelve years. That sounded wonderful. But when I exclaimed optimistically about the hope of years to come, Mick said,

'I can't say meeting him made me feel too keen on living for years. I got the distinct impression that he'd survived his life.'

On the night I came back from *Ghosts* his voice was slurred, a bit like a drunk's, but clear enough. I couldn't speak. After a pause he spoke. 'I can't say I feel too bad about quitting the scene.'

We were walking along Warwick Road to Earls Court tube station one day when he told me what they'd said about the end.

'You gradually get weak, the nerves fail, various muscles waste, you have to be helped to eat, go to the toilet, and so on. Probably. Then at some point you get pneumonia, and that's it. Doesn't sound too bad, really, does it?'

He had told me about the diagnosis on a Friday and the next day I went to a reading at Birkbeck, organized by Katharine Worth, to commemorate Samuel Beckett's death. Mick had known Beckett, so every word had a double sadness. After the buffet lunch, in a short break before the afternoon programme, I made some excuse and dashed over to Dillon's to look in a medical dictionary. One phrase struck me: 'A relentlessly progressive disease'. The language seemed flowery, as Scrooge would say, for a clinical description. It kept returning during the months that followed, and still impresses me.

I knew I hadn't done very well in finding words. In August and September we'd been through a period of low-level quarrelling. I was having problems with my new book. My mother was worried about her house, where the front wall was cracking, and I was worried about her, helping her cope with workmen, insurance, local authorities, wondering if she should move permanently to the Rhossilli cottage. I kept dashing up and down to Swansea, not able to give enough time and sympathy to Mick, not knowing he was so ill, impatient when he grumbled at my absences, and my silences when I was away.

The last time I'd been away I hadn't had the energy to phone him, and he wrote a letter saying he had been thinking about me a good deal, wishing I would keep in touch, and hoping I wouldn't stay there long. When I phoned to tell him not to keep harassing me, he replied mildly that not being able to talk or walk very well gave him lots of time to think about me and miss me. Up till then it had been mainly a weak neck and the weak voice, and I had assumed it was some throat infection. One of the doctors had murmured something about a virus. I said I hadn't known his walking was affected. He said his balance seemed a bit unsteady. I said I'd try to come down as soon as I got back, but the Swansea troubles were time-consuming. I talked on about the iniquities of Mother's insurers, who said the facade of her house had been inadequately bonded to the party walls, a hundred years ago, and wouldn't pay up. After years of taking her money. I hated insurers. He listened and his slurred voice was sympathetic. I said I was sorry to be so preoccupied.

I felt unsympathetic, didn't know why, and felt guilty. It was about this time he sent me the cheque for two thousand pounds that I sent back. He came up for a day and I wasn't very enthusiastic. Our usual games seemed to have gone sour. Then came the diagnosis.

On the Saturday evening when I came in from the Beckett readings I made myself a sandwich and sat down to write him a love letter. I wasn't going to type it, as I often did. I stared at the paper, as I'd never ever done with a letter to Mick. I started to write. I said how shattered I'd been by the news. I stared at the sentence, disliking it. I threw it away and started again. I found myself saying again that I was shattered, that he must know I was shattered. Then suddenly the block wasn't there. I was promising all over again to do anything he might want or need. I said I was sorry I'd been so unloving. I would go to Swansea as little as I possibly could. I'd come to Oxford as often as he wanted me to come. I'd cancel my trips to Italy and Poland. I'd be there when he wanted. I was all love, renewing the old vows. Mick had once told me that his loving wasn't selfish, that if I ever needed it, he would put me first. He wasn't promising to leave Ellen, or anything like that. I think he was just defining love. He said he could be unselved, if I ever needed him to be. I remembered that speech, and I felt unselved.

He wrote a very short letter in reply, saying he wanted me to be with him as much as possible, for us to make love as best we could, and as long as we could. That would be a big help.

He and Ellen stopped coming up for the weekends. For a while I went down every other weekend. Once he came up for a couple of hours, and I met his train, as I'd done a thousand times. He was feeling tired, didn't have the energy to come home with me, I couldn't get away for long, and he needed to talk to me about work.

We had coffee in the crowded coffee-room of the Great Western Hotel at Paddington, occasionally touching hands as we looked at two chapters of his Thackeray biography which I'd just read. One was an early chapter, much revised, the other was the last. He was racing ahead to get finished. We talked about his discussion of Thackeray's illness. Was it syphilis? I'd liked his account of Thackeray's funeral, attended by the great and the small, including all the painted ladies of the town. As we talked I noticed a food-stain on his blue pullover. His hands were very unsteady, but he was still using an ordinary knife and fork. Ellen wasn't up to sponging his clothes, which had always been immaculate.

He saw the direction of my stare and said he was sorry he was such a slob. Then he got back to the book.

'You don't think it's overwritten? No purple passages?'

'Not a bit. Lilac, perhaps. Like some of his, come to think of it.'

'What about the bit where Charlotte Brontë comes to call and he has to nip round to the club because it's heavy going? Nothing sexist there?'

'No, I thought that was fine. Sad little episode, isn't it? I hated it when he went out to the club, of course.'

We had gone together a couple of years before to look at Lawrence's great portrait of Thackeray in the Strangers Room of the Reform Club. I went on a bit about men's clubs and the Mall so grand and heavy, but I loved Thackeray looking down the elegant room, big and handsome with his lovely broken nose and his keen scornful expression. I went to lunch there two weeks ago, with a friend who was a member but didn't know the portrait. We went in search of Thackeray from great room to great room until we stood in front of him. I shut my eyes for a minute to hear my voice and Mick's.

I'd stood there arguing with him about Thackeray's poor mad young wife, who'd jumped from a boat into the sea, and ended up in a private hospital in Paris, with clubbable Thackeray becoming a single parent, helped and hindered by those governesses Charlotte Brontë unfortunately hadn't known about when she dedicated *Jane Eyre* to him. Mick surmised that Mrs Thackeray had been driven mad by sex, and I insisted the breakdown remained a mystery. Biographers can't have mysteries, they cut at the roots of their trade. Mick's speculations were scholarly, with a touch of inspired wildness. Once I said petulantly that he should have gone on writing poetry, instead of putting so much imagination into his biographies, and he laughed. His one volume had been praised, but he'd stopped writing poems when he got married, except for the odd occasional piece, like one he wrote for me about meeting at Albert Gate.

'Not very good, I know,' he said. 'But at least it shows close attention to you.'

We'd talked about his poetry then, walking in the park, looking at the ducks. I said they were mallards and he nodded vaguely.
He said it had been the poetry of a young man's desires. I was
amazed. It was so metaphysical. He said that was a thin disguise,
'When you are old and grey and full of sleep' in negative, made
abstract. And if he'd gone on writing poetry it wouldn't have
made money. I laughed and called him mercenary.

In the Reform Club the portrait drew us back from the argument about Mrs Thackeray. We looked at it for a long time, then
returned to our discussion, scholars plying their trade. We talked
about *Henry Esmond*, which I preferred to *Vanity Fair*, admiring
it as a highly original psychological novel, while Mick tended to
treat it as evidence about Thackeray's relationship with his mother.
But we could talk about literature without quarrelling. I loved
the way he wrote about Thackeray's letters to Jane Brookfield
after they had parted, letters full of harsh jokes, laconic allusions,
intimate understatement, bitter but always unselfpitying. Thackeray
was almost amused, Mick wrote, by his own survival of loss.

'Thackeray had beaten his demons,' he said, looking up at that
young-old face.

'Aren't we lucky, you and I, not to have demons,' I said. It
wasn't a question. I'd said to myself long ago that I was lucky,
after self-destructive Mel, to have Mick. He was not driven by
demons, but he recognized them when he met them. In his own
life and in the famous dead lives he contemplated. I wasn't sure
about my demons, but I thought they'd probably cleared off,
exorcized by Mick's passionate matter-of-factness. It was in control even now he was dying. He once said that a colleague of his
in Harvard – one of those two friends he'd told about me – hadn't
known as a young man what to do with his own brilliance. I
wondered more than once if Mick's composure came from knowing
precisely what to do with his brilliance. I was going to miss that
rational calm, which had given me such ease, and had been so
amusing.

He said, 'Very lucky. And lucky to have each other. Poor
Thackeray and poor Jane.'

He asked me if I was ready to send him some of the work on

my book, which was worrying me. It was a study of the English *roman-à-clef*, the genre for which the English have no name. I hadn't really started writing. I was floundering, puzzled about what to include, because there were so many borderline cases. I was doubtful about moving from the Victorians to the Moderns. I didn't even have a title. He told me to hurry up. I'd have plenty to say for myself.

We'd talked about every sentence of Mick's book, and a good many of Thackeray's. The manuscript had travelled from Oxford to London, in many drafts, and back again. It was the fourth big book he'd written while we were together, but the only one that mentions me in the acknowledgements.

'I shall thank you,' he said, in the Great Western coffee-room. He didn't need to say it was because the book wouldn't come out till after he was dead and it wouldn't matter any more. I racked my brains for something to say, and could only come up with, 'I thought perhaps you might.'

'Cheer up, darling. Don't look so miserable. Think of all you've done for me. After all, you're the only person to cook me Thackeray's favourite meal, the only dish that inspired him to write poetry. So smile!' I smiled.

'So it's finished. Congratulations. You've made it,' I said, as he slowly tidied the pages into a neatish pile, with hands that trembled, then put them away in his briefcase. All covered in my pencil scrawl, which only Charlie and Mick could read without swearing.

I was wearing a new grey trouser-suit, and in the middle of our talk about the book he leaned across, touched my breast, and laughed as he said he wished I could take my clothes off. As he did, somebody spoke, and I jumped. A smartly dressed smiling woman loomed up with her tray and asked if we minded her sitting at our table. We agreed reluctantly and uncertainly, and she settled down with a clash. We fell silent then so obviously that after a minute or two she apologized, got up and moved off. We didn't look a very romantic couple but something told her we weren't keen on company.

That was the last time Mick came to London, though I didn't know it at the time. A week or so later, I had my bathroom floor tiled. Some months before he'd given me the money to pay the tiler's bill, as a Christmas present. The tiler had taken his time, but now it was finished. There were huge matt blue tiles instead of the ancient dark green vinyl I'd never liked. I thanked him and described them and wished he could see the bathroom, and feel the new warmth since I'd had an extra radiator fitted. He chuckled and slowly said he was shivering for the past, and perhaps he could manage to come up again some time. Like my promised picnic lunch for Mick and Ellen, that visit didn't come off.

I was at Charlie's deathbed, after I'd stopped being his wife, but of course I never went near Mick's. Mick's last days were described to me by two friends, one English and one American. After Isabella wrote her condolence letter and we talked about it all, she told what she heard from a friend who knew Mick's daughter Maria. He'd been unconscious, apparently in the last coma, then had one of those sudden revivals before dying and talked to his children on the clever little tape-machine. He knew he was dying and wished they'd get on with living. And later on I heard from Jake, in Atlanta, that his colleague Arnold Hunter visited Mick in hospital and said seeing him die would help him face his own death.

I was glad to hear these stories. I didn't feel bitter. I didn't expect a dying message. I had known I couldn't be there. I hadn't been a friend of the family long enough.

TEN

Funeral Games

Death is like Christmas; it belongs to the family. I listened to my voice speaking to someone in the porters' lodge at Magnus College, where I'd phoned a thousand times, 'Can you tell me the date of the memorial service for Professor Michael Solomon, please?' My voice sounded calm in my own ears. I was listening to it.

The polite voice replied, 'It hasn't been decided yet, madam. Probably in two or three weeks' time. The funeral is tomorrow, but that is private, just for the family. The date of the memorial service will be in *The Times*. Or you could ring again. Next week, perhaps?'

I thanked the voice. I knew the funeral would be private. I hadn't asked about the funeral. I didn't phone the college again but bought the paper every day till I saw the announcement. Then next day I got a card addressed in Ellen's big square childish hand, which I knew from signatures in her books, and once or twice on Mick's manuscripts. I had met her five times, once at the party in their flat in Hans Crescent, once at the dinner party when I barely spoke to her, once at the airport, and twice at their house in Oxford when Mick was getting worse. Perhaps she sent cards to everyone in his address book, perhaps she sent it because I'd helped him with the last book on Thackeray, and had visited them twice, perhaps she guessed we were lovers, perhaps the card wasn't from her but from one of the children, whose handwriting looked like hers. I didn't know. I knew I didn't want to be invited to the memorial service by horrible Ellen, his widow.

I wanted to be the widow. I was the widow. I hadn't ever wanted to meet her during the fifteen years after the first meeting. But of course I had to in the end.

We were eating the chocolates I'd brought him in his awful posh hospital in the East End. I said the sentence in my head, then out loud, expressionlessly, as far as I remember.

'I think perhaps it's time I became a friend of the family.'

'Yes. OK. Come and have a drink when you're down next.'

The weekend after next. My heart banged against my ribs at the prospect.

Once he had said, 'Sometimes I think she knows all about us,' then with a shrug, 'and sometimes I know she doesn't.'

One afternoon, years ago, lying on the floor of his college room in full sunlight, I watched him buttoning his shirt and complained in post-coital sulkiness, 'If you suddenly dropped dead I wouldn't know.' The thought had just flashed into my mind.

'Well, darling,' he wrenched the comb through his thinning curly hair, pulling it out by the roots as usual, 'it would be in the paper, you know.'

'I hardly ever read the paper, you know.'

'Well, someone might mention it.'

'Well, that's exactly what I mean. Somebody might say, "Sorry to hear about Mick Solomon getting run over. Did you know him? Such a sweet man." And you'd be dead and buried without my knowing.'

I could hear my voice go Welsh. I was echoing what my mother had said once when I went to a conference in Newcastle, New South Wales, and as usual she was dreading the thought of the vast distance I was putting between us. She had commented that she could be dead and buried before I came back. I had reminded her that when I went on long trips I phoned frequently, and anyway the flight only took a day so she might be dead but probably not buried. She changed the subject.

Mick went on, pulling on his jacket, 'And just think. You wouldn't have to be bothered with any of the arrangements.'

I looked at Ellen's handwriting on the card, and felt a spasm of pure hate. I tore it in half and put it in the wastepaper basket where Mick had so often put Kleenexes and his hair combings. Joanna had enraged me by asking if I was going to send 'her' a condolence card or something.

I snapped, 'Certainly not. I wouldn't dream of it. I detest her. I was only polite to her because I had to see her to see him those last weeks.'

I hoped she'd know that not getting a condolence letter from me was a negative declaration, a message that we'd been lovers. I hoped she hadn't guessed and kindly sent me a card, like the *femme complaisante* she might or might not have been. If she'd guessed she'd surely have known that I wouldn't have needed to be informed of the occasion by her. Perhaps she had guessed and unkindly sent me a card. Perhaps she was being nasty to me, pulling rank as the widow. I tried to stop speculating. My daughter's question about a condolence letter treated me as a friend of the deceased. That was almost as bad as the widow doing the correct thing. The trouble was, I knew Ellen was simply going down a list of friends and acquaintances. I was invited with no sinister motive, as a matter of social routine. It was unendurable. I should have been sending those invitations. I should have been getting all those hundreds of condolence letters:

Dear Florence,
Words are useless, but I had to write to say how I feel for you. You have all your wonderful memories. Not many marriages are like yours. And you have the children and the grandchildren. . . .

Or

Dear Mrs Solomon,
We never met and you won't know my name. I am a great admirer of your husband's work and want to say how shattered I feel by his death, and how much I sympathize. . . .

Or

Dear Professor Jones,

I was a student of yours nearly twenty years ago, and meant to write to you when you and Michael Solomon were married. Now what should have been congratulation turns out to be condolence. . . .

I should have been sitting in the front row of St Magnus dressed in black, flanked by two daughters and two sons, smiling bravely, and listening to horrible old Sir Wallace Elliott mouthing his platitudes and apologizing for talking about Michael when others knew his work so much better. My mind strayed as he spoke. I couldn't decide what my name was on the envelope of the letters. Was I the woman who married him or was I myself, living with him after Ellen died? Had I married him, as he would have wanted, or not, as I would have wanted? Or had I changed my mind? Were the children mine or his or ours? In fantasy and fiction I'd been ringing the changes, imagining the end as death, and now death was here. I was sickened by it all.

I wasn't feeling grief any more. I was desperate with jealousy. I took my glasses off and made Ellen into a blur. I switched my attention to Sir Wallace. I wanted to get up and shout, 'Shut up, you old fool. Others did know him better. A lot better. Me for one. I'm the widow. I liked fucking him and she didn't. So why don't you fuck off!'

I hadn't imagined the service, or the invitation, but I had imagined the death over and over again. After a time it was evident that death was what would part us, so it was my death or his. I chose his, on the principle that what you imagine can't happen, at least not precisely in the way you imagine it. And of course all those years of kissing and nobly never telling made me long to tell. And to imagine telling. I imagined his death in the everyday fantasy, and of course in the novel that I was trying to write about the poet, his girlfriend, and his wife. There it happened suddenly, in the girlfriend's absence, as I'd fancied it happening years ago in that summer conversation about obituaries and funeral arrangements.

In the novel the heroine was Chloe, then Gite, after a

Frenchwoman I'd met and liked in Dijon, sometimes Belinda, then Flora, and in the end Clara. With its two syllables, Italian connection, and cluster of an 'l', a vowel and an 'r', it echoed Florence, as disguised names in books like to do. When her lover, Daniel Jacobs, died, Clara had been away teaching for a semester at Columbia where I had once given a lecture. She came home via Kennedy and Heathrow and Earls Court tube to find a pile of mail inside the flat door but no welcome home letter from Daniel. And after the first half hour, there was no phone call, either. Daniel – like Mick – always knew when his girlfriend would be getting home and always phoned to say hullo.

I sent Clara to Columbia about the time I'd been to Princeton. I'd been lecturing on Charlotte Brontë, she'd been lecturing on Emily Dickinson. I kept her interests near my own to make things easier. She didn't tell the whole story in her own voice, but half of it kept close to her point of view. She was the girlfriend. The other half of the story kept close to the wife's point of view.

Of course the novel was a prophecy. Of course it has turned into a memory. Everything does, unless it's sheer moonshine. I remember anticipating a future which caught up with the heroine and her author. I stopped writing the novel when Mick was given about a year to live. When he died I decided to write our story as it was, not as it might have been. I think he'd have liked me to. He took a professional care of our correspondence.

'If you don't mind, I'll send your letters back to your safe keeping,' he said.

He assumed I'd keep his and I did. I've kept the lot, his and mine, all unsorted, in boxes with labels saying the contents are private and should be destroyed unread. I intend to read them all again and then throw them away, but you never know.

And now Ellen's dead too. If she were alive I'd still write this, but I'd probably cut out some of the stuff about her. That would be hard, forcing me to change a lot of things. I'd been considerate while she was alive. I never breathed Mick's name to a soul, for her sake. He did tell, to my astonishment. He came back from the summer trip to the States after we first met telling me he had told his two closest friends about us.

'Unwise, I know, but I felt I had to.'

The pleasure in telling is the same, for fiction and fact. I put some things into fiction to stop them happening. It did and it didn't. Some of the events were the same – death and widowhood – but the illness and dying were new. My prediction of feelings was accurate enough. In fact and in fiction there was a flaming jealousy which made me weep with rage not sadness, a cold hostility to the mourning family and friends, a childish, fractious ache for public widowhood.

The mirror-image of the remorse I felt at Charlie's death was the delight that I'd behaved so well to Mick. As he had to me. It was easier to take his death than Charlie's, because there was no remorse. Only the grief of deprivation, and the common difficulty of believing in a death you don't witness. I couldn't believe it, especially after the abject ordinariness of getting a packet of my letters sent to me three days before he died. But the overwhelming feeling was jealousy.

When I tried to write the novel, long before his illness, I was partly driven by spite. Margaret Drabble once gave a talk to our students in which she said with candid humour that revenge was a neglected motive for the writer. A high-minded critic, I didn't believe her till I started work on my eternal triangle, and found myself whetting the knife. But as I wrote I got involved in the wife's character, and she changed from horrible Ellen to the woman I might have been, just as her husband became the man Charlie might have been, in a more advantaged and successful incarnation. Their marriage was the one we might have had if I had been less ambitious and successful, and if neither of us had been Welsh and lower-lower-middle-class, or working-class, or whatever we were.

Resentment and envy started me off. I don't feel them now. I still feel love. You can love the dead. I was surprised to find that. But I love dead Charlie as well as dead Mick. Distant happenings, like my marriage, have settled into the same time-set as my long love affair. They come close in a long perspective, to adapt the phrase Philip Larkin nicked from Thomas Hardy. But the daily sadness is there, being without Mick. I miss his steady affection, his constant presence, his arrivals and departures, his voice on the telephone night and dawn, and the daily telling as we planned and recalled nights and days.

In the novel Clara arrived home, didn't find the usual letter from Daniel, and sat down to go through her mail. She found a thick cream envelope with the embossed professional name and address of a solicitor on the back, and inside a short letter from someone called James Harrison, asking her to telephone him as soon as possible, and giving a daytime and evening number. She telephoned as instructed. A polite voice with a melancholy inflection told her he regretted being the bearer of bad news. He paused.

'I won't shoot the messenger,' she said.

She knew before he told her that Daniel was dead. He had died three days ago, suddenly, of a massive heart-attack. She wondered what a massive heart-attack was, as she heard the voice go on to say that he had been instructed a few years ago to break this news in this way in the event of a sudden death. She was grateful for Daniel's care that the news should be broken as gently as possible, so that she wouldn't open the paper and see the obituary or go hear a colleague say, 'Did you hear about Daniel Jacobs? What a loss!' Dear kind Daniel thought of that letter from his solicitor after dear kind Mick joked about me being spared a widow's troubles.

There was no letter from a lawyer, no arrival to absence, no sudden death. He took about a year to die, or rather to know that he was dying. I was there all the time, cutting down my visits to Swansea and Rhossilli, and cancelling lecture trips to Kraków and Bologna. I was in on the early innocent symptoms.

He came back from a trip to Toronto to get an honorary degree, saying he'd had some kind of a throat infection, and his voice hadn't been very good during the speech. He'd been a bit throaty. Some virus or other. The throatiness continued, and a slight slurring set in. Then there were cramps. He would jump into a seated position on the bed, hugging his legs and yelping. I remembered Auntie Mary occasionally groaning with the cramp at night. Then came fatigue, a slowing of the walk, a droopy weak neck. He went to his doctor and was referred to a neurologist for tests, but they didn't find anything, they said. Someone mentioned a virus again. He went for a second opinion to a new doctor, and he didn't find anything either. Mick told the doctor he didn't know that a recent symptom was a slight diminution in sexual desire and performance. It was very slight. Towards the end he reminded me that I'd joked about him coming back from each trip abroad slightly less potent, but while we continued to meet neither desire nor performance came to an end. Except for our very last meeting, when I was a guest for supper, and we did not go to bed.

Conversation was more impaired than intercourse though Mick never gave in. He persisted in talking right to the end, or to the end of our conversations, face to face or voice to voice. He still rang up morning and evening, and though in the early days of his voice failure I'd prattle away, thinking to bear the burden of talk, he would resist and persist. He was determined to finish his sentences for himself, like a stammerer. He would repeat his words till the mumble came clear, and the message fully formed. He never minded how many times I said 'Sorry, I didn't quite get that', or 'Darling, would you mind saying that again?' And I got so that I didn't apologize when I asked him to say a sentence or a phrase again. And again.

'Again, please.'

His mumbling didn't clarify quickly but I would get a couple more words on each go. We became endlessly patient, suffering each other's patience. We got very good at laughing down incoherence and misunderstanding.

Mick especially loved four things in conversation: gossip, pillow-talk, literary analysis, and jokes. I've never been able to remember jokes, nor laugh at them very wholeheartedly, but Mick's were either good jokes or good bad jokes, and he told them lovably. The last one he told me was a terrible joke about a wife-murderer and a Florida divorcée hell-bent on remarriage. A Florida joke, he said. It was the only one of its genre I ever heard. It took about fifteen minutes for the first telling, the requests for repetition, and the repetitions. When he'd finished and I'd paused and laughed, not quite as loudly as he did, he said something incoherent. After three tries I got it.

'Florence, you should go to Florida.'

I liked him making bad-taste jokes about death and sex but I also knew he was seriously thinking about my survival, so I shouted at him down the phone.

'I've told you a million times I don't want to get married. Again.' That was the only time during his illness that we mentioned my survival.

One May morning I telephoned his house and his daughter Sandy said, 'I'm sorry, but he's very ill.' There was a wobble in her voice. I asked her to give him my love and she said she would.

I hadn't seen Mick for two weeks and it was five days since we'd spoken. By then it was easier for me to telephone than for him, but right up to the last he would answer, if he was near the phone, or come when called. Sometimes it was answered by one of the friends who crowded round to them. Once the voice sounded familiar and recognized my voice, and it was somebody I'd met at Jake's party in Atlanta. Fortunately Ellen disliked the phone. After our third meeting, when we'd been to bed in his flat, Mick told me it was all right to phone him at any time, because his wife didn't like answering the phone. And during fifteen years, she never did.

When I had lunch with the family about three weeks before I'd promised to come again and bring them a picnic lunch. Mick kept reminding me, but I kept on postponing it.

I'd been to Swansea for the weekend to see my mother, and while I was with her I didn't feel like phoning him. When I got back she phoned me to say Daniel had tried her number, wanting to speak to me.

'Oh Florence dear, he did sound very bad. I told him you'd caught the 3.32, and would be back in London by the night. I said how very sorry I was that he was so ill.' She had spoken to him once before, very briefly and discreetly, and afterwards he said with a laugh he had the feeling she knew all about him. I'd told her about his illness.

The day after he spoke to my mother I got a big brown envelope addressed in his hand, containing a batch of my letters. He would send them back to me at intervals, and this last lot was obviously sent so it wouldn't be found among his papers. I wondered which of his relations and helpers had posted it. His small sloping hand looked uneven but clear. He didn't put in a covering note, but then he never did. I opened one or two at random. It's funny reading your own letters.

They were recent letters, when I was saying last things in truth and in kindness to the dying. One said half-truthfully that I'd hoped that Ellen would die first so that we could live together. It had been a hard letter to write, and I'd half expected a grateful reply, but didn't get one. It wasn't a big deal for someone dying. Another earlier letter contained a neatly folded cheque for two thousand pounds, sent after some mild squabble, for me to buy a present in celebration of our fifteen happy years. I returned it. It seemed too big and too small. Twenty pounds would have bought champagne or flowers, twenty thousand would have been a bequest, two thousand was somehow wrong. I sent it back, saying I was sorry but I didn't want to take it. He never replied, never said anything, never tore it up, just left it with the letter. I suppose he couldn't be bothered. I wondered if someone would see the cheque-stub, and if it was blank or had my name on it, but that didn't matter either. I'd been ungracious, but it was a storm in a teacup to a man expecting to die soon. I knew that, but a bit of unkindness was a relief from kindness. It broke the solemnity, too, reminding me of ordinary life.

I think it was the night before Mick died that the phone rang just after midnight, a time nobody else ever phoned. I hadn't spoken to him for a week or more, and since the conversation with Sandy I didn't expect to. I'd been lying awake, reading. I no longer kept the phone by my bed, so I had to get up and run into my study. When I picked up the receiver and said the number nobody spoke. I yelled into the silence, 'Mick, is it you?' I listened and tried again, then put the phone down and went back to bed, my heart beating like mad.

The next day I phoned his house again. When I asked how he was, an unknown Englishwoman's voice – one of their helpers, I supposed – said: 'I'm very sorry, but Professor Solomon died this morning.'

'Thank you,' I put down the phone, on the littered desk in my office.

You'd think I could remember what kind of day it was, but I haven't the faintest idea. I don't know what I was doing that day, either, except that it was the usual busy day in term-time. I must have seen students and colleagues and taken my classes. I know I decided to telephone the lodge at Magnus in three or four days' time to ask about the memorial service. Joanna was away but I told Susie when I got home. She said she'd come with me and asked me if we should wear black.

For the last memorial service I'd attended I'd worn a scarlet coat. It was for my friend Alec Whittington, a philosopher whom I met in my early teaching days at an aesthetics seminar run by Ruth Saw at Birkbeck. Everyone used to go from all over the university. Ruth was large, white-haired, benign, impersonal, tranquil, and radiant, the most relaxed teacher I've ever known. Alec was angular, intense, hard on himself and everyone else, his long bony face carved into a mask of misery. When we first met he explained that his range of aesthetic experience was limited to literature and architecture, as he was colour-blind and tone-deaf. He could manage a faint wretched smile when explaining Wittgenstein or quoting Wordsworth or looking at a Hawksmoor church.

He loved the City churches, and whenever I pass his beloved St Mary Woolnoth or St George's Bloomsbury, I think of Alec, as well as Charlie, with whom I first really looked at them. With Charlie the favourites were Wren and Gibbs. Alec was a difficult friend, never pretending to be cheerful, finding it hard to believe that other people also found writing troublesome, lamenting that he had to revise his manuscripts five or six times and not believing me when I said I did too. Instead of getting on with friendship, he explained in unnecessary detail that obviously he and I didn't find each other attractive. He was always in analysis, moving from Freudians to Jungians with appropriate shifts of dreaming, he told me with a flicker of humour. He was an uncomfortable companion who scrutinised every slip of the tongue or body with fervour. Once when he came to tea I dropped the tray, and felt guilty and self-conscious about Alec's interpretation of the accident as I stammered out that I had an irritating habit of always overloading trays.

He could maddeningly ignore the human in favour of the artistic, as he did once when we met to look round St Martin-in-the-Fields. I arrived early, and was sitting inside, looking at the pretty windows and ceiling when a roughly dressed man, probably one of the down-and-outs who shelter in that friendly crypt, rushed in, shouted some obscenities, and rushed out again. I was eager to tell Alec when he arrived but he brushed aside my story, made sure I'd taken in the chancel arch, and swept me outside to wonder at the great Corinthian portico and the West steeple.

He had an amazing recall of the poets, but no sense that you mightn't want to miss your last train while he finished reciting a whole book of *Paradise Lost* or *The Prelude*. But he had a mind that worked non-stop, a total intellectual availability, and a passion for the two arts he could respond to. He read his friends' work with zeal, raising details that you hadn't noticed yourself. When you asked him something about Descartes or Kant or Freddie Ayer, he would answer in pinpoint detail. When you asked him how he was he would answer in tormented particularity. He was impossible and I was fond of him.

When he took an overdose none of us were surprised, except perhaps by how much we missed him. I dreaded the memorial service at St Mary-le-Strand, most Italian of London churches, near King's College, where he taught. As I crossed the road I remembered Alec told me he stopped going to Italy because Rome and Venice were heartbreakingly full of young lovers, brown and happy. But once inside I was amused by the cellist playing Bach, to which Alec's uncompromisingly unmusical ghost would be deaf. When the music stopped there was plain unvarnished speech from his colleague Quentin Hadley, my ideal philosopher, a man who is capable of asking and answering any question with no touch of partisanship. He began by saying simply that Alec had been an extremely unhappy man, and went on to give that rare thing, a candid encomium. When he said Alec was a good teacher, I was startled but realized that was so. Quentin said there were no teachers of aesthetics any more; Alec was the last. He had a proper aesthetician's farewell. On Gibbs's small island in the Strand everything was purely beautiful: the curling street, the music, the architecture, the restraint, the truthfulness.

Nothing could be more different than the funeral games of my growing-up in Swansea. I remember thinking that as I looked at the colours. Everyone wore black. No scarlet, no architecture, no restraint, and something more or less than the truth. But they were great occasions. We never had formal memorial services, and the women didn't go to the funerals. My father and grandfather and uncles would rush home from work at midday, wash and shave noisily in the kitchen, shout for a clean shirt, run up-stairs and come down shining and transformed by their best black. The family chorus sat round wailing their memorial narrative.

'Poor old Llew. I never thought he'd go before me. Like a lion he was.' Or, 'I don't know what Willie the Hafod will do with-out Bron. He'll be a lost soul. He can't boil an egg.' Or, 'It's the children I feel for. Oh Bet will miss her Nana! I could howl.' 'Who'll look after the poor dog? Do you remember when he bought that pedigree Sealyham from the nurse in Morriston hospital?'

After the funeral, ham-teas with fruitcake made the memorial talk flow, even though in our family the dead were buried with tea. Our post-mortem ceremonies were always dry but the chorus got high on story-telling. As tales of the dead led to tales of the living, snivels and sobs became smiles and laughs. There were exceptions. I don't remember my father's funeral being very jolly, except when we were driving to the cemetery and Idris laughed at my black hat and said I looked like a Salvation Army lassie. My uncles looked disapproving, because women still didn't go to the cemetery, but I was delighted that my mother had asked me to go, as a special favour, though she didn't feel she could.

My grandfather's funeral party was hilarious. Charlie's mother was in her element. She'd come to help with the tinned salmon and sliced ham, and as she prided herself on telling people what she thought of them and never saying behind their back what she wouldn't say to their face, she was able to reproach my uncle Emmanuel for turning up though he didn't come near his father from one year to the next, concluding, 'If you ask me there's a lot of old hypocrisy about a funeral!' My mother shook her head, but Charlie insisted that his mother was only saying what my mother thought but was too polite to say.

Best of all were Uncle Bryn Ystradgynlais's stories of death and illness. Bryn was a prosperous baker who hadn't been on speaking terms with my grandfather, his elder brother, for years, but he was a large commanding figure with a gold watch and chain on his belly, and no one upbraided him. Charlie and I and Idris and our mothers and the uncles and aunts and cousins and one or two convivial neighbours listened to his reminiscences spellbound. He moved on from Grandpa's poaching days, and the accidental shooting of a swan, to his own son Gordon's first and last ride on a new motor-bike. He'd been riding it cautiously along the Ystradgynlais canal towpath when he came to a bend and accelerated instead of slowing down. As he whizzed by he caught sight of a child, then heard a scream. He stopped as soon as he could, turned and went back, but could find no child on the bank or in the water, not even a ripple. Nothing was moving on the surface except some old rubbish and branches. He looked up and down, but there wasn't a sign of the child. Had he imagined it? No, the cry was definitely a child's, loud and very near. Gordon hung about for ten minutes or longer, looking everywhere, walking up and down, and calling out. Then he got back on the bike and rode it slowly home. Didn't sleep a wink. Nothing in the *Evening Post* the next night. No drownings or missing children. There was a long pause, and we waited for the dénouement. I was dying to ask why he hadn't informed the police, but dared not ask.

'I tell you,' Uncle Bryn resumed impressively, taking a loud sip of my mother's dark brown tea, 'and you won't believe me, I know, but that boy was never the same again. Every nerve in his body was destroyed. Every nerve. All his hair fell out. Bald he was, completely bald, from that day to the day he went to

America ten years after. What that boy suffered nobody ever knew. He could never talk about it, not even to his Mam. That's why he went of course. Couldn't settle. Broke off his engagement to Edna. Remember Edna? Oh, she was a nice girl.' Charlie's mother was listening and nodding. Yes, she had known Edna's mother. A nice family. She'd been at school with Edna's father, in Brynmill Infants.

'There's a liar your uncle Bryn is,' my mother said after they'd all gone, and she was watching me and Charlie do the washing-up. I couldn't disagree. She shook her head contemptuously when Charlie asked her if she ever seen the bald and nerveless Gordon. She remembered him as a boy, but since the two brothers had been estranged, none of our branch of the family had seen him in adult life. All through Uncle Bert's story Charlie was making faces at me and I had a hard time keeping a straight face, even though I'd loved Grandpa. It had been an enjoyable funeral, once the burying was over, and after all he'd lived into his late eighties, without any serious illness, though with rheumatic aches and pains. Never been in hospital.

I wished I'd told Mick Uncle Bryn's story, but I hadn't thought of Gordon's ride along the Ystradgynlais canal for years, till I had to decide what to wear to Mick's memorial service, and my scarlet coat for Alec brought the best-black-clad Swansea mourners trooping back.

As Susie and I sat in the train, our books open, I thought of Mick's last words to me. We didn't have long conversations towards the end, and we didn't ring each other up so often. The sense of humour helps, but talking was a strain, though mostly in antic-ipation. I can't remember now everything we talked about on that last occasion, only that there was a lot of stopping and start-ing till Mick said, 'I like ... not talking ... to you'.

He had to repeat it four or five times. Because I couldn't hear the words clearly, I didn't see the joke. Or was it that I didn't see the joke so couldn't hear the words? In the end we were both laughing. I think that was one of the times he said I mustn't forget I'd promised to bring a picnic, and I said yes I would in a week or two. I had a graduate seminar on black women novelists, so different from the white Victorian women novelists, but only in some ways. I had a lot of new reading and thinking to do, and a strong disinclination to go back to visit Oxford as the family friend. Now it was a week or two later, and Susie and I were on the Oxford train.

Like an angel, she had come with me. So at least one person there knew I was mourning my dead. Mine not theirs, I said, anticipating the ceremony and the mourning family. I wanted to shout my claim aloud, because I was jealous, not because I really thought he wasn't theirs too. When we got outside the station, where Mick had met me in the car a thousand times, it was pouring with rain. We were early so we started to walk, but the rain got heavier and we stopped at a shop to buy an umbrella. I asked for the cheapest black one they had and it broke the next time I used it. We were so early that we looked round the clothes department and Susie bought a red sweater, which I came across when I was sorting things out for Oxfam last week.

It was suddenly late and we ran through the wet streets, and went in through the arch where I'd gone a thousand times, turning towards the chapel instead of the garden quad. Someone in a gown asked us for our names.

'Professor Florence Jones and Ms Susan Jones.'

'Why do they take our names, Mum?'

'For the paper I suppose.' I never looked in the paper to see. I hated the paper after the hateful obituary. I knew who wrote it because Mick had found out, with his nose for secrets, and though I thought it much better not to know, he was pleased by the choice. I was particularly infuriated by its half-heartedness because he'd voted for the anonymous writer's election as fellow of Magnus, liked him, and innocently expected him to sing his praise. It wasn't that the obituarist was hostile, but he praised Mick for all the wrong things, sound fact instead of bold speculation, range instead of wit. He had no loving detail; it was all generalized. And his language was banal, a rotten medium for Mick's encomium. But I daresay jealousy blurred my judgement. No obituary could have risen to my occasion. I've never been able to reread it, though it's filed away somewhere with Mick's letters and the reviews of his books.

The language of the memorial address was crashingly banal too. But that came late in the service, and so did my hostility. What I felt first as we sat down, and remember most sharply, was a physical nervousness, a fear of public exposure rapidly followed by a fear of invisibility. I can't remember the music or the hymns, only that unnerving. I tried to concentrate on the high vaulted roof and the brilliant windows. I'd only been there a few times before. The first was when we had made love, after a fashion, in Mick's room, then had a buffet lunch in the Turl. On later occasions we had a picnic in his room, but we hadn't got started yet and secrecy hadn't begun to seem imperative. At the beginning Mick even came on to the platform to see me off to Paddington. But as soon we began to accept that we were a fixture, we had to think about the conditions. It was clear that we must keep our affair a total secret, he for Ellen's sake, and both of us for our own sakes, since discovery would wound her and we'd almost certainly have to stop. So we didn't even use the cover of friendship. We were simply professional acquaintances, colleagues meeting at conferences, workers in the same field.

After that first lunch, when we were exhilarated, almost giggly, Mick took me on a lightening tour of Magnus, the gardens, the portraits, the hall and the chapel, the odds and ends of ancient statuary. He told me how famous the garden was, and pointed out a holm oak, the only tree, indeed the only natural object in nature, he ever correctly identified. I was misleadingly impressed with his knowledge, but soon got wise when we went for drives and short walks in the summer countryside. I started off thinking he was a lover of music and nature, to find that his subjects were literature and human relations, strictly urban contexts. Once in Ireland I tried to teach him a lark's sound.

'Listen. Like a hurdy-gurdy. Come on, it's too famous a tune for you not to know.'

For the rest of that day he recognized the lark, but by the next week he'd forgotten. Another summer there was meadowsweet everywhere, by all the roadsides and hedgerows of Oxfordshire. I thought I'd managed to get him to recognize it, but he mixed it up with Queen Anne's Lace and even elder. They were all white and frothy. He was hopeless, deaf and blind in the fields and by the sea, occasionally sweeping an appreciative arm towards a splendid view, as we drove fast through the Cotswolds, but only seeing land and sea as contexts for love and talk. It was an obtuseness I grew to love dearly, all his own.

The editor of his book on George Eliot and George Henry Lewes asked him to put in something about the Midland rural context. After a couple of days looking at her descriptions, and at paintings and photographs, with ice-packs on his head, he drove up there for a weekend. I didn't go because Ellen wanted to. They stayed in a hotel in Coventry and drove round the George Eliot country. It still didn't help and he asked me to help. But everything I could think of seemed wrong for him, and in the end he refused in mock despair, saying he was sorry but he couldn't do nature.

I was always surprised that someone who wrote poetry when he was a young man, and still wrote the occasional poem, was so unresponsive to nature. He would take me into the country for a treat, but it was always my treat. He would look at me looking at the land and sky and water, in a fond and puzzled way. Once we were driving up the west coast of Ireland, to Donegal, on one of our rare holidays, and the road dipped sharply so that we saw the sun rise twice. I exclaimed with pleasure, and he braked and asked me if I was all right. I toned down my rhapsodizing, and when we were having breakfast in a pub, I told him I was playing Fanny Price to his Mary Crawford.

'Nobody ever compared me to a Jane Austen character before. And a woman character. And such an attractive and witty one. Thanks.'

On that trip we stopped at Station Island, got out of the car, and looked down at the elegant pavilion and the pilgrims crossing for their three-day pilgrimage. He gazed for longer than I knew him look at any view. I realized that it wasn't the lucid gleam on the grey water, and the flying birds, but the scene's saturation in literature, Kavanagh, Yeats, and Seamus Heaney, whom he knew and liked. (He gave me Heaney's *Station Island* as a souvenir of that day.) We were secular onlookers seeing the place of pilgrimage from a great distance. Not candidates for purgatory, I thought, as I looked at him looking.

After Mick's death I got three condolence letters. The first was from Nest, Idris's eldest child. She happened to phone me the day he died, to tell me how she got on in her interview by the physics department of Imperial College. I was in a weepy state and told her why, and she sent me a nice little card, with a loving printed message of sympathy.

The second astonished me. It came two days after Mick died. It was from my old friend Isabella Rathbone, a colleague in Hull, asking enigmatically and affectionately if I was all right, because she had a feeling I might be in distress. Something on those lines. Isabella and her husband Colum had been our friends when Charlie and I were still living together, and they loved our children, and were loved by them. The Rathbones were younger than us and had their children later. We all stayed close until Charlie and I split up, and I saw them all without him. Isabella had known I had a long-term attachment, as she'd known about other lovers. She had several close friends in Oxford, where she had done her doctorate, and knew Mick and Ellen. The acquaintance was what gave her the clue. I can't remember what I told her, but she saw I was grieving. I may have said my lover was ill, I don't remember. When she heard about Mick's illness, the separate pieces joined together. Then she wrote me the extraordinary letter, which told me she knew without saying what she knew. She said she felt she had to write. The letter came immediately after his death, and I wrote back at once and told her everything. We met and talked. When she reads this, she'll remember how grateful I was. And am. It's a pleasure to send her this message of love, a message in a bottle I know will land safely at her feet.

The third letter came a year later, from Flora, another good friend. The name coincidence had first brought us together, joking about how you dislike people with a name close to yours. She lived in Ireland, I didn't see her very often, and we were both too busy to write, but the year after his death she came to London for a flying visit. We had dinner in my flat, drinking lots of white Rioja and eating fennel and peppers and smoked salmon and brown bread, and exchanging our stories as we'd often done before. But this time I told her more than usual. She told me about a new lover, I told her about my dead one. She'd known there was somebody, but not who. She had met Mick, so it was a warm, confiding and intimate conversation.

After she went back she wrote me a letter. She said all the right things, and I knew again how I'd missed the rites of widowing:

> My dear Florence,
> I was very moved by what you told me about Mick Solomon. It struck me that you couldn't have had many letters of condolence, which you deserved and needed. This one is late but no less sincere for that.

She wrote about how bright and attractive we both were, how well matched, how proud of each other we must have been, how I must miss all the meetings and prospects of meetings. She went on:

> It must have been lovely for him to have you right up to the end. And fifteen years of happiness is a lot to give someone and get from them. Since you told me I've thought constantly about you both: how right and happy a combination it was, as I always knew from the few things you said, obliquely. And when you spoke more directly, the other day, it made more sense. I wish he had not died, and that you were still together. But you are still, in your minds. I will think of you now even more affectionately, and think of you both together.
> With my love,
> Flora.

I loved her writing that about minds, though it was only half true. I'm not in his mind any more. But it was a great letter to have. It praised the beloved and the love affair, as a letter of condolence should do. Simply getting a letter of condolence, like the ones from Nest and Isabella, made me feel a proper widow. And here was another person who had known Mick. I looked forward to talking to her about him again when I went to Ireland for a holiday in August.

Three months later, in April, Terry, a mutual friend, rang me up from Dublin. He said he was very sorry but he had very bad news. Flora had been killed in a car crash. She had driven into a wall. Nobody else was hurt. She hadn't been wearing a seat-belt. I went to Dublin for her memorial service, only a year after Mick's.

It was a few weeks after the funeral. It was informal, a kind of Irish Quaker meeting, friends sitting and drinking in a private room in a pub. Her mother was there, warm and generous and easy. I'd dreaded meeting her grief. Her boyfriend was there, large and confident and clever and talkative. We had decided against a programme, and just sat there together, saying something about her or telling a story or singing or reading. Somebody sang 'Salonica', with the line I've always loved without knowing why, about the lad with a foxy head. One man told how she'd walked into a room, wearing a plain black dress, looking absolutely beautiful. One of her students said how she had known everything about Irish literature, and known them, and been a friend, and brought all the funny story-tellers and famous poets to the college. There were songs in Irish. Somebody said a bit about her life. She'd got a brilliant degree at Trinity College Dublin, worked as a whiz-kid in advertising, drove a white Jag, invented flower and herb cosmetics, then decided she wanted to be a scholar, and went back to university to write her thesis on Yeats. I read out a Yeats poem I heard her read in a lecture she gave on his late poetry, with the inexorable chorus: 'What then, said Plato's ghost, what then?' I could hear her slow deep English voice saying it. She was Irish but had an upper-class posh accent. She had just separated from her husband, settled her children in school and university, been made head of her department, started to make her name and enjoy the academic globe-trot. She had just moved into a new house of her own. My condolence letter had her drawing of it at the top, a Georgian house with a door right in the centre, five windows, a half-moon light over the door, and two bushes and a tree. Like the house and garden in the poem, I thought as I read.

Terry had told me, 'I went to see her in the mortuary. Her face was bruised, but she looked lovely. She looked like a baby. She looked innocent.'

Before she died she had opened her eyes and asked, 'Am I dead?'

Mick's memorial service wasn't like Flora's, or Grandpa's, or Alec's. Two hundred people in a fourteenth-century chapel. A trained choir. Hymns and music, none of which had anything to do with Mick, who never sang hymns and couldn't tell Bach from Vivaldi. A stiff and graceless address from horrible old Sir Wallace Elliott, who said with a little high laugh that he was about the least qualified person to talk about Michael's achievement, and went on to demonstrate it. It was drearily banal. It could have been about anyone. Self-deprecation and apology. Generalities about Mick's major contribution to Victorian scholarship. Emphasis on his marshalling of solid fact. Nothing about wit and style and daring. A rerun of the obituary. Joke about a Yank at Oxford. A brief mention of the early volume of verse. No bright detail. No flowering particulars. No feeling for the live man.

Nobody's memorial words could satisfy me. Des Mahony, a good Irish poet who'd been a friend of Mick's for years, wrote a poem in memory of Mick which was all about himself and his art and love. There was nothing about Mick except the dedication and one brief phrase about how he'd be missed. It was a good poem but I hated it as much as I hated the address in the chapel. In spite of the fact that I'd lectured on the necessary self-centredness of all good elegy, from Milton's 'Lycidas', all about his love and art, to Auden's poem, invoking the cold dark day of Yeats's death for a discourse on the powerlessness of art: it's different when the elegy is for your dead lover.

I would have been angry if horrible Sir Wallace had made a good speech. He had once been startlingly rude to me, in the loud resonant way of the upper, or pseudo-upper classes. Mick innocently introduced us at a party for the award of the Henry Mackenzie Fiction price. He had proposed me as one of the next set of judges, vague as ever, ignoring the fact that everyone was supposed to have an Oxford connection. When Mick murmured our names, and said I'd agreed to be a judge, loathsome Sir Wallace screwed up his small close-together eyes and his thin little mouth.

'There may be some difficulty, you know. I gather you weren't at Oxford. Strictly speaking, you know ... I'm afraid ... I don't know whether you've been told that our judges are required to have, or to have had, an appointment in Oxford.'

What was I supposed to say? 'I think you're charming too. Just blame Mick, who doesn't understand Oxford and will certainly not have read the small print, and shouldn't have proposed me as his successor on the panel because he is my lover.'

I said nothing, just nodded and walked off. I was furious with Mick, who ambled after me, laughing in his usual mild, ironic deprecating way, and taking my arm.

'Calm down, darling.'

He got me another drink and tried to amuse me by pointing out the willowy glamorous eighty-plus-year-old Lady Diana Cooper, in an enormous black-and-white hat, a perfect pale mask of make-up, and oddly animate dark glasses. No good. I would not be distracted. There were people all round us. I raved, in a low voice. I wanted him to apologize. I wanted him to make horrible Sir Wallace apologize. I wanted him to challenge horrible Sir Wallace to a duel. Of course I knew he would go on being good friends with him, forget how offended I'd been, and would absent-mindedly tell me again and again how kind Elizabeth Elliott was to Ellen. The Elliotts were such good friends and generous neighbours.

He smiled his sweetest smile. 'What does it matter, darling?' And I shut up.

Mick always listened to me very carefully. If he didn't wholly agree he would say, 'There's something in what you say.' But he didn't understand my deep-rooted social envy and touchiness, my superior inferiority, my jealousy of Oxford exclusions and assumptions, my pride and resentment at being outside those expensively preserved old walls. Like many clever Americans, he was an innocent in the English class system, surprised when I attacked him for mentioning the Oxbridge-public-school connection without seeing its politics. I told him how shocked

I'd been as a teenager when Charlie told me parts of Gower belonged to All Souls, and Mick was surprised at the facts and my fury. To him I wasn't a working-class Swansea girl with a Jude complex, but a successful middle-class professional woman, with an accent indistinguishable from the Elliotts', an expert on English usage when he wanted to know the proper pronounciation of 'Edinburgh', 'Thackeray', and 'perhaps', those traps for visitors from across the Atlantic. And in a way he was right. When I grumbled my hostilities I saw their unfairness as well as their justice. I was too mixed-up to go into a great class discussion with him. I could outline my story, but not all its history. South Wales was something mentioned in Auden. He could never come to Swansea and meet my family there.

I didn't return to the subject of Sir Wallace's bad manners. Nobody else brought up my lack of Oxfordness. After I got to know him, and we were chatting before a working lunch, I told the story to the chairman of the committee, Percy Haynes. He laughed sympathetically, and said Sir Wallace was a grocer. I didn't know if it was a metaphor or not, and never bothered to find out.

But I never forgave the old snob, as my mother would have called him. Here he was presiding, in at the death, boring us to tears, ruining the service, distracting me from sorrow, and proving how cultureless he was. 'What does it matter?' Mick had said, laughing it all away. I couldn't even look forward to telling Mick all about it. And the awful thing was that not only was he dead, but if his ghost was present it would be polite and grateful, smiling benignly, defending the speech, exaggerating its good points, praising it for understatement, shrugging at the neglect of his poetry, refusing to criticize. Horrible Sir Wallace droned cluelessly on.

I wished he'd drop dead in the pulpit. After the non-account of Mick's career, it got worse. Well, worse for me. It was probably fine for family and friends, the best part of the oration. He praised Mick's remarkable children, recalled his wonderful care for Ellen, their open house, their generous hospitality, their family strength. I wanted to shout out against the memorial service, its ignorance, its old hypocrisy. I wanted to beat against the high, august walls of Oxford. No, I didn't. I wanted to get up and explain with dignity, more fluently and vividly than Sir Wallace, that I had been an invisible pillar of that strong house for over a decade, that Mick was mine. No, I didn't. I just wanted to puke.

'Calm down, darling,' Mick's ghost mumbled in my ear. 'What does it matter?'